'He is an improviser, his work a performance on the page.
But experimental, improvisational, performative and dreamlike
as Aira's many marvellous books are, they also reveal him to be no
less of a traditionalist, responding to the most ancient custom
of storytelling as a way of passing the hours of the night'
Judges' citation, The Man Booker International Prize 2015

'Aira has written over seventy books. They are mostly novels,
mostly slim and mostly astoundingly good. He reminds me of
Philip K. Dick, of Honoré de Balzac, of Machado de Assis and
of Søren Kierkegaard . . . all of which is simply to say that he is
without compare' Rivka Galchen, *New Yorker*

'César Aira is writing a gigantic, headlong, acrobatic fresco
of modern life entirely made up of novelettes, novellas,
novellitos . . . In other words, he is a great literary trickster,
and also one of the most charming' Adam Thirlwell

'Aira's stories seem like shards from an ever-expanding
interconnecting universe. He populates the racing void with
multitudinous visions, like Indian paintings of gods
vomiting gods. He executes digression with muscular
lucidity' Patti Smith, *The New York Times*

'César Aira's body of work is a perfect machine for
invention – he writes without necessity or any apparent
forebears, always as if for the first time' Maria Moreno, *BOMB*

'If there's currently a writer who defies all classification that
writer is César Aira. Once you've read Aira, you don't want
to stop. Aira is an eccentric, but he's also one of the three or
four best Spanish-language writers alive today' Roberto Bolaño

'Aira's works are like slim cabinets of wonder, full
of unlikely juxtapositions. His unpredictability
is masterful' *Harper's*

'Aira's novels display a consistent engagement with the
importance of storytelling and the act of writing. The engrossing
power of his work comes from how he carries out these feats:
with the inexhaustible energy and pleasure of a child chasing after
imaginary enemies in the park' *Los Angeles Review of Books*

'To love the novels of César Aira you must have a taste for the absurd, a tolerance for the obscurely philosophical and a willingness to laugh out loud against your better judgment' *NPR Books*

'Aira's charm is subtle, unobtrusive, it doesn't try to seduce with cheap likeability. He takes a leisurely stroll through his scenes. It's as if Machado de Assis got redrafted by Bolaño and edited by Anatole France' *Bookslut*

'César Aira's novels are the narrative equivalent of the Exquisite Corpse, that Surrealist parlour game in which players add to drawings or stories without knowledge of previous or subsequent additions. Wildly heterogeneous elements are thrown together, and the final result never fails to surprise and amuse' *The Millions*

'In spite of the apparent randomness of his ideas and the pacing of his breaks, surprises and cuts in time, he inspires a sort of willingness in the reader to be taken aback; any reader – untrusting or submissive – might enjoy them as if they had pressed "shuffle" on their favourite pop band's discography' *Ox and Pigeon*

'What's really unique about Aira's output, considering the speed with which he "flies forward" (seemingly by the seat of his pants), isn't that he produces so much work, or that it's fanciful and odd, but that what he's produced forms a coherent body of work – and one that's consistently enjoyable to read' *The Argentina Independent*

'A manifestly gifted writer' *The Quarterly Conversation*

'Astonishing – turns Don Quixote into Picasso' *Harper's*

ABOUT THE AUTHOR

César Aira was born in Coronel Pringles, Argentina, in 1949, and has lived in Buenos Aires since 1967.

Three Novels

CÉSAR AIRA

Preface by Roberto Bolaño

Ghosts and *An Episode in the Life of a Landscape Painter*
translated by Chris Andrews
The Literary Conference
translated by Katherine Silver

PENGUIN BOOKS

PENGUIN BOOKS

UK | USA | Canada | Ireland | Australia
India | New Zealand | South Africa

Penguin Books is part of the Penguin Random House group of companies
whose addresses can be found at global.penguinrandomhouse.com.

Ghost first published as *Los Fantasmas* in 1990; published by arrangement
with the Michael Gaeb Literary Agency, Berlin
This translation first published in the United States of America by New Directions 2008
First published in Great Britain by Hamish Hamilton 2013
Copyright © César Aira, 1990
Translation copyright© Chris Andrews, 2008
An Episode in the Life of a Landscape Painter first published by Beatriz Viterbo Editora,
Argentina, as *Un episodio en la vida del pinto Viajero* in 2000; published by
arrangement with the Michael Gaeb Literary Agency, Berlin
This translation first published in the United States of America by New Directions 2006
First published in Great Britain by Hamish Hamilton 2013
Copyright © César Aira, 2000
Translation copyright© Chris Andrews, 2006
The Literary Conference first published by Ediciones ERA, Argentina, as *El congreso de literatura*
in 2006; published in conjunction with the Michael Gaeb Literary Agency, Berlin
This translation first published in the United States of America by New Directions 2010
First published in Great Britain by Hamish Hamilton 2013
Copyright © César Aira, 2006
Translation copyright© Katherine Silver, 2010
Ghosts, *An Episode in the Life of a Landscape Painter* and *The Literary Conference*
first published together in this edition 2015

001

The moral right of the copyright holders has been asserted

The preface, 'The Incredible César Aira' (*El increíble César Aira*) by Roberto Bolaño, was originally
published in *Entre paréntesis* in 2004 by Editorial Anagrama; © Heirs of Roberto Bolaño, 2004

Printed in Great Britain by Clays Ltd, St Ives plc

A CIP catalogue record for this book is available from the British Library

ISBN: 978-0-241-20292-0

www.greenpenguin.co.uk

Introduction

Preface

The Incredible César Aira
by Roberto Bolaño

IF THERE IS one contemporary writer who defies classification, it is César Aira, an Argentinean from a town in the
province of Buenos Aires called Coronel Pringles, which
must, I suppose, be a real place, although it could well have
been imagined by its most eminent son, who has given us
superlatively lucid portraits of the Mother (a verbal mystery)
and the Father (a geometrical certitude), and whose position
in contemporary Hispanic literature is equal in complexity
to that of Macedonio Fernández at the beginning of the
twentieth century.

Let me start by saying that Aira has written one of the
five best stories I can remember. The story, included in Juan
Forn's anthology *Buenos Aires*, is entitled "Cecil Taylor." He
is also the author of four memorable novels: *How I Became a
Nun*, in which he recounts his childhood; *Ema, The Captive*,
in which he recounts the opulence of the pampas Indians;
The Literature Conference, in which he recounts an attempt to
clone Carlos Fuentes; and *The Crying*, in which he recounts
a sort of epiphany or bout of insomnia.

Naturally those are not the only novels he has written.
I am told that Aira writes two books a year, at least, some

of which are published by a little Argentinean company named Beatriz Viterbo, after the character in Borges's story "The Aleph." The books of his that I have been able to find were published by Mondadori and Tusquets Argentina. It's frustrating, because once you've started reading Aira, you don't want to stop. His novels seem to put the theories of Gombrowicz into practice, except, and the difference is fundamental, that Gombrowicz was the abbot of a luxurious imaginary monastery, while Aira is a nun or novice among the Discalced Carmelites of the Word. Sometimes he is reminiscent of Roussel (Roussel on his knees in a bath red with blood), but the only living writer to whom he can be compared is Barcelona's Enrique Vila-Matas.

Aira is an eccentric, but he is also one of the three or four best writers working in Spanish today.

GHOSTS

ON THE MORNING of the 31st of December, the Pagaldays visited the apartment they already owned in the building under construction at 2161 Calle José Bonifacio, along with Bartolo Sacristán Olmedo, the landscape gardener they had hired to arrange plants on the two broad balconies, front and rear. They climbed the stairs littered with rubble to the middle level of the edifice: like the other apartments, the one they had acquired occupied a whole floor, the fourth. Apart from the Pagaldays there were only six other owners, all of whom made an appearance on that last morning of the year to see how the work was coming along. The builders were conspicuously busy. By eleven, there were people everywhere. It was in fact the day on which, according to the contracts, the apartments should have been ready to move into; but, as usual, there had been

1

a delay. Felix Tello, the construction company's architect, must have gone up and down fifty times, allaying the owners' concerns. Most had come with a tradesman of some kind: a carpet layer to measure the floors, a carpenter, a tiler, or an interior decorator. Sacristán Olmedo was talking about the dwarf palms that would be arranged in rows on the balconies, while the Pagalday children went running through rooms, which still had no flooring, doors or windows. The air conditioning units were being installed, ahead of the elevators, which would have to wait until after the holiday. Meanwhile materials were being hoisted up through the shafts. Perched on their high heels, the ladies were climbing the dusty stairs scattered with pieces of rubble; since the banisters had not yet been fitted, they had to be especially careful. The first basement level was to be used for garages, with ramps up to the street, which had not yet been covered with their special anti-slip surface. The second level was for box rooms and storage space. On top of the seventh floor, a heated swimming pool and a games room, with a panoramic view over rooftops and streets. And the caretaker's apartment, which was no more finished than the rest of the building, but had been inhabited for some months by Raúl Viñas, the night watchman, and his family. Viñas was a reliable Chilean builder, although he had turned out to be a prodigious drinker. The heat was supernatural. Looking down from the top was dangerous. The glass panels that would enclose the whole terrace were not yet in place. The visitors kept their children well away from the edges. It's true that buildings under construction seem smaller before the windows, doors and flooring have been put in. Everyone knows that; and yet somehow the opposite also seemed to be true. Domingo Fresno, the architect in charge of the interiors on the second floor, was walking anxiously through that capacious labyrinth, as if across the sands of a desert. Tello had done his job well enough. At least the building was standing firm on its foundations; it could have melted like an ice cream in the sun. No one had come to see the first floor. The Kahns, an older couple with two young daughters, were on the fifth floor with their decorator, the extraordinary Elida Gramajo, who was calculating aloud, working out the quantities of fabric required for drapes. Every detail had to be taken into account. And no detail could be specified without measuring both the space it would occupy and the surrounding space. Consequently, that big concrete cage was measured exhaustively, in three dimensions, millimeter by millimeter. A woman in violet was catching her breath on the stairs between the sixth and seventh floors. Others didn't have to make an effort: they floated up and down, even through the concrete slabs. The owners were not bothered by the delay, partly because they didn't have to make the last payment until they took possession, but also because they actually preferred to have a bit more time to organize the furnishings and fittings. The measurements were expanding the space that had been shrunken by illusion; similarly, the duration of the move was expanding. Besides, there would have been something violent about taking possession on the last day of the year. On the sixth floor, Dorotea and Josefina Itúrbide Sansó, two girls aged five and three, were kicking up cement dust with their little sandaled feet while their parents chatted placidly with Felix Tello. Tello excused himself to greet the woman in violet and accompanied her up to the next floor. They met the Kahns coming down from the games room and introduced themselves. Meanwhile the Pagaldays looked out from their balcony at the large plane trees growing in the Calle Bonifacio. Although not yet fitted with security grilles, the balconies with high balustrades were, for the moment, the safest place for children. It was a morning of high childishness. Everything belonged to the children. The expansion produced by the measurements and the feeling of contraction that goes with fear were overlaid by the world of childhood. The real universe is measured in millimeters, and it is gigantic. Where children are present, dimensions are always mediated, scaled down. The decorators were crafting miniatures. Besides, all these powerful people and this profitable business were operating for the benefit of the children; if not for them, the parents would have chosen to live in hotels. Horrible and half-naked, the builders came and went among them. The frontier between rich and poor, between human beings and beasts, was a line in time; the space occupied by one group would soon be taken over by the other. In spite of its symbolism, the 31st was a crude and obvious allusion to this state of affairs. It was also indisputably true that the poor had a right to be happy too, and could even exercise that right. The mediation between large and small sums of money is effected by use and especially the diversity of users; possession, on the other hand, is as transitory as the gathering that was taking place that morning on the building site. Fresno was planning to put as many plants inside as Olmedo was putting outside. In a way, they were all landscape gardeners. And indeed, for the time being, the whole site was outside. The building would be finished when it all became an inside. An intimate, armor-plated little universe. Felix Tello himself would vanish like a puff of dust blown away by the passing years. The children would grow up here, for a while at least. The López family, who would occupy the first floor, had small children; they were in their square patio at the back, where the red paving stones had already been laid. The owners of the third floor, who arrived at midday, were the parents of the lady in violet who was going to live up on the seventh; they arrived with her children. There could hardly have been more children; each would have a private landscape, one on top of the other. Ms Gramajo had spent three hours taking notes, writing down figures extracted from space. Mrs De Itúrbide said she had seen a horrible fat monster like a sumo wrestler. He was from Santiago del Estero. A tray with buckets on it was rising up the elevator shaft, hoisted by a little motor. Around one, as the owners were leaving, there was an impromptu meeting on the first floor, where it was cooler. From the top floor you could see into the yard of the police station, which was around the corner, on the Calle Bonorino. An old gentleman, the López's cabinet maker, had measured various walls for bookshelves and cupboards. Since the owners had bought their apartments off a plan, they had all preferred to have their cupboards specially built. The construction company had suggested a firm of cabinet makers who were looking after four floors: their workshops would take orders directly from the decorators. Downstairs, while the parents were talking, various kids watched the workmen filling a big metal dumpster in the street with rubble. They were wheeling their barrows up a sloping plank that was blocking the sidewalk; women coming back from the supermarket on the corner with their trolleys full of provisions for the New Year's Eve feast had to go onto the road, a manoeuvre they accomplished reluctantly. Domingo Fresno was talking with a bearded young architect, an acquaintance of his, who would be doing the interiors on the seventh floor. The moment for swinging into action was, they felt, dizzyingly imminent: although the building seemed utterly incomplete and provisional, with so much rubble and empty space, any day now it could be finished. Elida Gramajo, who had already left, was thinking the same thing. Less mindful of what lay ahead, the owners were thinking something else. But if anyone should have been imagining the disappearance of the builders, seeing them vanish into thin air, without a trace, like bubbles bursting soundlessly, it was them. The electricians stopped working at one on the dot, and left. Tello spoke for a moment with the foreman, then they went to look at the plans, which kept them busy for a good quarter of an hour. Putting in the wiring wouldn't take long at all; the power points and all the rest could be finished off in an afternoon. The parents of the lady in violet climbed up with the children to see the games room on top and the swimming pool, which was already lined with little sky-blue tiles. An extremely thin, badly dressed woman was hanging washing on a line, in what would be the patio of the caretaker's apartment. It was Elisa Vicuña, the night watchman's wife. The visitors looked up at the strange, irregular form of the water tank that crowned the edifice, and the big parabolic dish that would supply television images to all the floors. On the edge of the dish, a sharp metallic edge on which no bird would have dared to perch, three completely naked men were sitting, with their faces turned up to the midday sun; no one saw them, of course. On the fourth floor, the Pagaldays were leafing through the contents of a large oblong portfolio, listening to Sacristán Olmedo's explanations. The children wanted to express their opinions too. Generally, though, what the children wanted was to look out from the balconies: wherever they came from, the difference in height was exciting. Even if they were moving from one third floor to another, there was a difference. What you could see from that height was different. The children were coming up with strange and sometimes illogical ideas about where they were. They resumed their races through the rooms, over the bare cement floors. Light penetrated to the farthest corner. It was as if they were in partitioned fields, raised to a certain height. After exchanging congratulations and best wishes for the year to come with a family that was about to leave, Felix Tello expressed his justifiable confidence that "they would be happy in their new home."

The owners of the apartments had their own idea of happiness; they imagined it wrapped in a delay, a certain developmental slowness, which was already making them happy. In short, they didn't believe that things were going to proceed as planned, that is, quickly. They preferred to think of the gentle slope of events; that was how it had been since they paid the deposit and signed the settlement a year earlier. Why should they adopt a different attitude now, just because the year was coming to an end? True, they knew there would be a change, but at the last moment, beyond all the moments in between. It wouldn't be today, or tomorrow, or any day that could be determined in advance. Like the spectrum of perception, the spectrum of happening is divided by a threshold. That threshold is just where it is, and nowhere else. They were focusing on the year, not the end of the year. Needless to say, they were right, in spite of everything and everyone, even in spite of right and wrong.

The union of the year and the moment was like the ownership of the building. Each owner possessed a floor, a garage and a box room, but nothing else: that was all they could sell. And yet at the same time they owned the whole building. That's how a condominium works.

Standing still on the dumpster's higher side, in the street, was a builder, a young man named Juan José Martínez, with an empty bucket in his hand. He had been distracted by something that had happened on the corner. There was nothing special about the corner or about him. An ordinary sort of guy, who wouldn't normally merit a second glance. Various people looked at him, but only because of where he was standing, perched up there, motionless, looking toward the corner, holding that position for the sheer, childlike pleasure of balancing all on his own in a high place (he was very young). The only unusual thing about him was that stillness, which is rare to see in a person at work, even for a brief spell. It was like stopping movement itself, but without really stopping it, because even in those instants of immobility he was earning wages. Similarly, a statue sculpted by a great master, still as it is, goes on increasing in value. It was a confirmation of the absurd lightness of everything. The people distracted by the sight of him, as he was by the sight of something a certain distance away, knew that future moments of daydreaming would be nourished by the poetic argument they were absorbing, an argument about eternity, about the beyond where promises are set.

The worst thing is the way they lie, Felix Tello was saying, but to judge from the broad smile on his face, he wasn't worried in the least. The architect's words met with a most attentive reception. Such attentiveness is not unusual when the lies of a third party are at issue. Tello was referring to the builders and by extension to the proletariat in general. They lie and lie and lie. Even when they're telling the

truth. Enthusiastic up-and-down jerking of heads, to sig-
nal assent. Felix Tello was a professional from a middle-class
background. From a certain point on in his career, he had
associated almost exclusively with two opposite fringes of
society: the extraordinarily rich people who bought parts of
his sophisticated buildings, and the extremely poor workers who built them. He had discovered that the two classes
were alike in many ways, and especially in their complete
lack of tact where money was concerned. In that respect the
correspondence was exact. The very poor and the very rich
regard it as natural to extract the maximum benefit from
the person they happen to be dealing with. The middle-
class principle, natural to him, of leaving a margin, a ghostly
"buffer" of courtesy, between the asking price and the maximum that could be obtained, was foreign to them. Utterly
foreign. It didn't even cross their minds. Having associated
with both groups for so long, and being both intelligent
and adaptable (if that is not a pleonasm), he had learned
how to mediate with a fair degree of efficiency. He took
advantage of the perfect trap that the rich and the poor
had set for each other. Once he had secured the means to
sustain a respectably comfortable way of life, all he wanted
was to live in peace. The only thing that surprised him,
when they confronted each other with their home truths,
wearing those stupid expressions, was the sincere perplexity on both sides. It was like the episode in his favorite
novel, *L'Assommoir*, in which the heroine, Gervaise, stops
paying back the money she owes to the Goujets: "From

next month on, I'm not paying you another cent," and soon she even starts charging them for the work she does. What a rude surprise for the bourgeois reader! How could this good, honest, hardworking woman refuse to pay a debt? So what? Why should she pay, just because of some moral obligation? But what about manners? No, manners didn't even come into it, in her situation; she was poor and had an alcoholic husband, and all the rest. That Zola, the man was a genius! (But with this expression, which Tello formulated silently, clasping his hands and lifting his eyes skyward, as if to say "Even I couldn't have come up with that," he un-wittingly confessed that he was fifty thousand times more bourgeois than those who were scandalized by the behavior of the pretty laundress with the limp.)

Except for the oldest couple and the youngest, all the others had embarked on their second, that is to say, defini-tive, marriages. Which is why they had invested in comfort-able, pleasant dwellings, where they could settle down and live for years. That was Tello's style: sensible, child-friendly, family-oriented design. And good business sense, of course.

The little group hanging on his words, those remarried couples with their shared project of happiness, had been infiltrated by two individuals, two naked men covered in fine cement dust. They were listening too, but only as a pretext for bursting continually into fierce, raucous laugh-ter. Or not so much laughter as vehement, theatrically sar-castic howling. Since the others didn't hear or see them, the conversation continued at its polite and leisurely pace.

The naked men shouted louder and louder as if competing with each other. They were dirty like builders, and had the same kind of bodies: rather stocky, solid, with small feet, and rough hands. Their toes were spread widely, like wild men's toes. They were behaving like badly brought-up children. But they were adults. A builder who happened to be passing by with a bucketful of rubble on the way to the skip stretched out his free hand and, without stopping, grasped the penis of one of the naked men and kept walking. The member stretched out to a length of two yards, then three, five, ten, all the way to the sidewalk. When he let it go, it slapped back into place with a noise whose weird harmonics went on echoing off the unplastered concrete walls and the stairs without marble paving, up and down the empty elevator shafts, like the lowest string of a Japanese harp. The two ghosts laughed more loudly and frenetically than ever. The architect was saying that electricians lie, painters lie, plumbers lie.

Most of the visitors were already leaving when a truck loaded with perforated bricks arrived and backed into what would be the lobby on the ground floor. The architect was impressed to see the delivery being made, given the half holiday. He explained to his audience that it was the final load of perforated bricks for partition walls, then indulged in a subtly cruel quip: if anyone wanted to make a last-minute change to the floor plan, they should speak now or forever hold their peace. Things were becoming irrevocable, but that didn't worry the owners; in fact, it enriched their sense of well-being. For the builders, however, the delivery came as an unpleasant surprise, since they had no choice but to unload the truck, and their half-day would have to be extended. They lined up quickly, forming a human chain, as they do for unloading bricks. The two ghosts had taken up a new position in the air above a round-faced electric clock hanging from a concrete beam above the place where the elevator doors would go. Both of them were head-down, with their temples touching; one vertical and the other at an angle of fifty degrees, like the hands of a clock at ten to twelve; but that wasn't the time (it was after one). Tello suggested going upstairs, so as not to get in the way, and to show the late arrivals the games room and the swimming pool, which were the building's prime attractions. Those who were not going up said good bye. When they got to the top, where it was scorchingly hot, they said what a good idea a swimming pool was. The metal skeleton rearing above them required some explanation: the solarium would be roofed with sliding glass panels, moved by a little electric motor, and a special, separate boiler would send hot water through that tangle of pipes, because of course the pool would be used much more in winter than in summer, when people generally go to the beach. A huge number of glass panes had to be fitted: the whole roof and most of the sides (not the south side, facing the street, because that was where the dressing rooms, the bathrooms and the caretaker's apartment would be). The laminated glass, with an interlayer of pure crystal, had already been delivered; the packages were waiting in the basement. The fitting of the panes would be one of the last jobs. They went to the edge to look at the view. It wasn't truly panoramic (after all, they were only at seventh-floor level), but it was fairly sweeping, and took in the impressive rampart of buildings along the Avenida Alberdi, with its crazy racing traffic, a hundred yards away, plus a broad expanse of houses and gardens, and a few scattered high-rise buildings in the distance. And overhead a glorious dome of sky, the cobalt blue of summer midday. Except in the early morning, the sun would be visible from the pool all day long. As they had noticed a number of children watching them, they started talking about the night watchman and his family. News of his drinking had reached them, but it was not a cause for worry: the proximity of the police station, which they could see from where they were, had insured them against theft during the construction of the building, in spite of the watchman's distractedness and hangovers. Within a few weeks, the family would be gone. They're Chileans, did you know? Yes, they had thought so. Chileans were different: smaller, more serious, more orderly. And in the architect's experience they were also respectful, diligent, excellent workers. Naturally Raúl Viñas was in the habit of getting drunk with his Chilean relatives, some of whom had been employed as laborers on the site. Very soon they would all disappear forever, them and the others. They had been living on the site for a year. The owners found all this curiously soothing. Someone had to be living there before they came to live definitively. They could even imagine the happiness of being there, provisionally, balancing on the edge of time. During the first months, while the frame went up, the night watchman's family had lived on the ground floor in a very flimsy shelter with cardboard walls, then they came up to the top. In a way it was a rather poetic existence, but it must have been terribly cold for them in winter, and now they were roasting. Not that Raúl Viñas cared, of course. And, naturally, they had lied: for a start, they weren't legal residents; they didn't have work permits. On the other hand, they were paid practically nothing, although it was a lot for them, because of the exchange rate. Apparently they already had somewhere to live afterward, and in fact they'd been asked to stay a few weeks more, because it wasn't worth hiring another night watchman for such a short time. "They're better off than us," said Mrs De López. At least as far as timing was concerned, they agreed.

Meanwhile, on the third floor, the carpet layer, a short, chubby man, was checking his notes for the last time, room by room, and sometimes taking the measurements again, just to be sure that he hadn't made a mistake. After reading off the number, he flicked his wrist expertly and the metal tape retracted itself, dancing about briskly, making a sheathing noise. All the measurements were right. All of them, from the first to the last. He could have carpeted the ceilings. Before going down, he leant over the balcony to see if his mini-van, a yellow Mitsubishi, was still where he had parked it. Directly below him the snout of a big truck

César Aira

was sticking out, the truck from which the bricks were being unloaded.

The builders were in such a hurry they had made two chains instead of one. Eight of them were busily at work. Two men in the back of the truck took the perforated bricks three at a time and threw them down to a pair below, who threw them in turn to two more builders, who threw them on to the last pair, who piled them up against a wall. Each flight of the bricks through the air was the same as the previous flights, down to the way they separated slightly and were clapped back together in the hands of the catcher, making a sound like castanets. People with time on their hands are often fascinated by the sight of this operation and spend hours watching from the opposite sidewalk. In this case the only spectator was a fat little four-or five-year old boy with blond hair, who had walked in beside the truck. After watching the synchronized movements for a few minutes, he approached Raúl Viñas, who was juggling bricks in one of the chains, and asked him: Aren't the kids here, Mister? Viñas, who was in a particularly bad mood because lunch had been delayed, didn't even look at him. It seemed he wouldn't answer, but then he did, with a mono-syllable, through the smoke of his cigarette (he was managing to smoke while catching and throwing bricks, three by three): No. The kid insisted: Are they upstairs? Another silence, bricks going and coming, and the boy: Huh? Finally Viñas said: José María, why don't you fuck off home? The builders burst out laughing. Offended, José María stepped

aside and stood there watching, quite calmly. Offended, but
pleased that his name had been pronounced. Besides, he
really was interested in Operation Bricks. He was in no
hurry, because lunch was late at his place, and anyway, he
always waited until his grandmother, a little old lady with
a powerful voice, whose shouts had made his name known
throughout the neighborhood, came to fetch him (she lived
around the corner). But then he saw one of the naked individuals, white with cement dust, at the back of the building,
and went tearing out the way he had come in. The fat guy
from Santiago del Estero on the back of the truck, dripping sweat as he heaved the bricks, remarked: How strange.
Which made the others laugh again, partly because of his
accent and partly just to prolong the fun. They laughed mechanically, without losing concentration, which was all that
mattered until the job was done.

Meanwhile, Raúl Viñas' young nephew, Abel Reyes,
was at the supermarket on the corner buying provisions for
the builders' lunch. As usual, he was keeping it simple and
quick: meat, bread, fruit. As youths of a certain age often do,
he refused to use the shopping trolleys provided, and since
he didn't have bags either, he was carrying everything in
his arms. Barely out of childhood, he wasn't really a youth
yet. Although fifteen years old, he looked eleven. He was
thin, ugly, awkward, and his hair was very long. On arriving in Argentina with his parents two years earlier, he had
been struck by the way young men wore their hair long, as
common in the new country as it was rare back home: he

thought it was sublime. Being young, foreign and therefore naïve, he didn't realize that the Argentineans with long hair belonged to the lowest social stratum, and were precisely those who had condemned themselves never to escape from it. But even if he had realized, it wouldn't have mattered to him. He liked the look, and that was that. So he let his hair grow; it already reached half way down his back, below his flat shoulder blades. It looked truly awful. His parents, who were humble, decent people, had unfortunately tried to reason him out of it; if they had threatened him or issued a decree, he would have submitted to the scissors straight away. But no, they began by telling him he looked like a girl, or a lout; and once they had set off on that path, there was no end to it. They couldn't retract their reasoning, which was sound. Besides, they were kind and understanding. They said: "He'll get over it." Meanwhile their son went around looking like a little woman. Since his hair got in the way when he was working, he had thought of putting it in a pony tail with an elastic band, but for the moment he didn't dare. On the building sites no one remarked on it, or even deigned to notice. It really was very common; at least he had been right about that. In Chile, he would have been interviewed on television or, more likely, thrown into prison.

The supermarket was bustling. It was peak hour, on a peak day. The place had been seized by a buying frenzy. People were stripping the shelves bare, to make sure they wouldn't run out of food on New Year's Eve. In the freezers down at the back, he was lucky to find two big packets

of beef ribs, which chilled his hands. He was also carrying a bunch of grilling sausages, a rib cap roast folded into
four, and twelve steaks, all sitting in little white trays and
wrapped in transparent plastic film. He went to the fruit
section and chose two small bags of peaches that seemed
to be fairly ripe, and a dozen bananas. All this was complicated to carry without a bag. And the worst was still
to come. Before getting the bread he went to look at the
ice creams, which were in a deep, trough-like refrigerator. There would have been no point getting ice cream, of
course, because it would have melted well before the time
came to eat it; but those eight-serve tubs of butterscotch
would have been perfect. Two of them would have done
the job. He decided to tell his uncle: maybe someone could
come back for them at the appropriate moment. It was
risky, though, because everything was getting snapped up.
He could only hope that the price would put people off; it
was very high, after all. Now, yes, the bread. It was essential
not just as an accompaniment, but also for resting the meat
on, country-style. To eat like that you need a very sharp
knife, so to keep their blades honed they were always having to call one of those knife sharpeners who go around
blowing on flutes (except that the man who worked in
that neighborhood used an ocarina: he must have been the
only one in Buenos Aires). Every day, Abel was annoyed by
the way they only sold bread in small loaves, barely nine
ounces. Four of those little loaves in plastic bags went on
top of the packets of meat and the fruit, making a precari-

ous pile; they kept slipping off. But what could he do, short of making two trips? Like a father carrying a big baby in his arms, he headed for the drinks section. Unfortunately, since there was no refrigerator on the site, the builders had to do without cold drinks. But you got used to it, the way you get used to all sorts of things. Abel took two big plastic bottles of Coca-Cola, picking them up by the tops with the index finger and thumb of each hand, which was all he had free. The shoppers had increased considerably in number, and movement along the aisles was obstructed by the supermarket employees, who had begun to mop the floor. Abel looked rather out of place among the other clients, with his torn shirt and long hair, holes in his shoes and cement dust on his trousers. It was amazing how skinny he had stayed, with all the strenuous physical work he had to do. At first glance you could have mistaken him for a girl, a little housemaid. His heart sank when he saw the checkout queue: it stretched the full length of the supermarket, about thirty yards, down to the back, around the corner, and all the way up the next aisle to the front again. Although there were three checkouts, only one was in operation today, and the woman operating it was extremely incompetent; even Abel, who was notoriously dopey, had realized that. In fact, the whole supermarket worked in an inefficient and rather arbitrary way. It wasn't run as a commercial enterprise; its aim in serving the clients wasn't to make a profit but to do something else, something religious, though what exactly wasn't clear. It was part of a chain that belonged to an evangelical sect; you could tell by the lack of business sense. Or rather, you could tell by considering any aspect of the supermarket, right down to the finest details, since the whole place was pervaded by the quintessence of the ineffable: religion. It was rumored that attempts were made to indoctrinate young workers from the neighborhood who happened to venture into the supermarket: they were accosted and presented with a videocassette showing the finest performances of the sect's patriarch, a North American pastor. Abel Reyes had not been accosted, although he was the only young worker who went there every day: either they had picked him for a Chilean, and therefore a diehard, fanatical Catholic, or decided he wasn't much of a catch, because of his hair and what it suggested about his character, or, perhaps, they had thought he wouldn't have a video player at home (or that he didn't know English and wouldn't be able to understand the sermons). He went to the end of the queue, slightly hunched, as always, and started moving forward little by little. It was then that he saw his aunt with the children.

It was getting on for midday, a fateful hour for the housewife, and up in the solar oven, Elisa Vicuña was needled by the feeling that the supermarket on the corner, her sole source of provisions, on which she depended absolutely, might shut at twelve: it wouldn't have been surprising, not only because most people were taking half the day off, but also because that supermarket was unpredictable; it could be shut already, or it could stay open till five to midnight. Now, if it was shut, she was in trouble, because she hadn't done even half the shopping for the celebrations that night; so she decided to go and check, although she hadn't planned to do so, in order to avoid a catastrophic surprise. She tried to go on her own, to save time, but the children simply refused to stay with Patri, who she was leaving in charge of the food while she was gone. She had to put shoes on the barefooted ones, and since some of them hadn't even washed their faces and wouldn't cooperate, it took her fifteen minutes to make them more or less presentable (combing their hair and so on). She would never get used to those stairs without banisters, covered with rubble, stones and dust. She carried the baby girl in her arms and the others went down on their own, leaping about, but none of them had ever fallen. There were four children, two boys and two girls; the oldest (a boy) was seven and the youngest (the baby girl) was almost two. She thought they were very pretty, and no doubt they were, with something of their father's manner, and something from their mother's side as well. Elisa was a lady of thirty-five, slim and rather short (slightly shorter than her husband, who wasn't tall), and naturally, given the family's economic status, not very elegantly dressed or presented. On the first floor, where she noticed that the visitors who had been wandering around the site all morning had disappeared, she exchanged a few words with her husband. Then she left, with the children in tow. She made the baby girl walk, which meant she had to go very slowly. The supermarket was just down the street, no more than thirty yards away, on the same side. Still, it was an outing. As always, the children went running around the columns of the brick façade along the side of the supermarket.

As soon as she reached the door she was stunned by the number of people inside. She might have foreseen something similar (although she wasn't given to such predictions), but not so many people, or even half as many. Reality usually outstrips predictions, even if no one has made them. All she could do was remind herself why she had come: to check if they were shutting at midday. Since there was no notice to be seen, she went in to ask. At the counter where they gave coupons in exchange for containers, ten people were waiting, all carrying huge loads of empty bottles and complaining; there was no one to serve them. The kids had already gone down the aisles, as they always did, and disappeared into the crowd. Unruffled, their mother went to look for them, and find someone to ask while she was at it. Elisa Vicuña was that anomaly, not nearly as rare as is often supposed: a mother immune to the terrifying fantasy of losing her children in a crowd. Reality kept proving her right, since she always found them again, if they were ever lost in the first place. She was still holding the baby girl, Jacqueline, by the hand. In the first aisle she went down, threading her way among trolleys and shoppers, she came across the boy who usually served at the bottle counter; he was mopping the floor, with great difficulty because of all the people coming and going. She was relieved when he told her that they would be shutting at four. That meant she could come back after lunch. She continued in her search for the children, looking at packets of food on the way. She was trying to make a mental list. She had to pick up Jacqueline, who had started to whine, and then wanted to get down again as soon as she saw the other kids. The three of them were standing in front of a supermarket employee in a red apron, wearing too much make up, who was handing out little sample cups of coffee to anyone willing to try them. The kids obviously wanted to ask for some, but they didn't dare; she wouldn't have given them any, of course, and they didn't even know what it was. They had never tasted coffee. But they had been overcome by childish curiosity, that craving to receive. Since she was there in the supermarket, Elisa took a bottle of bleach off the shelf, thinking she had run out, or was about to. She consumed a great deal of bleach, because she used it for all her washing. It was a habit of hers. Which explained why all the family's clothes were so faded and had that threadbare look, humble and worn and yet beautifully so. Even if an article of clothing was new, or brightly colored when she bought it, from the very first wash (a night-long soak in bleach) it took on the whitish, delicate and somehow aristocratic appearance that distinguished the clothes of the Viñas family. As soon as she picked up the bottle, however, she realized how absurd it would be to queue for an hour to buy just that; she would go straight to the checkout and ask the person at the head of the queue to let her in, since she only had one item. She gathered the children and told them it was time to go. Whether out of obedience or boredom, they followed. But as it turned out, she didn't even have to go through with the manoeuvre, which often caused a fuss if there happened to be one of those argumentative women at the head of the queue, because she spotted her nephew Abel near the other end, with his arms full of packets and the two big bottles of Coke hanging from his fingers. Poor thing: what an ugly, ridiculous-looking kid, with his hair falling all over his shoulders. He had seen her too, and greeted her from a distance with his polite little smile, reserved, of course, for members of the family. She came over and asked him to do her a favor: buy the bleach (she gave him an austral from her purse) and then bring it up to her. Abel accepted graciously. She looked at what he had bought, and judged it to be insufficient. Tactlessly, she told him so, leaving him there downcast and worried, with the bottle of bleach on the floor, between his feet. Off they went. On the way out, the kids ran into José María on his bicycle. They pleaded raucously with their mother to let them stay and play on the sidewalk for a while, especially the older boy, Juan Sebastián, to whom José María was going to lend the bike. But she took a firm stand, because, as she said, "it was already time for lunch." That little brat was always hanging around in the street. She didn't want to have to come down again in half an hour to look for them. They went on whining, interminably, and in the end she spent fifteen minutes on the corner, talking to the florist, while they ran around. When she went up, dragging the children with her, there was still no sign of her nephew with the bleach.

Abel Reyes was still queuing patiently; his arms had gone numb from the weight. There were some very pretty girls in the queue, and he was watching them to pass the time. But in the most discreet way. He could truthfully have said that girls were what he liked best in the world, but he always admired them from a certain distance, held back by his pathological, adolescent shyness. He also felt that the inevitable stillness of a supermarket queue put him at a disadvantage. Movement was his natural state, albeit the movement of flight. To him, stillness seemed a temporary exception. He advanced step by step, as the train of full trolleys made its very slow way forward. Many of them were full to capacity, with what looked like provisions for a whole year. The people behind and ahead of him in the queue were talking continually. He was the only one who was silent. He couldn't believe that the neutron bomb really existed. Here, for example, how could it eliminate people and not things, since they were so inextricably combined? In a situation like this, a supermarket queue, things were extensions of the human body. Still, since he had nothing better to do, he imagined the bomb. A silent explosion, lots of radiation. Would the harmful radiation get into the packets of food, the boxes and tins? Most likely. An analogy for death by neutron bomb occurred to him: you're at home, listening to the radio, and a song begins to play; then you go out, and you hear the same song coming from the window of a house down the street. A block further on, a car drives past with the song playing on its radio. You catch a bus, the radio is on, and what do you hear but the same song, still going—without meaning to, you've practically heard it all. Everyone hears the radio (at some point during the day) and many people have it tuned in to the same station. For some reason this struck him as an exact analogy, supernaturally exact; only the effects were different. These thoughts helped him to while away the time. As usual, the trolleys just in front of him took longer than the others; the woman at the checkout even went to the bathroom and left them standing there for ten extra minutes. But everything comes to pass. Finally, it was his turn. It was a relief to put his shopping down on the metal counter. The cashier pressed the wrong buttons on the electronic register a couple of times, as she had done with almost all the clients. Every time she made a mistake she had to call the supervisor, who pushed through the hostile multitude and used a key to cancel the error. It came to forty-nine australs. Abel paid with a fifty-austral note, and the cashier asked if he didn't have any change. He rummaged in his pockets, but of course he had no change, not a cent. The note he had given her was all the money he had brought. The cashier hesitated, looking grief-stricken. Don't you? she asked. She stared as if urging him to check. Abel had noticed that the cashiers at this supermarket (maybe it was the same everywhere) made a huge fuss about change. They always had plenty, but they still made a fuss. In this case there was really no reason: she only had to give him one austral. He was waiting, holding the one-austral note his aunt had given him, folded in four. The cashier looked at the note. So that she could see it wasn't hiding forty-eight others, Abel unfolded it for her. In the end she lifted the little metal clip holding down the one-austral notes in the register (there were at least two hundred), extracted one with utter disgust, ripped off the receipt and handed it over without even looking at him. He went straight for the door, forgetting his shopping, which was still on the counter. The woman behind him in the queue, who had started to pile her purchases on top of his, called out: Why did you pay for this stuff if you don't want to take it away? Back he came, mortally embarrassed, and gathered it all up as best he could. He dropped the little loaves of bread, and various other things. By the time he got back to the site, the truck had gone, and they were waiting for him with the fire alight under the grill. His uncle and another builder, an Argentinean named Aníbal Fuentes, or Aníbal Soto (curiously, he was known by both names), who were the designated grillers, tossed the meat onto the grill, a rectangular piece of completely black wire mesh. What's that? Viñas asked him, pointing at the bottle of bleach. It's for Auntie Elisa, Abel replied, I'll just take it up to her. They asked him to get some things while he was there, glasses and so on. He disappeared up the stairs. Since the architect had left, Viñas decided to close up the wooden fence, and put the chain on, but not the lock. Now, at last, they could have their lunch in peace.

It's strange that they hadn't bought any wine, isn't it? Especially since some of the men were committed wine-drinkers. But there were two reasons why the builder's young butler hadn't even thought of buying any: first, they didn't drink wine at lunchtime as a rule, except occasionally on a Saturday, when as well as knocking off early they had something to celebrate, like a birthday. The second reason was that Raúl Viñas bought all the wine himself at a store in the neighborhood, where they had a special bottling system, and recycled the bottles over and over, which worked out to be very practical and cheap. He had already laid in provisions for that day, and for the next day as well. It was an extra special occasion: for a start, they were stopping work early, so they could drink their fill if they wanted to. Afterward they would be going to their respective homes to get ready for the party that night, a big family do. There was also something to celebrate, of course, because it was the end of the year. Overall it had been a memorable year, a year of work and relative prosperity; they couldn't complain about that. It could even have been called a year of happiness, although not straight away; they would have to wait some time for that to become apparent, in retrospect. It wasn't over yet: there were ten hours left, to be precise. So Raúl Viñas was keeping fourteen bottles of red wine cool, with a system he had invented, or rather discovered, himself. It consisted of resolutely approaching a ghost and inserting a bottle into his thorax, where it remained, supernaturally balanced. When he went back for it, say two hours later, it

was cold. There were two things he hadn't noticed, however. The first was that, during the cooling process, the wine
came out of the bottles and flowed like lymph all through
the bodies of the ghosts. The second was that this distilla-
tion transmuted ordinary cheap wine, fermented in cement
vats, into an exquisite, matured cabernet sauvignon, which
not even captains of industry could afford to drink every
day. But an undiscriminating drinker like Viñas, who chilled
his red wine in summer just because of the heat, wasn't
going to notice the change. Besides, he was accustomed to
the wonderful wines of his country, so it seemed perfectly
natural to him. And, indeed, what could be more natural
than to drink the best wines, always and only the best?

When Abel Reyes reached the top floor (curiously,
climbing the stairs never seemed to cost him any effort: he
let his mind wander, and before he knew it, he was there)
he found his uncle's children in the middle of their lunch.
The caretaker's apartment had been minimally fitted out,
ahead of the rest of the building, to make it livable for Viñas
and his family. But not much had been done, just the bare
minimum. No tiles on the floor, no plaster on the ceiling,
or paint on the walls; no fittings in the bathroom, or glass
in the windows. But there was running water (although it
hadn't been running for long), and electricity from a pre-
cariously rigged-up cable. That was all they needed. There
were two medium-sized rooms, plus the kitchen and bathroom. All the furniture was borrowed and rudimentary. The
children were sitting around a homemade table, with chops

and peas on their plates. They didn't want to eat, of course. In front of Patri were four glasses, a bottle of soda water, and a carton of orange juice. She was looking severely at her half-siblings, who were looking at the glasses and whimpering. The idea was to make them understand that unless they ate, they wouldn't get anything to drink. They were dying of thirst, they said. Their mother was making macaroons in the kitchen, and had switched off for the moment. Patri, being younger, had more patience; in fact, since she was still a child in some ways, she was patient to a fault, and rose to the children's challenge, refusing to yield a drop. Trying all their options with a wicked cunning, they cried out to their mother. But Elisa didn't respond, not just because she was in the kitchen; her mind was elsewhere. All of a sudden Patri filled the glasses with juice and soda and distributed them. The children drank eagerly. She finished her chop and peas, and had a drink as well. The baby girl, sitting by her side, wanted to leave the table. Patri picked her up and began to spoon-feed her. The others started getting rowdy. Juan Sebastián, the eldest, had eaten more than the others, but still not finished his meal. The older girl, Blanca Isabel, hadn't even started, and was already asking for more to drink. The heat in the dining room was intense, but the light was very mild, because the window was covered with a piece of cardboard. The sun was beating on the cardboard, which was thick, but seemed to be slightly translucent. That summer light is incredibly strong.

What could you do to cool off up there? Well, nothing.

It was pure heat, perfectly real and concrete. Beyond the shadow of a doubt. And yet, if not shored up by eternities of faith, it would have crumbled to a puff of ice-dust. Having drunk a glass of soda water and juice, not so much because she was thirsty, but to set an example for the children, Patri was suddenly covered in perspiration. Blanca Isabel, who didn't miss a thing, said, Did you go for a dip? Thinking it wouldn't have such a spectacular effect, Patri helped herself to another glass. Feeling she had done it to taunt them, Juan Sebastián leapt to his feet and ran to the kitchen to tell his mother, who paid him no attention. They all started crying out for more to drink. You'll have to make do with tap water, because that's all there is left, said Patri, showing them the remaining soda. She gathered up the glasses again to make orangeade, with the dregs, in equal quantities, but only for those who would eat. They made an effort, and she even had to cut the remains of Ernesto and Blanca Isabel's chops into little pieces. Elisa looked out and asked if they had finished. The meat, said Patri, but not the peas. Sebastián was the only one who had polished off his meal, but what a performance it had been. His mother asked him if he wanted any more. He replied with a groan: he had eaten so much, he was full, stuffed. Patri distributed the glasses. The children emptied them in the blink of an eye. She left Jacqueline on her chair and went to the kitchen to get the grapes. It's the same every day, she said to Elisa: they just don't want to eat. It's because of the heat, Elisa replied, poor things. She asked Patri if she wanted to finish the peas. Echoing the children, she said she couldn't. But wasn't Elisa going to have anything? She hadn't even sat down. No, she said, she wasn't hungry. Although, in the end, she ate the plate of leftover peas, because she hated to waste them. Patri went back into the dining room with the grapes and a clean knife, with which she cut them in half and took out the seeds. Each child received one grape at a time, and Jacqueline's took a bit longer, because she had to remove the skin as well. Luckily she was good with her hands.

Abel went straight to the kitchen and put the bottle of bleach on the bench for his aunt. There was a big skylight in the ceiling, and at that hour of the day, the sun was shining straight into it. Elisa had covered it with a blue towel, which had been wet for a while. That might have afforded some protection from the heat, but in any case it was stifling, especially since she had been cooking. She asked Abel if he was going to stay and eat with the men. Well I'm not going to leave now, am I, he said, as if it were obvious. Have you told your mother? No, he hadn't, why? Because she'll be expecting you, she said. It hadn't occurred to him. But Abel said he didn't think she would, since he hadn't told her about the half-holiday. She might have worked that out for herself, said Elisa. I don't think so, I don't think so, said Abel impatiently. His aunt didn't really know his mother, he thought. She didn't realize that his mother didn't look after him the way she looked after her children, or even her nieces and nephews. Like all adolescents, he believed that any family was preferable to his own. The belief was entirely unfounded, but he held it all the same. Elisa had guessed all this, and let it pass. She asked him who they had invited for the New Year celebrations. Abel replied: his elder brother's girlfriend and her family. And he launched into a detailed description of those potential relatives, making them out to be the epitome of all the virtues and powers. His brother's future brother-in-law had an auto-repair shop, and Abel liked to portray him as a big shot, someone who could do just what he liked, whatever took his fancy, because he had the means. He ran through a detailed catalogue of the big shot's properties, exaggerating outrageously. Because of some subtle bias in the subject, or subjects in general, property led on to food. Abel believed that he had very special tastes, worthy of careful study, without which they might seem a mere jumble of preferences. Elisa let him go on, but her mind soon wandered. There was no point feeling too sorry for him just because he was ugly and stupid. She made a suggestion: it would be best not to drink wine at lunch. They're all going to end up trashed, those animals, she said. I never drink wine, said Abel, with a characteristic lack of tact (he was speaking to the wife of the biggest drunk in the family!). When Patri came in to get the grapes, they greeted each other with a kiss. She thought he was ridiculous, but was quite fond of him. They always laughed about him behind his back, because of his hair. Her hair and his were the same length, and even the same kind: slightly coarse, straight and black. When the girl went out, he chatted on and on with Elisa, until, fed up, she told him to go down, because the men would probably have started eating already.

When they had finished the grapes, the children escaped, without shoes, and went to play in the empty swimming pool, which was in full sun. But they loved it, almost as if the pool were full and they were splashing about in cool water. The three older children were always playing make-believe adventure games, and the baby girl tagged along. She was always there, and was sometimes useful, as a victim, for example, a role that didn't require much skill, or none at all. After various days of other scenarios, they had returned to car racing. They had a number of little plastic cars. Their childish instincts had alerted them to the silence below, where the builders had stopped working, so they ventured down the stairs to the sixth floor, and then to the fifth. The cars went down the stairs in little hands and parked in the farthest rooms. Excited to have the whole building to themselves, or at least the upper floors, the children complicated their game, leaving a car on one floor and going down to the next, then coming back up to look for it, taking unfamiliar routes. A building site was the least appropriate place for a car race (although ideal for hide and seek), and yet the adverse conditions made the game special, giving it a novel, impossible flavor, which made them forget everything else. They felt they had gone straight to the heart of truth or art. Jacqueline kept getting lost and crying. Ernesto, who was specially attached to her, went to the rescue, up or down, depending on where he was. The only interruption occurred when Abel said, Careful not to fall, and continued on his way down to the ground floor. When he was two floors below them, they began to call out "Mophead!" Then they resumed their game with the toy cars, going up and down. A breeze was blowing over those superposed platforms, but it was slight and not very refreshing; in any case the heat would probably begin to ease off once the sun began to go down. The light must have been changing, gradually, but it wasn't noticeable; the brightly-colored toy cars were the light-meters in the children's game. They went down to the third floor, but didn't dare go any further, because they could hear the men's voices.

All the builders had, in fact, gone downstairs a fair while before, and since they wouldn't be returning to work, had washed and changed, to make themselves more comfortable for lunch. The radicals among them had hosed themselves down and dried off in the sun, out in the back yard. They had taken off their work clothes, which, once shed, were so many dusty, torn and mended (or not even mended) rags, and packed them away in their bags. Clean now, hair combed, they sat down around a table made of planks to wait for lunch. They had put the table as far away as possible from the grill, where Aníbal Soto was checking on the progress of the meat. There were ten of them in all. As well as Viñas and Reyes, there were two other Chileans: Enrique Castro and Felipe Rojas. Rojas was known as Pocketman because he was in the habit of keeping his hands in his pockets, even when he was sitting down. It was a pretext for endless jokes. Now, for example, he was sitting with a glass in his left hand and his right hand in his pocket. Next to him was the fat guy from Santiago del Estero, who although by no means an ingenious joker, could get a laugh by dint of sheer ingenuity. He put his hand into the Chilean's pocket to find out what was so nice in there, as he put it. This made all the others laugh, and gave Pocketman a start, making him spill a few drops of wine, which he complained about. The master builder, a short man with grey hair and blue eyes (he was Italian) was convulsed with laughter, but he knew how to change the subject in time. They had all served themselves a glass of wine and were drinking it as an aperitif. Luckily it was cool down there; it was almost like having air conditioning. They drank a toast, and so on. The meat was soon ready, but they had clean forgotten to make a salad. Reproachful gazes converged on young Reyes, who almost always forgot to buy something or other. But, since it was the last day of the year, it didn't matter. Anyway, the meat was first-class.

As well as the Chileans, there was another foreigner, a Uruguayan called Washington Mena; he was an insignificant person, without any noteworthy characteristics. The other one with long hair was a young Argentinean, about twenty, called Higinio Gómez (Higidio, actually, but he said Higinio because it was less embarrassing), who was spectactularly ugly: he had what used to be called a "pock-marked" face, due in fact to a case of chronic acne, as well

as that long hair, almost as long as Abel's, but curly. Then
there was one they called The Bullshit Artist behind his
back, although his name was Carlos Soria. While the others
laughed at the fat guy's joke, he just mumbled and ended up
making openly sarcastic remarks. The joker from Santiago
del Estero turned out to be the most curious character of
them all, partly, in fact mainly, because he was spherically
fat. That transformed him. He also fancied himself as a wit
and even a Don Juan. His name was Lorenzo Quincata; he
spoke very little and always gave careful consideration to
what he was going to say, but even so, no one would have
mistaken him for an intelligent young man.

Soria started running down Santiago del Estero and its
inhabitants. They let him talk, but teased him all the while.
He said that in Santiago they drank hot beer. Really? How
come? He'd been there, of course, passing through; nothing could have persuaded him to stay on those sweltering
plains. One day, in a bar, he had sampled that strange bev-
erage (strange for him, anyway). They used a wheelbarrow to bring the beer in from the yard, where it had been
sitting in full sun; it was hot like soup, he said. Someone
asked him: Why the wheelbarrow? To bring the cartons
in, of course, what else could they use? How many cartons, they asked, suspecting him of exaggerating. First he
said thirty-six, then he said eight, but it wasn't really clear
which number he meant. He pointed out that there had
been twenty people drinking. Some of the builders were
laughing so hard they cried. That'd have to be a record,

wouldn't it, they said. If he drank thirty-six cartons of hot beer all on his own.

Only in Santiago del Estero . . . , said Raúl Viñas, laughing too. He clinked his glass with Quincata. Viñas was a Santiago man himself, he explained, but from Santiago de Chile, which made all the difference.

Soria pointed out once again that there were twenty people drinking, a whole team of road workers. The cartons of bottles were sitting in the yard, out in the sun. Did they know what his belly was like, after drinking it? Well, round, of course. As for how it felt, best not to imagine that, or even try. And yet they did.

Castro reminded Viñas about a famous liar they had known in Chile, a man who, whenever he met someone, would say that that he had just crossed the Andes from Argentina, braving extremely risky or at least unusual conditions, coming through unlikely passes, or right over the mountain peaks, crossing snowfields, always on foot, alone, setting off on the spur of the moment. Each time he ran into someone he knew, he came out with the same story, or rather, a variation. But sometimes he ran into the same person again quite soon afterward, and then he had to invent the opposite journey, since he couldn't always be crossing from Argentina into Chile, without crossing back the other way at least occasionally, indeed just as often, even in the world of the imagination with its somewhat flexible laws. It was a pretext for doubling his lies.

"Lorenzo", they felt, was an incongruous name. They all

thought it suited its owner, but at the first stirring of doubt, they flipped over to the opposite opinion. It was the same with "Washington," and again with "Higinio," and so on through the names, even the commonest ones, like "Abel," "Raúl" and "Juan." It would have been absurd to claim that people looked like examples of their names, and yet, in a curious way, they did. The worst (or the best) thing was that in any given case you could convince yourself of a name's appropriateness or inappropriateness simply by listening to the other person's arguments, and if that became the norm, even within a small community of friends or colleagues, it would be like seeing ghosts emerge. They were pouring out wine for familiar ghosts. (The real ones had disappeared a while before, as they did every day when the smell of meat rose from the grill, as if it were detrimental to them. But they would reappear later on, more active than ever, at siesta time, which was the high point of their day, in summer at least; in winter, it was dusk.)

This reminded the master builder of certain regrettable episodes from the past; some of the men present had been working with him for quite a few years, and they joined in the reminiscing. There was the time they had put up a building, like this one, or even bigger, with materials and tools that were hopelessly inadequate, especially the tools. You know the way there's always some liar exaggerating outrageously, he said. Well, it was really like that. But in this case, the witnesses, including Carlitos Soria (The Bullshit Artist), were not going to let him get away with lying.

Which building? they asked him. The one on Quintino Bocayuva. Oh, that one! They all remembered how terrible it had been. Torture. Instead of ... just about everything, really, they had had to make do with, well, anything at all, whatever came to hand. Instead of wheelbarrows, they used some old baby carriages they found dumped in a vacant lot. Instead of buckets, flowerpots (they had to block up the hole in the bottom). And it was the same with everything else: a truly abject scramble for makeshift solutions, which had scarred them for life.

In less than an hour, and the time flew by because of the interesting conversation, every last mouthful of food disappeared, including the bananas and the peaches and the bread. There was really nothing strange about that: the whole idea was to eat it up. With the wine, however, it was different. In a sense, drinking it was not the whole idea. And yet that is what they had been doing, and they continued: instead of coffee after the meal, they had a glass of wine, or two. The drinking, in fact, had become absolute. Inevitably, though, some drank more than others. The three adult Chileans (young Abel Reyes was drinking Coca-Cola) were the quickest, and so attained the highest level of stupefaction, to the point where they could hardly say a coherent good-bye when the others began to leave. And yet they still had some more drinking to do. They did it sitting down, staring into space, smiling vaguely. The others finally vanished, and the three of them underwent a kind of collapse. They felt as if they had imbibed the whole world, but in tiny doses, or as if a joy outside of them had begun to spin, sweeping them up. And, what is more, although they were off their faces by now, it seemed they could go on drinking, go on filling the glasses and lifting them to their lips. At least they still had that feeling, like a giant smile inside each one of them.

At four in the afternoon, just after the last of the builders had gone, Elisa came down to see what state her husband was in. She had to look around twice to find him, slumped as he was. She wasn't too alarmed, but she did check to see if there were any others left. And sure enough, the other two Chileans were there. As it happened, Pocketman emerged from a brief spell of unconsciousness and volunteered to help get her husband upstairs. She accepted: Raúl Viñas had come around sufficiently for the two of them to suffice. Almost restored to his normal lucidity by the climb, Pocketman offered to chain up the gate from the outside, although he wouldn't be able to lock it. After saying good-bye, he went back down. The remaining Chilean, Castro, was still sleeping, but when Pocketman gave him a shake, he woke up completely, if in a bad mood, and since they were both going in the same direction, and a fair way (they had to take the train), they headed off together, placidly, though not entirely steady on their legs. Pocketman kept his promise of chaining up the gate, so unless someone took the trouble of looking for the absent lock, the building appeared to be securely shut. It wasn't really, but there weren't any passersby. It was siesta time, the quietest and most deserted time of day, and the hottest. The silence was complete.

When the man of the house was peacefully unconscious in bed, covered only with a fine sweat of wine, Elisa asked Patri if she could do her a favor, a big favor (she stressed these last words with a certain irritation), and go fetch the children, who shouldn't have run off in the first place. Patri, who was a model of good manners and respect, repressed a "huh!" but couldn't quite stifle a sigh, which made her feel immediately ashamed, although it had been as faint as a breeze in the far heights of the sky. Elisa, who was deeply Chilean in this as in all other respects, could perceive the subtlest shades of an intention. So she added a comment, to compensate for the unfortunate tone of her request—or, at least, to unhinge it and let it swing loose beyond, where the real words are, which have no meaning or force to compel. It was amazing, she said, that even in this heat they still had the energy to run off. Playing excited them so much they just couldn't get enough. It was the equivalent of "living" for adults: you're not going to decide to die when night comes just because you've been living all day. Patri smiled. Also, they had been up early, said her mother; and lack of sleep, which makes adults slow and drowsy, makes kids restless. But they'd have to take a nap, or they'd be unbearable at night. Patri couldn't promise that she'd be able to get Juan Sebastián to go to bed, or even his buddy Blanca Isabel. The older boy hated the siesta. Elisa thought for a moment. She had, in fact, seen them when she was coming upstairs with her husband. She regretted not having told them to follow her. Each time they saw their father in that state, they thought he was sick and about to die; she could have exploited that momentary terror and shut them away in the dark. With a bit of an effort, they could get to sleep. If they ran off, it was hopeless. Luckily there was no danger of them getting out into the street. For some reason, that danger didn't exist. There was the possibility of a fall, from any of the floors, since the building was still a concrete frame, with just a few internal walls in place, not all of them, by any means. But neither mother nor daughter mentioned that possibility; it didn't even enter into their private reflections. They had once said that an adult was just as likely to fall as a child; there was no difference, because the planet's gravitational force worked in the same way on both. It was like asking which weighed more, a kilo of lead or a kilo of feathers. And that's why they were vaguely but deeply revolted by the way the owners of the apartments took such care not to let their children approach the edges when they visited, like that morning. If that was how they felt, why were they buying the apartments in the first place? Why didn't they go and live in houses at ground level? "We're different," they thought, "we're Chilean."

But there was an easier way to do it after all, said Elisa, and that was to take away the toy cars. Without them, there would be no reason to remain at large. If she knew her children, and she was sure she did, it was bound to work. It had sometimes worked for her in the past. Patri said they would hide them. Her mother bent down calmly (they were at the door of the little apartment, talking in hushed voices, unnecessarily, since Viñas was sound asleep), and picked up the cardboard box full of toys. With an expert hand, she began to rummage through it. She knew every one of her children's toys. "The big yellow one, the red one, the little blue truck . . ." She calculated that exactly four were currently in their possession. She even told Patri which ones. But Patri wasn't paying much attention. She didn't think it would be possible to recover all the cars, and so bring in the children. As long as they still had one, just one, Juan Sebastián would stay awake all through the siesta, the little devil.

She went downstairs to the sixth floor. The quickest way to do it was to check the floors one by one, room by room. If they heard her, they would try to hide. She set about it systematically, but it was hard to concentrate because the heat and the time of day had dazed her. The sixth floor seemed endless. Her chances of finding anything in that void perpetually full of air were minimal, given the terrible brightness, which she had grown so used to, living up there as summer set in, that her pupils had shrunk permanently to pin-points. She didn't understand the arrangement of the rooms, which wasn't clear at that stage of the construction; but she felt there were too many of them. The trend toward having more and more rooms was, she felt, absurd. A family couldn't observe the protocol of a royal court. If people started multiplying rooms by their needs, they could float away into the infinite and never touch the ground of reality again. One for sewing, another for embroidery; one for eating, one for drinking, one for each activity, in short. The same room reproduced over and over, each one fulfilling some silly requirement, as if in a perpetually receding mirror. Her mother had put it very well, except that she hadn't gone far enough in her generalization. Because the illusion of exhaustivity affected things as well as people. In any case, the children weren't there.

When she went down to the fifth floor, she was already tired and her eyelids felt heavy, which surprised her slightly, since she didn't like the siesta—she was still a child in that respect. Having washed the lunch dishes and left the miniscule rooftop apartment impeccably clean and tidy (in so far as they could, given that it was still under construction), she and her mother had watched television. She would have liked to go on watching, but the time slot for the kind of show they preferred had come to an end, and the ones that were starting required a different kind of attention.

It might seem odd that at lunchtime, when Abel Reyes came up, his cousin Patri had greeted him with a kiss. A kiss on the cheek was a normal enough greeting; what might seem odd is that they needed to greet one another, when he had been working in the building since early that morning. But, as it happened, they hadn't seen each other, which was not unusual, because she hardly ever went down. Her mother did the shopping, and rarely needed help. Patri went down once a day, if that. She helped a lot around the apartment, watched television, and looked after her half-brothers and -sisters. She was pretty much a homebody, like all Chileans, except when they are tireless travelers (she was a bit of both). She was fifteen; her surname was Vicuña, like her mother's, because she had been born when her mother was single. Very quiet, very serious, pretty hands.

They weren't on the fifth floor either, as she was able to verify (or so she thought), by checking from the front to the back, room by room. The children weren't there, but the other characters, those bothersome ghosts, were legion. They were always around at that time. To see them, you just had to go and look. Although they kept their distance, with an air of unaccountable haughtiness. For some mysterious reason, they had started shouting, bursting into thunderous peals of laughter that shook the sky. Patri wouldn't have paid them any more attention than usual, if not for two rather particular circumstances. The first was that there weren't just two or three or four ghosts, as one might have expected, given their characteristic and constitutive rarity, but a veritable multitude, appearing here and there, then moving away, laughing and shouting all the while like exploding balloons. The second circumstance was even more remarkable: they were looking at her. Normally they didn't look; they didn't seem to pay attention to anything in particular, or even to have attention. They were like that now too, except that they seemed to be making an exception for her, as if she were the object of their ostentatious, senseless amusement. She didn't take offence, because it wasn't serious. It was more like a flying puppet show, an out-of-place, unseemly kind of theater. She had seen naked men before, of course (although not many); she didn't find that especially frightening. But there was something implausible about it, since you wouldn't normally see men without clothes except in particular situations. The way they were floating in the air accentuated the ambivalent impression. She had occasionally heard them speak, and wondered about it afterward, for a while. It seemed easy enough to take them by surprise, to slip past behind them. But perhaps it wasn't so easy.

She leant out over the front balcony and looked down at the empty street. A car whizzed past. She went through the apartment, searching for the children, until she reached the back, and looked down from there as well. The sun was beating in; it was an oven. She thought she saw a body falling, even faster than they normally do, the naked body of a ghost, covered with fine, white dust. It might have been an optical illusion, but she knew it wasn't when she heard another volley of guffaws, a great choral outburst of laughter so loud it was almost desperate. When she turned back toward the stairs, they were there again, or had just appeared, some swinging back and forth stupidly, like garlands, others perfectly balanced—they all were, in fact, it was just that they were using different methods. A quick movement behind her and a touch that felt particularly real made her swing around suddenly. It was Blanca Isabel, looking at her with a fading surprise. She was a pretty girl, an exception in the family, lively, and very intelligent according to her parents. Although she was startled and must have guessed why her sister had come downstairs, a smile was hovering around her lips: she thought she had caught Patri peeking at a forbidden sight. She looked as if she were about to start humming. Patri didn't feel that she had been "peeking" at the ghost's genitalia, not at all. Their laughter proved her innocence. "Now we're going to take a nap," Patri said energetically, although she too was disconcerted. It was a bad tactic, because Blanca Isabel didn't feel like a nap, and ran away. She reached the stairs before Patri, and started going down, whispering something to the others, who must have been nearby. Patri knew she had to hurry if she wanted to catch them, but she was half-hearted about it. It was too hot, and she was tired. So she listened, helplessly, as they scattered. Nevertheless her momentum carried her to the stairwell. Juan Sebastián was looking up at her from the next landing, ready to go down to the third floor. "Let's go," she said, "or Mom will come and get you." "Why?" he replied. Children always ask why. "Because you have to take a nap." "I don't know how. How do you do it?" "Where are the others?" "How should I know?" Patri started going down and the boy took off. He was already down on the next floor. She'd be able to corner him eventually, if he went all the way down. But the rascal knew hiding places with two escape routes, so the chase could go on forever. It was no good. She raised her voice again hoping to scare him into submission. She was irritated and couldn't understand why he had to run away. She wasn't going any further. What a stupid, childish thing to be doing, chasing kids around at siesta time! If they didn't want to sleep, why should they? It made no difference to her, or to their health, why would it? But since she had come down to the fourth floor, she could fetch the baby girl, at least.

Luckily for her, little Ernesto was there, looking at her with his beautiful big, dark eyes. Hi, he said, as if hiding something. There was a wet patch on the wall, at a height that indicated clearly what had happened. The children were forbidden to urinate anywhere inside the building, but they did it anyway. She shook her head disapprovingly. I took out my weenie and did it, said the boy. I know how it works, but your dad's going to tell you off. My dad did it too. Here? she asked him. He looked around, mildly perplexed. He seemed to mean two things: first, "all the floors look the same to me" and, second, "they all take out their weenies." He was letting his thoughts show in that gentle, docile way because sleepiness was overcoming him irresistibly. And both aspects of his excuse were reasonable, in a way. The mood of summery exhibitionism prevailing on the site, accentuated perhaps by the imperfect, deceptive repetition from one floor to the next, didn't shock Patri (even she wasn't that naïve) so much as intrigue her. She'd seen the gangs of ghosts shaking their sturdy members and aiming the jets of urine at the sky, showering it over the first-floor patio (their favorite place for this sport) until rainbows with a metallic sheen appeared in the siesta's white glare. The day the big satellite dish was installed on the terrace, they spent hours doing it, perched on the edge.

You get to bed, or Mom's going to smack you, she said. Compliantly, half-asleep, Ernesto headed for the stairs. Where's Jacqueline, she asked? The two youngest children were never far apart. He shrugged his shoulders. Patri called her. I'm going, she said finally. She followed the little boy up the stairs. When she was half way up, Blanca Isabel appeared behind her, with the baby girl in her arms, intending to move her to a safe place on the third floor. Patri turned around and started back down. The movement was enough to make Blanca Isabel deposit her sister and take off alone, jumping down the stairs three at a time. Jacqueline burst into tears. As soon as Patri picked her up, she calmed down. She put her arms around Patri's neck and rested her head on her shoulder. She weighed nothing at all. Amazingly, she was still the size of a doll at the age of two. But, in fact, it was like that with all children. They might be relatively big or small for their age, but, compared to an adult, they were always tiny. They were human in every way, but on another scale. And that alone could render them unrecognizable, or give the impression that they had been produced by the baffling distortions of a dream. As Ernesto had said a moment ago: the weenie. That must be why children were always playing with scaled-down models of things: cars, houses, people. A miniature theater, with its doors opening and closing, over and over again. The previous night, on television, they had seen *The Kiss'n Cuddle Love Show*, in which two puppets, a frog and a bear recited the names of the birthday boys and girls, and those who had written in. They never missed the show, although they had never written in themselves. Anyway, the puppets appeared on a tiny scene, with two window shutters instead of a curtain, which opened when their act began, and closed again at the end. In the course of normal distracted viewing, Patri had assumed that the shutters opened on their own, as they seemed to do, or were pushed from the inside, or something like that. But last night a problem with the lighting or the general clumsiness of the production had allowed her to see that the white shutters were opened by hands in white gloves, which were supposed to be invisible. The children didn't realize, but she did. Her mother noticed too, and although they said nothing, both she and Patri thought of the ghosts. They said nothing because it wasn't worth the effort of opening their mouths. But now, in retrospect, Patri felt that the incident had a sexual significance, or connotations at least.

She asked Ernesto what game they had been playing. We were pretending that the people who came this morning were our parents. She sighed in disapproval. Appalling! That must have been the older two children; they were always coming up with ideas like that, the little devils.

The third floor was the same, yet different; it wrapped the three of them in a fresh layer of silence. They say that silence increases with height, but Patri, who lived at altitude most of the time, wasn't so sure about that. Anyway, if it was true, and if there was a gradual increase, the difference between one floor and the next should have been perceptible, at least for someone with a sensitive enough ear, a musician, for example, listening in reverse, as it were. As she went from the fourth to the fifth floor, she felt the silence thicken, but that didn't prove anything, because the data of reality, as she had observed in the past, were produced by chance, or rather by an inextricable accumulation of chances. Also, since it's well known that sounds rise (which must be because "they're lighter than air," as the saying goes, or a lighter kind of air), you should hear more noise as you go up; it should be quiet on the ground. True, sounds fade progressively as they rise, because height is a kind of distance. But under normal circumstances, human beings are at or near ground level. If a man were placed at a great height, and he looked down, somewhere near halfway he would see two corresponding limits, floating like magnetized Cartesian divers: the limit of the sound as it passed into imperceptibility, and that of his own hearing range. But those divers ... men floating in the air ... she knew what *that* was about. And speaking of noise (and magnetism too, come to think of it), the most clamorous and disturbing noises she had heard in her months on the site had been made by cats. The neighborhood was populated by strays. Their survival and proliferation were favored by the gardens of the Theological University, the car bodies that the police left permanently parked all along in front of the station, the square a hundred yards away, the convent school's enormous park (the size of a whole block) with its luxuriant foliage, and, above all, the empty buildings, each with its clientele of old witches who came twice a day to put out milk and hamburger steak. The way the cats howled was beyond belief. At first she had thought they were children gone crazy. But that wouldn't have been so bad. The inhumanity of the cats' screams gave them something extra. And their speed, because those sounds were produced in the course of races and escapes, as opposed to the karateka's shout, which issues from a still body. (Patri had taken karate lessons in Chile, on the advice of her stepfather. For various reasons, including her innate distaste for perfection, she had neglected to sit the exam which would have given her a blue belt. Even though blue was her favorite color.) The astonishing activity of the cats, obscene as it was, reminded her of the ghosts, who manifested themselves as the opposite of obscenity, as a kind of innocence.

In fact, they were manifesting themselves at that very moment. They were emerging from the light, from transparency: they were opaque, definitely opaque, but because of the whiteness of the cement dust, they were hard to distinguish from the light. Where could their covering have come from? It was true that everything was dusty on the building site, but the strange thing about the ghosts was how evenly covered they were with that white dust, every square inch of them. And there was quite a lot to cover because they were tall like Argentineans, and solidly built, even chubby. Although well proportioned in general, some of them, the majority in fact, had big bellies. Even their lips were powdered; even the soles of their feet! Only at odd moments, from certain points of view, could you see the foreskin at the tips of their penises parting to reveal a tiny circle of bright red, moist skin. It was the only touch of color on their bodies. Even birds fluttering around in ashes don't achieve such a uniform result. Patri traversed the air through which they had flowed, unworried by the thought of her breath mixing with theirs. She was walking on the ground. What a destiny: unwittingly, unwillingly thrust into the midst of a nudist colony.

Tired and annoyed, she paid them no attention. She was sleepy too; since she was barely out of childhood herself, she still needed quite a lot of sleep. She felt she had wasted time, but, on the other hand, it was time that was good for nothing except being wasted. That was in the nature of siesta-time. The mysterious men were watching her from a certain distance, but she couldn't really be bothered returning their gaze. The laughter, at least, had dissipated. There was something aloof and severe about those insubstantial gangs. They were simply there.

Elisa was waiting for them at the top of the stairs. What about the others? was the first thing she asked. Ernesto started to explain, but Patri shrugged her shoulders. I couldn't catch them, she said. They got away. Mother and daughter were silently resigned. Elisa took the children inside. It's so hot! said the boy, yielding to the truth. She put them in the bedroom, where their father was snoring. She didn't even wash their feet; in a few seconds they were perfectly quiet. In the dining room, Patri saw the bags left out, and remembered that there was shopping to do. When Elisa came out of the bedroom, she offered to go and do it, with a list. No, said her mother, I have to do it myself this time, because I still haven't worked out exactly what I'm going to buy; it'll depend what's there. No one made a fuss about meals in that family, as long as they were nutritious and tasty. On the way, Elisa added, I'll look for the other two and take them along. That was a good idea. But then she said: Since they're not going to sleep, I'll take them for ice cream. Patri frowned as if to say: Well that's a great way to punish them for misbehaving. *She* didn't get any ice cream, even though she loved it. You lie down too, said her mother. I guess that's what I'll be doing, she replied. Elisa put on her shoes and picked up the bags. Back in a bit. See you, said Patri.

Off she went. Patri removed the crochet rug with which she covered the sofa that was her bed. She pushed the chairs up against the table. She took off her dress and got under the sheet. It was uncomfortable, because of the heat, but it was the prudent thing to do, because that room was the entrance to the little apartment, and anyone could have come along. It was boiling hot. The silence had deepened and was almost complete, with a just a vague echo of cackling, which made her even sleepier. She shut her eyes straight away. And fell asleep.

She dreamed of the building on top of which she was sleeping, not as it would be later on, not seeing it finished and inhabited, but as it was now, that is, under construction. It was a calm vision, devoid of troubling portents or inventions, almost a verification of the facts. But there is always a difference between dreams and reality, which becomes clearer as the superficial contrast diminishes. The difference in this case was reflected in the architecture, which is, in itself, a reciprocal mirroring of what has already been built and what will be built eventually. The all-important bridge between the two reflections was provided by a third term: the unbuilt.

The unbuilt is characteristic of those arts whose realization requires the remunerated work of many people, the purchase of materials, the use of expensive equipment, etc. Cinema is the paradigmatic case: anyone can have an idea for a film, but then you need expertise, finance, personnel, and these obstacles mean that ninety-nine times out of a hundred the film doesn't get made. Which might make you wonder if the prodigious bother of it all—which technological advances have exacerbated if anything—isn't actually an essential part of cinema's charm, since, paradoxically, it gives everyone access to movie-making, in the form of pure daydreaming. It's the same in the other arts, to a greater or lesser extent. And yet it is possible to imagine an art in which the limitations of reality would be minimized, in which the made and the unmade would be indistinct, an art that would be instantaneously real, without ghosts. And perhaps that art exists, under the name of literature.

In this sense all the arts have a literary basis, built into their history and their myths. Architecture is no exception. In advanced, or at least sedentary, civilizations, building requires the collaboration of various kinds of tradesmen: bricklayers, carpenters, painters, then electricians, plumbers, glaziers, and so on. In nomadic cultures, dwellings are made by a single person, almost always a woman. Architecture is still symbolic, of course, but its social significations are manifest in the arrangement of dwellings within the camp. The same thing happens in literature: in the composition of some works, the author becomes a whole society, by means of a kind of symbolic condensation, writing with the real or virtual collaboration of all the culture's specialists, while others works are made by an individual, working alone like the nomadic woman, in which case society is signified by the arrangement of the writer's books in relation to the books of others, their periodic appearance, and so on.

But in Patri's dream the architectural analogy was developed a little further. In Africa there is a curious race of pygmies, the Mbutu, nomadic hunters without a chief or social hierarchies. They look after themselves, and everybody else, without dramas. Their communities are relatively small: twenty or thirty families. When they decide to set up camp, they choose a clearing in the jungle and the dwellings are arranged in a "ring," which, according to the anthropologists, is typical of egalitarian societies. The huts form a circle with an empty center. But anthropologists are dreamers too, sometimes. How could this ring be visible except from a plane? Needless to say, the Mbutu pygmies don't fly; if they were meant to fly, they would have been born with wings. Also it's debatable whether or not the center is empty, since it's occupied by the space that makes it a center. "Whoever speaks in the center is heard by all," say the anthropologists, alluding involuntarily to dream ventriloquism. The huts are isotopic shells, in which an opening can be made anywhere. The Mbutu make just one: a door, facing the neighbors they like best. Say the lady of the house is cross with her neighbor for some reason or other. No problem; they block up the door and open another one, facing the neighbors on the other side. The researchers who have observed this system fail to draw the logical conclusion: the house of a truly sociable Mbutu would be all doors, and so not a house at all; conversely, a finished and complete construction presupposes hostility.

A contrasting example: the Bushmen. They too are nomadic and their camps are arranged in a "ring". Except that there is something in the middle of their ring. They place their little houses around a tree; under the tree the chief of the group builds his hut; at the door of the hut the chief lights a fire. What was lacking from the Mbutu camp was not a center, but its symbol. Providing a symbol engages a process of symbolic accumulation: the tree, the chief, the fire ... Why not a rose, a stuffed giraffe, a sunken boat, a mosquito that happened to alight on the earlobe of a Nazi spy, a downpour, or a replica of the Victory of Samothrace?

The little Bushmen are comical, but it's the same with the extremely serious Zulu, who are formidable hunters and warriors. Those who have had the misfortune of facing them in battle (for example, the son of the Emperor Napoleon III and Eugenia de Montijo) can confirm that they form a semi-circle, "enveloping" the enemy troops before annihilating them. This is a reproduction of the method they use for hunting. And their camps are arranged in the same way: a semi-circle of huts. When the method is transposed from hunting to war, there is a transition from the real to the symbolic, without any loss of practical efficacy. It's not that one level replaces the other; the levels can coexist, and a Zulu might even try hunting a tasty zebra with a technique tried and tested on the imperial prince. The architecture of the camp, whatever its degree of realization (interpretations and intentions must be taken into account as well as actual huts), constitutes a return to the real, because life is real, and the Zulu have to live, as well as hunting and making war. But they return involuntarily, as it were, without any plan, the way dreams unfold. The centre of the village is a void elegantly furnished with a bloody suction.

The architectural key to the built / unbuilt opposition, which analogies fail to capture, is the flight of time toward space. And dreaming is that flight. (So it wasn't a pure coincidence that Patri's dream was about architecture). Except in fables, people sleep in houses. Even if the houses haven't yet been built. And therein, perhaps, lies the origin, the original cell, of the sedentary life. While habits, whether sedentary or nomadic, are made of time, dreams are time-free. Dreams are pure space, the species arrayed in eternity. That exclusivity is what makes architecture an art. Beyond this point, the timeless mental material of the unbuilt is detached from the field of possibility, ceases to be the personal failure of an architect whose more daring projects stalled for want of financial backing, and becomes absolute. Even the mixture of the built and the unbuilt becomes absolute. The construction at whose summit Patri was sleeping was a real model of that mixture, by virtue of its incomplete state and everything the decorators were still planning to do. It was a step away from the absolute, waiting only for bricks, mortar and metal to expel time from its atomic matrix in a fluid maneuver. That was the purpose of the girl's dream.

Now if the unbuilt, or the mixture in which it participates, can be considered as a "mental" phenomenon, like dreaming or the general play of intentions, the mind, in turn, can be seen to depend on the phenomenon of the unbuilt, of which architecture is the exemplary manifestation.

There are societies in which the unbuilt dominates almost entirely: for example, among the Australian Aborigines, those "provincial spinsters" in the words of Lévi-Strauss. Instead of building, the Australians concentrate on thinking and dreaming the landscape in which they live, until by multiplying their stories they transform it into a complete and significant "construction." The process is not as exotic as it seems. It happens every day in the western world: it's the same as the "mental city," Joyce's Dublin, for instance. Which leads one to wonder whether unbuilt architecture might not, in fact, be literature. In urbanized societies, city planning doubles architecture, robbing its symbolic function. If, in nomadic societies, the arrangement of the camp performed a function that was not performed by the construction of houses, that is, symbolizing society, in the planning of large contemporary cities, where the buildings require the convergence of skills and know-how from a great range of social sectors, urban planning repeats a function already satisfactorily performed, and ends up having no function of it own (or rather it symbolizes the ·policing of society). But perhaps it would be better to say that it leaves a "symbolic vacancy," an energy unemployed by any current necessity. The Nias come to mind with their twin deities, Lowalani, who represents positive forces, and his enemy, Latura Dano, god of the negative. According to the Nias, the world is layered, made up of nine superposed planes, on the highest of which resides Lowanlani, sleeping with his consort, a nameless goddess (let's call her Patri), who is a kind of mediator. The planning of the Nia villages "represents" this construction, horizontally of course, the high, for example, corresponding to the right-hand side, and the low to the left, or whatever. Now the condominiums, the skyscrapers that the Nias haven't built (negating the negation of the unbuilt, as it were), would represent symbolism itself. From which it could be deduced that for every building there is a corresponding non-building. On the same principle, the natives of Madagascar make pretty wooden models of multi-story houses, crammed with little people and animals, which are used as toys. If those models represent anything, it is "the children's house," another form of the unbuilt.

But the Australians, what do the Australians do? How do they structure their landscape? For a start they postulate a primal builder, whose work they presume only to interpret: the mythical animal who was active in the "dreamtime," that is, a primal era, beyond verification, as the name indicates. A time of sleep. The visible landscape is an effect of causes that are to be found in the dreamtime. For example the snake that dragged itself over this plain creating these undulations, etc., etc. These "intellectual dandies," these "spinsters," these curious Aborigines make sure their eyes are closed while events take place, which allows them to see places as records of events. But what they see is a kind of dream, and they wake into a reverie, since the real story (the snake, not the hills) happened while they were asleep.

The dreamtime, as giver of meaning or guarantor of the stability of meanings, is the equivalent of language. But why did the Australian Aborigines need an equivalent? Didn't they already have languages? Maybe they also wanted a hieroglyphic script, like the Egyptians, and they made it from the ground under their feet.

The elements of Australian geography are as simple as they are effective: the point and the line, that's it. As the Aborigines proceed over plains and through forests, the point and the line are represented by the halt and the journey. With a line and a point, a line that passes through many points in the course of a year, frequently changing direction, they trace out a vast drawing, the representation of destiny. But there is something very special going on here:

via the point, the precise point in space, the nomads can pass through to the other side, like a dressmaker's pin or needle, through to the side of dreaming, which changes the nature of the line: the hunting or gathering route becomes a mythic itinerary. Which adds a third dimension to the drawing of destiny. But the passage through the point is happening all the time, since no point is specially privileged (not even waterholes—contrary to the anthropologists' initial assumptions—although they serve as models for the points of passage, which can, by rights, be found anywhere, at any point along the line), so the food-gathering route is always taking on a mythical significance and vice versa. There is something dreamlike about the points that provide a view of the other side, but they belong not so much to the dreamtime as to dream work. The nomads enter the dreamtime not by setting off on some extraordinary, dangerous voyage, but through their everyday, ambulatory movement.

To symbolize the point, the Australian Aborigines have a "sacred post" (a rough translation, of course, because it's not sacred in the western sense), which they carry with them and drive into the ground when they camp each night, at a slight angle, like the tower of Pisa, to indicate the direction they will take the next day. This post is decorated with carvings, which allude to the mythic itinerary, and in this way it combines the two contrasting motifs of the halt (signaled by the place where the post has been driven into the ground) and the itinerary (doubly represented by its inclination and the carvings, since the itinerary has two aspects, relating to food-gathering and to myth, while the point is single in its nature—it is always a point of passage.)

But Patri's dream went further, higher, taking in different systems, which were increasingly original and strange. In some cases the construction of the landscape, common to a great variety of carefree indigenous peoples, was simplified to the extreme. For example by certain Polynesian islanders, whose landscape consists entirely of those specks of earth or coral emerging from the sea, which seem to be adrift . . . They have a simple fix for this, using two lines that are not so much imaginary as utilitarian: one from the island down to the bottom of the sea, like an anchor, the other up to a star at the zenith, to stop the island from sinking.

And even the Polynesian system is complicated compared to some others, especially virtual systems, which start from humanity and proceed toward thought—an itinerary which, in turn, is doubled with dreaming.

After non-building comes its logical antecedent, building. As a real practice, building is decoration. In architecture, decoration is always an expansion, expanding anything and everything, until only the process of expansion remains. In agricultural societies, the accumulation of goods and the management of social inequalities gives building the function of creating an "artificial world," in which the privileged are confined by their status, whatever it may be (even the status of pariah). At which point architecture (paradoxically) becomes "real"; and if, until then, the world—the landscape or the territory—had been humanity's artistic miniature, its little dream-lantern, now the opposite phase begins, the phase of expansion, which gives rise to decoration, which is everything.

The development of "real" architecture, that is, of the decorative elements, is directly linked to the possibility of accumulating provisions for the workers or the slaves who do the building, and don't have time to go hunting or gathering food. Such accumulations result in inequalities. There is a mechanism for reducing excessive accumulation, and regulating wealth (without regulation there would be no wealth): *potlatch*, the festivity that involves squandering food and drink and other sorts of goods in a brief, crazy splurge, and so reducing the stocks to a satisfactory level. By staging a grand and brilliant spectacle, comparable to a temporary or perishable work of art, the festivity performs the function of attracting the greatest possible quantity of people. The size of the audience on the day is crucial, since this artistic manifestation will not endure in time. Art, in all its forms, has an inherent economy, and this case is no exception.

The *potlatch*, of course, belongs to the prehistory, or the genealogy, of festivities and partying, because with the passage of time, an alternative must arise at some point: instead of more and more people being present, a subtler form of sociability limits attendance to special people, the people that matter. The logical conclusion of this process is the single-person party, and the best model for that is dreaming.

In Patri's dream the building on the Calle José Bonifacio was under construction. Standing still yet seized by an interior, interstitial movement. Suddenly a wind, a typical dream-wind, so typical that dreams might be said to consist of it, arose and blew the building apart, reducing it to little cubes the size of dice. This was the transition to the world of cartoons. The building was reconstructed somewhere else, in another form, its atoms recombined. Then it disintegrated again, the wind scattering its particles, one of which came to rest on Patri's open eye, and in its microscopic interior, an entire house was visible, with all its rooms and furniture, its candelabras, carpets, glassware, and the little golden mill that spins in the wind from the stars.

Two hours after going down, Elisa Vicuña came back up the stairs, laden with bags full of shopping. The heat had not eased off in the least; on the contrary. It was the time of day when one suspects the climate of malevolence. She climbed the last flights of stairs on her own, because Juan Sebastián and Blanca Isabel went to get the toy cars they had left behind and resumed their games; not that they really wanted to go on playing, but they were still scared that their mother would put them to bed. There was no danger of that any more, because the hour of the siesta had passed, but just in case, and out of sheer willfulness, they ran away. They had been to an ice-cream shop with air conditioning, where they had stayed a fair while. The cool interlude had refreshed them a bit, but the contrast when they came out made the persistence of the heat all the more terrible. Elisa saw that her eldest daughter was asleep. She didn't wake her up. She went to the kitchen, and took the shopping out of the bags, but didn't put anything in the fridge, because they didn't have a fridge. Then she started washing. They didn't have a washing machine either, but that didn't bother her too much, although she would have liked one. In fact she enjoyed washing, and spent quite a lot on soaps and special products, as well as the bleach. Oddly, for someone who was so fond of this pastime, her hands were not ruined. So what if those two brats didn't want to sleep. She hadn't taken a siesta today either; she didn't feel like it. For various reasons, the washing had built up. She filled the two washbowls and the two plastic buckets, and began to make a mixture of various products, which she always finished off with a healthy squirt of bleach. She started scrubbing some of the kids' little T-shirts. She felt depressed, because of the heat, because of all the work she had done already that day, and what remained to do, because of the end of the year, and her husband, and so on, and so on. It wasn't a momentary low. She was going through a period of depression due mainly to the fact that they hadn't moved, as she had hoped, or rather planned. Her husband had been tempted by the special bonus they had promised him if he stayed until the building was finished. By now, she thought, she should have been in the new place. Not that it was better, but she had got used to the idea, and no one likes having to give up an idea, even, or especially, if it doesn't have have any intrinsic merit. She would buy something with the extra money, but it wouldn't be the same: money and new things, they were explicable, whereas her idea of moving before the end of the year was beyond explanation; it belonged to the world of whim. Anyway, it was Raúl's decision, and today he would get to hit the booze twice. He often scored a double: lunch and dinner. What a liver he must have! thought his wife. It's incredible, it must be made of iron. Drunks were tougher all round, or in a different way from normal people; she liked the feeling of being protected by that superhuman vigor. What other protection did she have? She liked a lot of things about her husband and had no desire to complain about him, not even in the privacy of her ruminations. For example, she couldn't imagine herself married to a sober man.

As she put some of Patri's clothes into the wash, Elisa's thoughts turned to her daughter: now *she* was a more serious worry. Elisa had never known such a mixed-up girl. No one could say how she would turn out, least of all her mother. It was partly her age of course, but even so, she was a particularly worrying case. She never stuck at anything; she had no perseverance, as if she didn't really know what she liked. If only she would fall in love! Proceeding mechanically through the washing, Elisa set out the problem point by point. Like many Chileans, she had the secret and inoffensive habit of addressing long, casuistic explanations to an imaginary interlocutor, or rather a real but physically absent person. In her case it was a friend she hadn't seen for years, not since she had come to Buenos Aires, even longer, in fact. Nevertheless, it was to this friend that she explained the case of her eldest daughter. Look, she didn't even stick with the karate; that was my husband's bright idea, typical! But at least it was something. And those mother-of-pearl buttons she used to polish so nicely, she gave that up too, even sooner. I can't really blame her for that, though, because we moved here. OK. But what about school? Same again: she refused to sit the equivalence tests. She wanted to be an electrician. Crazy! *I'd* have as much hope of doing that. As Elisa explained to her absent friend, the fundamental problem and the source of all the others, was Patri's frivolity. Was there ever a more frivolous girl in the world? It was hard to imagine. She didn't take serious things seriously because she was always serious about something else. She was a little dreamer, living in a looking-glass world. Not that she wasn't intelligent; but her frivolity made her come across as silly. She had talent, and plenty of it. She was a talented seamstress, for a start. She could have been earning a living already from her sewing, if she'd wanted to. There was some hope, then, for the future, faint though it was, because sewing was a frivolous occupation. All that mattered was the result, not the intentions, which could be supremely whimsical. And Patri's whims were limitless. For example, six years ago, when Blanca Isabel was born, she had prevailed against Elisa and insisted on choosing the baby's name. It was the name of a famous fashion designer: an Argentinean woman, but the daughter of a Chilean, who in turn was the daughter of a woman who had been the godmother of Raúl Viñas's grandfather. Elisa's heart had been set on baptizing the child Maruxa Jacqueline, a desire she had partially satisfied later on, with her youngest girl.

Her soliloquy was interrupted by a feeling she often had, the semi-epileptic impression that someone was passing behind her. There was no one behind her in the kitchen, and no room anyway, but through the open door she could see a band of ten ghosts watching her from the terrace, between the apartment and the stairs. What were those floury clowns doing there, she wondered crossly. She didn't like it when they interrupted her conversations with an intimate friend, all the more intimate for being in her mind and nowhere else. (Elisa didn't know it, but a few months earlier, a horrific derailment in Concepción had claimed her friend's life.) Anyway, it wasn't their normal time. Were they going to start showing up around the clock? Or was there something special happening because it was the last day of the year? That could have explained why they were staring at her with their round eyes open wide in their stupid faces. As if they had something to propose to her. It was odd, because they were meant to be seen rather than to see. And since she was in the relatively dark interior of the kitchen, she may not have been visible from outside. But she couldn't be sure about that, because even if the shadows hid everything else, her thick, twelve-diopter spectacles could reflect or condense enough light to make them visible (she had been caught out like that before): two shining circles, like the eyes of an owl suspended in the night. In any case, she could see *them*, and that must have been their way of watching. But was she really seeing them, or was it a waking dream? Ah, that was another question. Seeing ten naked men with their dicks dangling while washing clothes in the kitchen wasn't exactly the most realistic experience. Although for a married woman like her, the scene had a special significance, not a promise but a confirmation: men were all the same in the end. They had nothing to hide. It wasn't just that all men had the same bits; they also had the same value. Which was, admittedly, considerable, but it was shared out among a multitude that was almost beyond the grasp of the imagination, like the idea of "everyone." The only thing that bothered her was the bad influence the ghosts might have on her children, particularly on her frivolous elder daughter. Since Patri was given to building castles in the air, certain chimerical spectacles could lead her to the utterly misguided belief that reality is everywhere. It was just as well that the family would soon be leaving the building site. They would have left already, if her husband had listened to her. Meanwhile those jerks were still staring at her. Or was it the other way round? She turned away and went on with the washing, trying to concentrate; what with the distraction she'd probably gone and put in too much bleach. She was always doing that.

She was nearly finished when the apparition of Patri at her side gave her a start. Heavens, I didn't see you come in, she said, to hide her agitation. A little sleep and look at me, said Patri, displaying her arms, shoulders and neck, covered with sweat. They spent a moment complaining about the heat. Hey, I'd like to have a shower, said Patri, if that's OK with you. Of course, said her mother, I'm just about finished anyway, see. Just wait till I rinse this out ... there ... just the sight of that cold water running ... I'll have a shower, too, after ... and this one ... there we go. She turned off the faucet. All yours; careful not to wake the kids. They had to take all these precautions because when water was coming out of one faucet, it wouldn't come out of another, and if they turned on two at once it didn't come out of either. It was something they had discovered simply by living there. No doubt some problem with the plumbing, or rather with the general design of the building, which would have disastrous consequences for its occupants later on. Raúl Viñas felt it was best not to tell the architect. Why did he need to know? So he could get uptight about it? The Chilean builder regarded the problem as insoluble, so what was the point? As for them, they managed all right, turning off one faucet before they opened another, politely asking permission. It wouldn't be so simple when the apartments were occupied, but they would be gone by then. Patri went to the bathroom and turned on the shower. Elisa heard the beatific murmur of the water. She took the buckets full of rinsed and wrung-out washing and went out to where she had strung up a line on the terrace, in front of the big frame for the games room and the pool. The sun's force was brutal, even though it had begun to go down. The clothes would be dry in a flash, she thought. Pity there wasn't the slightest breeze. The ghosts were still hanging around. They had scattered now, but there were more of them. Some were sitting on the sharp edges of the parabolic dish, as they liked to do; it was a bit of a shock to see them there, but of course they didn't feel the sharp edge. And even to say they were sitting was a fiction as Elisa could tell by the way they were "seated" all around the edge, even on the bottom, that is, upside down. Perhaps because there was something different about them at that hour of the day, she was vaguely troubled, for the first time, by a serious concern: they were *like* men, and you couldn't help seeing them as such; but there was also the possibility of seeing them as *real* men, while knowing they were images. As she hung out the washing, it struck her that with so many men available, the key was to choose the right one. But how? She discussed it with her imaginary friend. It's not that there's a shortage of men, she said, with a chuckle that was imaginary too, but they're never there when you need them. The sun was already making her feel faint and giving her a headache, so she finished hanging out the washing and went straight back inside without even glancing at those creatures, leaving the dining room door slightly ajar in the hope that some air would flow through. She went to the bedroom to have a look: Raúl Viñas was sleeping soundly, the two little one as well. She half-closed that door too, and switched on the television, with the sound down low. Patri came out of the bathroom with wet hair, fresh and smiling. Do you feel better now? Sure, see the difference? I could have spent hours under that shower. Well, when we fill up the pool, you can splash around in it all day long, huh? Has it started already? asked Patri. I don't know, I just put it on; OK, let's see, it's about to start, I think.

There was a soap opera that they watched at six. They loved the story, although, since they weren't completely stupid, they realized how bad it was. But that didn't really matter, as long as they didn't lose the thread, and, surprisingly, they never did. Women lived in a world of stories, according to Elisa, surrounded, smothered, submerged by fascinating stories. Mother and daughter had watched a good many soap operas over the years and could safely say that they were all the same, but they didn't regret having watched them. The plots always revolved around pregnancy and money. The link between the two themes was a woman who became wealthy, immensely wealthy, the better to scorn the man who had got her pregnant when she was poor. The charm lay in the incongruous balance between the superfluous and the important. With the benefit of her experience, Elisa could easily dismiss the questions of money as secondary and concentrate on the rest. Moving from the relative to the absolute, if only in fiction, made her happy. (For her daughter it was very different, although equally enjoyable.) Almost every evening at that time, they would sit down, just the two of them, in front of the television, to watch the story of young Esmeralda, who had risen from being a slave, held in secret on an anachronistic plantation in Costa Rica, to owning vast oilfields on the

Arabian peninsula. They discussed the issues as they arose in the story. Elisa would try to point out certain things to her daughter, who obstinately refused to see them, or would only see them from her own point of view. It was a little one-student school, in which practically nothing was learned, although you never can tell. The question of pregnancy, for example, was more complex than it might have seemed at first. Elisa had got pregnant with Patri when she was as old as Patri was now. The father, so she said, was the best man in the world. He had disappeared from her life, like most childhood memories. That was the problem with men: they weren't definitive, they weren't right. But Mom, objected Patri, I'm going to find the right man in the end, like Esmeralda, I hope. In the end, yes, in the end, said Elisa emphatically, in the end . . . maybe. But not before. And when you think about it, what's a pregnancy? She pointed to the screen: Do you suppose that actress was really pregnant when all this was happening in the story? Of course not. You have to be very careful not to mix up truth and lies, reality and fiction. Yeah, but you really got pregnant, didn't you? Or were you just an image, a hypothesis? Elisa laughed. It was true, in a way; that was what she had been. Amazingly her adolescent daughter had touched on a very deep truth, and yet, at the same time—there's always another side to things—it was a truth composed of silences and suppositions. For example, she had never confessed the identity of "the best man in the world" to her parents. They had made an incorrect supposition. In fact, she thought, during a commercial break between chapters of the soap opera, she had made an incorrect supposition herself. Because later, a few years later, Raúl Viñas had appeared in her life, and everything had changed.

There you go, said Patri, as if she had hit on the most convincing argument: Isn't he the right one? Her mother replied with a smile. All her friends and acquaintances knew what a loving couple Elisa and her husband were, a real example. For just that reason, there was something elusive about their love. If her daughter found that disconcerting, well, she was sorry, but there was nothing she could do. Some things took time to understand. And Elisa was as quick as anyone to recognize her husband's faults, such as his fondness for drink. It was no more justifiable than any other vice, but Elisa came up with good explanations for it. For example, that by drinking glass after glass of wine, in interminable sessions, Raúl Viñas was gathering momentum in his quest for the infinite. It was like swallowing the sea, as they say, and what was wrong with that? It might be terrible to have that kind of thirst, but for those who don't, it's a magnificent spectacle. And another thing: Raúl Viñas was one the few happy men left on earth, or at least in Chile, where they would have stayed if Elisa Vicuña's opinions had carried any weight. Happiness always brings happiness, and plenitude, in its wake.

But we're poor, look at how we live, Patri replied, pointing to the stifling, cramped, unfinished apartment. But that doesn't matter, girl, why should that matter? We're healthy aren't we, we have enough to eat, and beautiful children playing happily, and loving relatives and friends? You are *so optimistic*, said Patri, with the expression of someone confronting an utter impossibility. Her mother was laughing. Don't you see, girl. I've been lucky. It's not funny, Mom. But I'm not joking, sweetie. The thing is to find a real man, even if he has all the faults in the world. A real man. A real man. She repeated the phrase mechanically as their conversation languished—the story was beginning again. In all the splendor of her incredible beauty, the heroine signed the papers that would make her the legal owner of the Palace of Versailles, which the socialist government of France had sold to raise money for the development of advanced technology. This is so absurd, said Patri under her breath. Just like our lives, said her mother, who hadn't taken her eyes off the screen. A number of typical soap-opera clues had led them to suspect that the heroine's lover, a Japanese magnate whom she had supposed dead after a crash landing in the Azores, was about to reappear, and both of them knew that when he did, when he opened the door . . . they would cry.

It must have been around seven, the soap opera had finished on a note of suspense, relating, of course to Esmeralda's reproductive system (if she could be said to *have* one since, in a sense, she *was* an exquisite and luxurious reproductive system), and they had switched off the television, when they heard a din rising from below. Someone's coming, said Elisa, announcing only one of the possibilities, although it was rather early for the guests to start arriving. But as the old saying goes: "Evening's guests arrive by day." If they do, she remarked, they'll get a splendid reception, with half the family asleep. Within seconds she recognized the voices of the children, who didn't even give them time to get up from their chairs: Juan Sebastián came running in shouting: Look what Aunty Inés brought me, one for each of us, this one's mine, etc. etc. With urgent sign language Elisa implored him to lower the volume. It was as if the kid had a megaphone in his mouth. Can't you see the others are sleeping? Yeah, yeah, OK, he conceded impatiently; but they had to understand, he was thinking about the presents. He had already put four toy cars on the table; they were made of plastic and all the same, down to the color: red. Blanca Isabel came in like a whirlwind and pounced. This one's mine! They started shouting again, inevitably. The eldest child had of course taken the initiative of opening the packet. Each of them seized a car; although the cars were identical, there was an obvious advantage in being able to choose while the other two children were asleep. What a surprise they would get, poor suckers, when they found they could only choose between the two remaining toy cars, which where indistinguishable from the others! Juan Sebastián and Blanca Isabel reveled in their triumph. Elisa went to the door, which had been left wide open, and waited for her sister-in-law, who, influenced somehow by the soap opera's delaying tactics, or simply because the children had come rocketing up, seemed to take forever

79

to appear. Elisa's curiosity was particularly piqued because her sister-in-law had arranged to come with her boyfriend, who still hadn't met the family. If he had come too, it was odd that she couldn't hear them talking. Or maybe they had stopped to look at the apartments? Maybe she had come early to help, and he'd be turning up later.

At last the extraordinary Inés Viñas made her appearance. Predictably, she had climbed the stairs at a leisurely pace and wasn't even out of breath. Are you on your own? said Elisa as soon as she saw her. Roberto's coming later, dear, I came early to give you a hand. But you didn't need to bother, etc. etc. They gave each other a kiss without interrupting their conversation. You couldn't find two more typical Chilean women. And seeing them together, it was striking the way they realized the type, almost to the point of caricature. The coincidence was especially notable because they were so physically different. Inés Viñas was quite short and petite. Her skin had a more olive tone; her hair was a shinier black, and her cheeks were sunken (while Elisa Vicuña's were round and somewhat childlike). She was quite pretty and rather flamboyant, within the demure limits imposed by her family and nationality. She was wearing stylish white sandals, an Indian skirt and a blue cotton tee shirt. And long earrings. You look really well. Not as well as you. No you do, really. Come off it, can't you tell I had a cough? What do you mean, a cough? Like I said, one of these days I'm going to catch pneumonia. She's so funny this girl, she kills me! Hi Patri! Patri was extraordinarily Chilean too. Seeing the three of them together made it even more noticeable. You washed your hair? See how awful mine is? Come on, mine's much worse. I told you to be quiet, you kids! The older children wanted to make off with the toy cars that belonged to the others. No, said Elisa Vicuña, You leave them there. Oh, poor things, said Inés Viñas, I'll wrap them up again. No, don't, this little devil ripped the paper. It was already ripped, shrieked the boy. Are they asleep? asked the guest lowering her voice, which, since she was Chilean, was already very soft. Your brother too, said Elisa. The three of them put on highly stylized laughing expressions. They found it seriously funny. Still napping at seven! All right, off you go, said Elisa. Silly of me, wasn't it. Four exactly the same. I didn't know what to get them. You shouldn't have bothered, dear. It wasn't much of a bother: the same thing for all four! Inés dear, it's perfect. Before I forget, I brought something for you too, Patricita. For me?! Listen, Elisa, Roberto is going to bring some bottles of wine . . . That's too kind! But you don't have to, you know, I'm not a little girl any more. Look, it's just something small. Patri removed the gift with great care from the little paper envelope: it was a bracelet of colored beads. Her pleasure and gratitude soared to indescribable heights. She put it on straight away, and it looked very nice on her. What a cute bracelet! They moved on to more general topics. How about this heat? said Inés Viñas. It doesn't let up, does it? asked and confirmed her sister-in-law. There must be a bit of breeze here, though. Don't you believe it. Isn't there? Well, yes, but only sometimes. That was understandable. What I can't understand, said Inés, is why you came to live in this birdcage. They laughed.

Meanwhile, the children had woken up. A bit of crying and moaning: here we go, said Elisa Vicuña. She went into the bedroom and came back with the two little monsters, one under each arm, naked and crying, covered with perspiration. Their aunt gave them a kiss, laughing at the way they were carrying on. She had an easy manner with children, which calmed them down, and even these little ones were alert to the word "present." The two toy cars had been wrapped up again, and the parcel was on the table. A little bath first, said Elisa. I'll give you a hand. No, don't worry, it won't take long ... you'll see ... I'll just give them a splash ... She went into the bathroom and poured some water over the children, which woke them up properly. Patri, she called from the bathroom: Go and tell the others to come for their snack. Patri went out. Hey, is Javier coming? In a minute, said Elisa. With the whole family. The two children, with wet hair, were deposited on top of the table, and Ernesto began to open the parcel. Aunt Inés cuddled them. The little girl was so tiny and sweet. She's always smiling, isn't she! She's lovely! Elisa was preparing something in the kitchen. How can I help? asked her sister-in-law. I'm fine, in a minute I'll give you their shoes and you can put them on. Where are they? Hold on, said Elisa, heading for the bedroom, I'll get them for you now. As she took the children's shoes, Inés said: And that man is still asleep, is he? Uh huh, like a log, takes a fair bit to wake him up. The two older children came in. You haven't gone and broken the cars already, have you? said their mother. No, no! See! They displayed them, intact. Patri had come in quietly and was looking at the bracelet on her wrist. Inés Viñas finished putting on the children's shoes, and told them each to sit on a chair, with their red toy cars, if they liked (but the best thing, said Juan Sebastián, is crashing them), while their mother poured them each a big glass of milk. So you must have bought a fridge, said Inés, looking at the glasses . . . No, no. They're going to lend us one. This is special milk, it keeps without a fridge. Oh yes, I know, said Inés.

While the children were busy with their afternoon snack, Inés Viñas made the following remark: The last time I was here, not even ten days ago, you could see right through each floor, but today on the way up . . . Her sister-in-law interrupted: So you saw the partition walls? They've put most of them up already; they might even have finished. Hey, can we look at them? At what? At the apartments, dear. Sure, straight away! The owners won't come? Why would they come, at this time of day, on New Year's Eve? Anyway, Patri put in, they were all here this morning. Were they? Why? I don't know, said Elisa . . . I think there was a meeting. You wouldn't believe how many people there were. We stayed in here, while they came and went.

Then they told the children to finish their milk while they went down to look at the apartments. But they could have saved their breath: the four of them guzzled down what was left so they could come along. They began the descent chatting brightly. They guessed at the layout of the rooms from what they could see. The upper floors were more finished. Patri was quite amazed by their suppositions, which would never have occurred to her. She knew that those rooms would be bedrooms, dining rooms, bathrooms, or kitchens, but she had never wondered which would be which. The other two were even doing imaginary swaps: I wouldn't put the living room here; I'd make this my bedroom. Other aspects of the apartments made them laugh. They'll have to put up huge drapes, said one, and the other replied: Except they don't have neighbors looking in, that's the advantage. They went down from the sixth floor to the fifth, and from the fifth to the fourth, talking all the way. They ranked the floors according to preference. Look at the way these rich people live, said Inés Viñas. And they're going to splash around up there too? Elisa looked up at the ceiling, bewildered for a moment, until she remembered the swimming pool. How do you like that, she remarked, a pool on the rooftop terrace! I couldn't *believe* it, until I saw it with my own eyes, or rather till I saw they were building it. It's just incredible, said Inés. Isn't it? said Patri, who was taking a very small part in the conversation. Some things are unbelievable, said the visitor, but when you see them with your own eyes, you have to bow to the evidence. Yes, said Patri.

As they visited the apartments methodically, from one end to the other, the question of evidence led to two topics that were, not unreasonably, dear to their hearts: medicine and marriage. Inés Viñas swore by homeopathy and warmly recommended it at every opportunity. She saw her little old homeopath as a kind of shaman whose precise and parsimonious doses could cure anything. Her sister-in-law Elisa, while not a supporter of allopathy (it didn't deserve supporters, she admitted, since it was just a business) favored conventional medicine, because she had a problem with belief. There are people who just can't believe, she said, and I'm one of them. But you could make an effort! said Inés. If it was only a matter of making an effort, I would have done it already, if only to please you, replied Elisa. Well *don't* make an effort, then, just believe! Elisa: The thing is, you *have* to make an effort. And not believing is simply not being able to do that. Elisa dear, I really can't follow you, although I'm trying, I swear. Come on, what if you gave it a go? This whole conversation was abstract, in a manner of speaking, because neither of them was ill or thought she was. Which probably explains why they could reason about it. Look, Inés, homeopathy, or any other kind of magical medicine, only works for those who believe. That's where you're wrong, Elisa! Lots of people who didn't believe have been cured. Is that so? But didn't they believe afterward? Of course, why wouldn't they? That's what I mean: you have to believe, either before or after. But it's not the same thing! It doesn't matter: I'd only be convinced by someone who didn't believe at all, someone who had been cured, and went on not believing. But that's impossible! Exactly, you see what I mean?

While talking about medicine they were also talking about marriage. If there was any disagreement on that topic, it was subtler. Because all women, or nearly (all the ones they knew, anyway) got married, sooner or later. It was a kind of universal homeopathy, which sent belief leaping wildly, all over the place, with nothing to guide it. Patri, whose part in the conversation was limited to an odd monosyllable or chuckle, was listening carefully. Inés Viñas sensed this attention, and looked thoughtfully at the girl.

When they had seen enough of that layered, multi-family mansion, and there was nothing left to criticize in their good-natured, skeptical way, they started going back upstairs, without so much as a moment's pause in their chatter. Which, come to think of it, was, in itself, something to be marveled at, a challenge to belief: how is it that conversation topics keep coming up, one after another, inexhaustibly, as if they weren't tied to objects, which are finite, as if they were pure form? It went to show that life had hidden recesses. When they reached the top of the building, the heat, which had not eased off in spite of the late hour, reminded the hostess of something they still hadn't bought, because they were leaving it till the last minute: ice. She asked Patri if she would do her a favor and fetch it. Patri went to get the bag, and her mother told her to take some money from her purse. Patri was thinking: Where does all the money come from? We're always spending it, but there's always some left. Her mother had a reputation in the family as a good housekeeper. And she was in fact fairly good, but the reputation was based on a misunderstanding: seeing the whole family dressed in faded clothes, the relatives supposed that Elisa Vicuña was extremely thrifty and economical. To tell the truth, they couldn't understand how clothes that were so faded, almost white, and therefore, they supposed, very old (when in fact they might have been bought the week before) remained in one piece: it could only be explained by infinite care and vigilance. When Patri came back with the bag and the money, Inés Viñas, who was at the edge of the empty swimming pool, admiring that huge absurdity, offered to go with her. No, there's no need; it's not far, just round the corner. We'll get two bags then, to make the drinks extra cold, replied Inés, laughing. Don't worry, don't worry, said mother and daughter, but she insisted. Since she had come to bother them so early, she might as well help with something.

Inés and Patri went downstairs and out into the street, which was coming back to life. Inés asked if she had friends in the neighborhood. No, replied Patri, I hardly ever go down. This is the first time I've been down in two days. Inés was amazed. She couldn't imagine it. And how are you going to find a boyfriend like that, my girl? Patri laughed in reply, and Inés joined in.

Hey, don't laugh, I'm serious. Didn't you hear what we were saying, your mom and me? Yes, but I still don't know who I'm going to marry. Inés took a few steps in silence, wondering what to say. Never say you don't know. Why not? Because. Patri chose to respond with a chuckle. Tell me, said

Inés, You're not a virgin, are you? No, not any more. Uhuh, but weren't you worried about getting pregnant? This time it was Patri's turn to ponder her reply. Eventually she came out with: More or less. What a funny answer! said Inés and burst out laughing. But you're a funny girl all round, aren't you, Patricita! Hearing her laugh made Patri laugh too. They went into the store that sold ice, made their purchase, and, when they came out again, started talking about love. It's the most important thing, the only thing there is in the world. Yes, yes, of course, said Patri. Why do you say you don't know who you're going to marry? Because it's true. Even so . . . They walked a while in silence. The trees in the street were as still as plaster statues. It's so hot, said the younger of the two. It's a heat wave, really, said the other, then added: You know what that means, don't you? There'll be a big, long storm afterward and then it'll be cold. Are you sure? It's hard to believe. That's how it is. That's what always happens in Buenos Aires. The weather does one thing, then the other. I think it does that everywhere, said Patri with a certain irony. Yes, but here, said Inés, it's more pronounced and it happens every time. What does? The downpour. Ah, said Patri, looking at the spotless blue sky. No, not now, but you'll see. Changing the subject abruptly, Inés remarked: There are some really good-looking men. Yes, there are some I find very attractive. There are some I find *extremely* attractive. Well, me too, if we're going to extremes. But, you know, they can turn out to be bastards. Yeah, of course; that's always happening on TV. But that's fake. Didn't you just say . . . ? No, what I'm saying is they *can* be bastards. Like they can be anything, Inés added. Oh, OK, all right. But the really important thing, in love, is to find a real man. Not the real men again! exclaimed Patri. That's what mom's always telling me. Well she knows what she's talking about, I promise you. How does she know? Inés shrugged her shoulders. They went around the corner and glanced at the building, which didn't look like anything special from the outside.

At that moment, a typical Argentinean beauty walked past: broad weight-lifter's shoulders, pumped-up breasts, narrow hips (viewed from the front, because side-on she was markedly steatopygous), dark skin, almost like an African, indigenous features with certain oriental characteristics, thick protuberant lips, black hair dyed a reddish color, a very short denim skirt showing off her long, strong, lustrous legs, sandals, which she was dragging along languorously, and a key-ring dangling from her hand. Inés and Patri, petite and delicate, slipped past her like two ants beside an elephant. The Argentinean woman didn't even look at them; her big, dark Japanese eyes were half closed, and she wore an expression of disdain. That's what they're like, said Inés Viñas when they were certain distance away. What do they do if they can't get a real man, smack his head off or something? Patri didn't reply, but the image of a real man without a head remained with her for a few steps. Inés added: We don't have that athletic determination . . . and, besides, we can't dress like that, there aren't any clothes that suit us that well. Then Patri said softly: It's because we're different. We're Chilean.

Before going in, Inés pointed out an old red and white van covered with mud, parked on the opposite pavement, a certain distance away. Isn't that Javier's? she asked. Yes, it was. What a wreck! Then both of them thought: They've arrived. A pretty straightforward deduction, really.

Any doubts they might have had disappeared when they went in: an unusual racket of children's voices was echoing down from the top floors. Not that Javier and his wife Carmen had lots of children (they had two and were expecting a third); it was because of the multiplying effect that children produce when they get together. Right now, said Inés, I'd appreciate an elevator. Each of them was carrying a bag of ice. Patri glanced at the electric clock hanging from the beam on the ground floor: it was seven twenty-five. Two ghosts were floating in the air, in line with each of the clock's hands: because of the time, they were both head down, like the branches of a Christmas tree. Come on, or it'll all melt, said Inés. What's the hurry? It's going to melt anyway.

As they climbed the stairs, Patri, who had been thinking about what they had said when the Argentinean woman went past, asked: Don't you think they're more vulgar? Inés Viñas didn't want to be categorical, although it was perfectly obvious what Patri was thinking: Well, my girl, they're different, just like you said. To us they seem primitive, savage, like those tribes ... For example, they have codes of appearance: you can always tell at a glance whether an Argentinean woman is married or single; it's as if they put a bone through their nose when they got married, or shaved their heads, or something like that. But with us ... we all seem married, or all single, if you like. We're always the same. Patri agreed as they climbed the stairs.

The situation on the terrace had changed substantially. The assembly of women had become a general meeting, buzzing with attention, tacit family understandings, news, the roughness of men, and a good quantity of joy. For a start, they had taken some chairs from the dining room to a part of the terrace shaded by the neighboring building. It was even possible to imagine that a cooler breeze was beginning to stir, but that was just the impression naturally created by open air and altitude combined. Here's the ice! cried Raúl Viñas. Javier Viñas stood up to greet the women. He was thinner than his brother, and taller too, although still short, more reserved, more distinguished-looking, but he also smiled more and had a more affectionate manner, although he was not so mysterious; perhaps, all in all, he was more ordinary. He hugged his sister and then addressed an elaborate greeting to Patri, with whom all the family were especially polite. Raúl Viñas had risen to his feet to greet his sister and apologized for having been asleep when she arrived. Carmen Larraín, Javier's wife, also exchanged salutations with her sister-in-law and Patri, while her children, Pablo and Enrique, paragons of politeness, patiently waited their turn. What about Roberto? Carmen asked Inés Viñas.

He'll be right along. They proceeded to talk about him in his absence. Unlike the hosts, Carmen and Javier had met Roberto. They lavished praise upon him, while the interested party expressed prudent reservations. Roberto was a Chilean-Argentinean, a traveling salesman for a small cigarette paper manufacturer. The engagement had been formalized only a few weeks before; they were planning to get married at the end of the coming year, which would begin in a few hours' time. The Viñas brothers (Inés was the youngest child, by a fair margin; Raúl and Javier were twins) were observing the developments with interest. A man's entry into the family was apparently more important than a woman's; they had each brought a woman in already, and in Raúl's case, a prior daughter as well: Patri, that enigmatic supplement. In fact the opposite was true, but the apparent was more important that the real. They considered the prospect at leisure, in a gentle, affectionate, futile way, since it was one of those things that is only a matter of time (which are the things that make time matter). With all the chatting it got quite noisy up there, thirty yards above street level. The presence of the men made a difference: it was more international, not as strictly Chilean as when the women had been talking amongst themselves, less of an artificial enclave, not so much a gathering of exiles, and yet at the same time more Chilean too, in a certain way. Differences like that made the women feel that the men were irreplaceable.

Elisa took the bags into the kitchen, and Carmen Larraín went with her, asking the usual question: Did she need any help? It was customary to reply in the negative. Raúl Viñas had suggested that they bring glasses for the first toast. Your husband's eyes are so red, dear, said Carmen, they're like slices of raw ham. Elisa laughed uproariously. Her sister-in-law was renowned for her witticisms. In case it wasn't obvious, she explained that he had been celebrating with his workmates at lunchtime. Ah, well, it's understandable then. Of course it is! A transition: Tell me, what are you cooking? Oh, nothing special, chicken, and the salads there, see what I bought. Perfect, perfect, said Carmen Larraín without even looking. Who's hungry in this weather? Hey, what do your kids like? Everything, but they don't eat much; don't make anything special for them. You've brought them up so well, your kids, said Elisa Vicuña. Mine just refuse to eat. Wait till they grow a bit, dear. I guess that's all I can do: wait. They laughed. Patri came in, like a shadow. Her mother asked her to take out cups for all the children and put an ice cube in each one. The girl counted out six orange plastic cups and placed them on a tray of gold-colored cardboard. The mothers started talking about Carmen's pregnancy. The experience of pregnancy was always interesting; though repeated often enough to be envisaged by all women, it still retained an exceptional character, which set it apart from, and above, normal repetitions. Outside, the men were talking about oceanography: the return of the catastrophic El Niño current. The children rushed for the cups, and were disappointed to find that they contained only little ice cubes, and nothing to drink. Reluctant to waste the opportunity to do something, they started shaking the cups to make a noise, and naturally some ice came out and fell on the floor. Inés Viñas called them to order and took them all to a tap so they could rinse off the cubes, which were covered with dust. Even those who hadn't dropped their ice wanted to rinse it. I'm bringing the Coke, said Patri. Hey, Patricita, bring our glasses, don't forget, will you, said Raúl Viñas. She smiled: Mom brought them already. What a good girl, remarked Javier. The heat seemed to have diminished with the approach of night. Perhaps it hadn't really, but at least the light was not so harsh. Elongated shadows hung in the air above them, and the sun was sinking toward their homeland.

The grown-ups helped themselves to two or three ice cubes each, which they put into the good glasses. They were abundantly served with soft drinks and wine, and began to drink immediately. What about the toast? asked Inés Viñas. The first drink's for thirst, said her brother Raúl. Anyway, remarked Elisa, Roberto still hasn't arrived. Well, said Raúl, accommodatingly, what about we drink an interim toast? Let's just wait for the sweat to break out. His joke was a great success, because they had all noticed that almost as soon as the drink went down their throats, they were wet from head to foot. Apparently it was hotter than they had thought. Or perhaps their bodies had dehydrated without them realizing, and now had to go through a phase of re-adaptation. For a moment all of them, even the children, remained still, dripping with perspiration. The climate of Buenos Aires was different; it still had surprises like this in store, although they had been living in it for years. Elisa went back to the kitchen to start preparing the chicken. The children broke the spell, and began to shout and run around again. A big white piece of paper came floating through the still air from somewhere and fell onto the men. Javier Viñas shook it off, and then examined it. With a few precise movements he folded it into a boat; it was a skill he had perfected. He gave it to the children, who had never played with such a big paper boat and immediately wanted some water to float it in. How could we get enough water? asked Carmen. Put it in the pool, suggested Javier, and when they fill it up, it'll float. So they did, for a bit of fun, and since fun always finds a way to go on, the older cousins climbed down the metal ladder into the pool, although they had been forbidden to do so, on the pretext that the boat had fallen on its side, and they wanted to leave it upright, waiting for the flood. Rock music emerged from a neighboring house.

When Elisa looked out from the kitchen, Raúl Viñas seized the opportunity to propose a first toast. He called his wife, and since there was a general desire to formalize the little ceremony, everyone, including the children, picked up their refilled cups and glasses. All eyes converged on the host, who had lifted his glass and was gazing absently at the wine. We're waiting, said Javier. Raúl Viñas raised his eyebrows, as if he were about to speak, yet a few seconds of silence ensued. Could he have been thinking? Possibly, because when he finally uttered the toast, they were struck by its aptness. He said simply, "To the year." And they all approved. If it had been a year of happiness, it was worth drinking to. And if not, it didn't matter, because the three words had a deeper or higher meaning: the prodigious gift of a year's time, loved and respected by all. But it *had* been a year of happiness, thought Patri, and in that sense the toast concealed a secret, not shared by the others, known only to them, Elisa, Raúl and Patri (the children didn't count, although they were an essential component of the happiness). The others were left out, but they didn't know. It was immediately suggested that the children should also propose toasts, and Patri was invited to open the proceedings, as the oldest member of the next generation, so, without much thought, she said: To my mom and dad. Then, thinking that the last word of the sentence might lead to confusion between her progenitor, "the best man in the world," and Raúl Viñas, she added: "That is, Raúl Viñas." This was considered very fitting; the grown-ups smiled. The children followed her example, each proposing a toast, "To my mom and dad, that is Raúl (or Javier) Viñas," even baby Jacqueline, who babbled it out, parroting the words of her siblings and cousins. The adults listened seriously right to the end, smiling a little as well. Then they knocked back the wine. The conversations began again, with an extra degree of joy and liveliness.

But Patri went on worrying that she had put her foot

in it. She hadn't; on the contrary, if she had been able to read the adults' thoughts, she would have seen that she had their full approval. But it wasn't what she had said that was worrying her so much as a familiar yet troubling anxiety, which had been mounting for a few minutes. It was like approaching the void. She left her glass on the ground and walked over to the edge of the pool, on the bottom of which the giant paper boat was lying, forgotten now, right in the middle, on the dry cement. She walked all the way around the pool until she came to the rear of the building. From there, the sunset was visible, becoming intensely yellow and red. The sun was setting, and the year was setting. The "Year of Happiness," as Raúl Viñas had suggested. They had drunk the sun in one gulp, and the originator of the toast had a special reason for doing so: it wasn't just that he had spent the year drinking, or even that he was going to continue from now until midnight; the reason was that drinking allowed him to stretch time, without in any way altering its punctuality and precision. Also, by virtue of a curious linguistic habit, "New Year" was an instant, twelve midnight, the minute when the sirens went off. And happiness was, precisely, an instant, not a year.

When Patri lowered her eyes, still dazzled from looking directly at the sun, she thought she saw human-shaped shadows flying through the air and into the sixth floor, just below her feet. Who could they be? Her anxiety gave way naturally to a feeling of curiosity, and she could see no reason to suppress it. So she continued her circuit of the pool, walking along the other side now, more quickly, heading for the stairwell. To get there she had to pass in front of the others, who were chatting away noisily, but no one noticed her. She went down the stairs. Although the sixth floor was empty, it seemed different. In the several minutes or half-hour since she had come up with Inés, the configuration of light had changed. The shadows had thickened toward the front, and an intense yellow light was coming in from the back, through the passageways. The perfection of the silence was accentuated by the faint, far-sounding noise of conversation and laughter coming from the terrace above. Paradoxically, a frightening intimation of the unknown was creeping in from the bright side.

Stepping lightly, Patri ventured toward the back. This is not unusual. When a woman, in a film for example, approaches a mysterious room where the bravest spectator wouldn't dare set foot, fear counts for nothing. In this case, it's true, there was no possibility of supernatural danger or any other kind (although the gate in the fence had been left unlocked and unchained). She reached the back landing, onto which the bedroom doors opened; the empty spaces were outlined with strong yellow light. There was not a sound to be heard. She went into the middle room. Somewhat dazzled, she took two steps, and two ghosts passed her saying, "We're in a hurry, a big hurry," then disappeared through the wall. She turned around, went out, and rushed into the adjoining room, so as not to miss them. They were already passing through another wall, and their legs seemed to be sinking into the floor. "Why?" she asked them. She went onto the landing. One of the ghosts had turned toward her. "Why what?" "Why are you in a hurry?" "Because of the party," the ghost replied. They had been tracing a downward curve through space and now they were sinking into the floor and the base of the bathroom wall. "What party?" she asked. Before his head went under, the slower ghost had time to reply: The Big Midnight Feast . . .

Patri rushed to the stairs, realizing there was something entirely new and unprecedented about the ghosts. In her surprise all she could do was hurry, without stopping to think about what they had said. The novelty was precisely that they had spoken to her, and answered her questions.

Although she hated running (and was aware that whatever disappears will reappear), when she got down to the fifth floor, Patri ran to the place where, according to her calculations, the ghosts should have emerged from the ceiling (it still hadn't dawned on her why she was hurrying), but they were already gone. She plotted the curve approximately with her gaze, down to the point where the floor should have swallowed them up. She hesitated for a moment, and then, through a doorframe, saw a group of five or six go by, floating half way between the ceiling and the floor. Although momentary, the vision struck her as even stranger than what she had just seen, almost as if she were in the presence of real men. She took a few steps in the passageway; on this floor there were a number of bedrooms in a row. She could see ghosts in the next bedroom, and in the third. "Are you going to the party too?" she asked, finally. One of the ghosts turned his head and said, "Of course, Patri," but a second later they were disappearing through the wall. These ghosts were moving along a curve as well, but it would only have been visible from above, since they were maintaining a constant altitude. They passed briefly through the corner of the third bedroom, and came out into the big living room at the back, which was flooded with light. There the velocity of their movement increased. Patri got her first good look at them, as they traced an increasingly rapid arc in front of her. "Why did you say 'of course'?" she asked, continuing the conversation. A different ghost, not the one who had spoken before, asked in turn, "Who'd miss the Big Midnight Feast?" but didn't look at her (indeed he seemed to be facing the opening at the back, the source of light). And when they were already disappearing through the wall on the left, she heard one of their characteristic peals of laughter, which, for some reason, sounded incongruous now. She wanted to ask who was throwing the party, but was too shy. Instead she followed their circular path all the way to the big living room at the front (corresponding to the one at the back) where they scattered like a squadron of fighter planes.

Since she had ended up near the stairs, and various ghosts had been following downward paths, she decided to go down to the next floor. From one floor to the next, the light diminished. Since fewer partition walls had gone up on the fifth floor, she could see through to the back, where some of the ghosts were floating in empty space, beyond the edge. It wasn't really accurate to say that they were floating. It looked to her more like they were standing, on something that could not be seen. She went toward them, with a sleepwalker's clear innocence. And they were watching her.

There was something architectural about the dusk as well. It was a construction, not governed by chance, as one might have supposed in the case of a meteorological phenomenon, but well thought out; or rather, it was itself a kind of thought. The largest conceivable spaces were transformed into instants, and under covering layers like roofs or paving stones, grids of shadows, light and color formed. But it couldn't be called a real construction, not in the usual sense of the word, not as the building was real, for example. The dusk was provisional, indifferent, subtle; its compartments of light were home to no one, for the moment, but anyone could see their image cut out of a photograph and stuck to the beautiful heavenly roof. Within the imaginary Great Construction, minor, real constructions reared, gloriously useless and incomplete, provisional too, but in their own way, hinting at permanence. And the strangest thing about it was that all this was a time of day, or night, but really more a time of day, and nothing else.

Absorbed by the sight of the ghosts, Patri had come almost too close to the edge. When she realized this, she took a step back. She observed them in the half-light, although they were a little too high, relative to her line of sight, for her to study them in detail. She could tell that they were the same as ever; what had changed was the light. She had never seen them so late in the day, not in summer. The unreal look they had in the saturated light of siesta-time, at once so shocking and so reassuring, like idiotic bobbing toys, had evaporated in the dramatic half-light of evening. They rose up in front of her quite slowly; but, given her previous experiences, Patri had reason to believe that their slowness was swarming with a variety of otherworldly speeds. Seen from the right distance, what seemed almost as slow as the movement of a clock's hand could turn out to be something more than mere high velocity; it could be the very flow of light or vision.

In this new, late apparition, their bodies had become three-dimensional, tangible; and what bodies they were, such depth and strength! The dust that covered them had become a splendid decoration; now that it didn't have to absorb tremendous quantities of sunlight, it allowed the dark golden color of their skin to show through, and accentuated their musculature, the perfection of their surfaces. Here were the bulging pectorals she thought she had seen in normal, living men, the well-proportioned arms, the symmetrically sculpted abdomens, the long smooth legs. And their genital equipment, somewhat curved, but also slightly raised by the sheer force of its own bulk (it's true she was looking from below), was different from anything she had seen, as if more real, more authentic.

They watched her as they rose, since they were rising

and moving forward, toward the fifth floor, at the rear of the building. They looked down at her and smiled an indecipherable smile.

Who's throwing the party?

We are.

They were no longer laughing as if possessed. They were speaking, with warm voices and words she could understand, in a Spanish without accent, neither Chilean nor Argentinean, like on television. They were speaking to her, and it was like being addressed by television characters. She was even more surprised by the way they seemed to be rational. Her surprise crystallized the feeling that had made her come downstairs; that vague, indefinite worry and alarm were becoming a specific torment, a pain, which was indefinable too, but for different reasons, as if it were impossible for her to touch the most genuine reality, the reality of a promise that eluded her grasp. Not that the ghosts had aroused her desires; that was, of course, impossible; and yet, in another sense, they had. Some desires, while less exact and practical, are no less urgent, or even less sexual. She told herself she shouldn't have heeded her curiosity, she should have resisted. But it was useless. She would do it again, a thousand times, as long as she lived.

They had disappeared over her head. The last she saw of them were their heels. She had tipped her head so far back that when she reassumed her normal posture she felt dizzy and teetered perilously on the brink, which she had approached again unawares. She turned around and headed for the stairs, intending to go up. In the darkest part of the apartment, at the front, a ghost appeared before her, moving diagonally (which seemed to be the fashion) and upward. It reached the roof before she came near and began to pass through it head first, slowly. So slowly that it seemed to stop halfway through the process (mutations within the movement transferred the velocities to other dimensions). When Patri got there, the bottom half of the ghost's body was hanging from the concrete ceiling, like some dark, nondescript object. She climbed the stairs and went to the rear of the building again, where she had a feeling they would be gathering in greater numbers. And as it turned out, a large group was waiting for her, or seemed to be, by the edge, but outside, in empty space, bathed in the last light, against a background of intense, end-of-evening air. Within the dark visibility of that air they were waiting for her, specifically for her, because one of them called her by name. What? asked Patri, stopping three yards away.

Don't you want to come to our party tonight?

If you invite me . . .

That's what we're doing

A silence. Patri was trying to understand what they had said. Finally she asked:

Why me?

She was bound to ask that. They didn't answer. All things considered, they couldn't. They left her to work it out for herself. There followed a somewhat longer silence.

So?

I'm thinking it over.

Ah.

There seemed to be something ironic in their attitude. They began to withdraw, without making the slightest movement, like visions affected by a shift in perspective. Nevertheless they withdrew, treating the innocent explorer to a sight that could not have been more extraordinary. As if inadvertently, they were entwined by a kind of luminous helix, enveloping them in invisible yellow. The dust on their skin was barely a hint now, a down. At the sight of those men, Patri could feel her heart contracting . . . as if she were truly seeing men for the first time. Stop! cried her soul. Don't go, ever! She wanted to see them like that for all eternity, even if eternity lasted an instant, especially if it lasted an instant. That was the only eternity she could imagine. Come, eternity, come and be the instant of my life! she exclaimed to herself.

Of course you'll have to be dead, said one of them.

That doesn't matter at all, she replied straight away, passionately. Her passion meant something apart from her words, something else, of which she was unaware. But it also meant exactly what she had said.

They seemed to be very still as they watched her. But were they? Perhaps they were traveling at an incredible speed, traversing worlds, and she was in a position from which that movement could not be perceived. That didn't matter either, she thought. In any case, they slid fluidly down to the next floor, leaving her there looking out into the emptiness, where the big city was, and the streets with their lights coming on.

Since she found that spectacle uninteresting, she turned around and went back to the stairs. But when she reached the landing, she realized that she didn't know whether to go up or down to find them again. It was as if, having accomplished their mission, they had disappeared. Anyway, there was no point chasing them up and down the stairs. It would just tire her our and make her legs hurt. You had to really watch your step on those bare cement stairs without banisters. She'd already had plenty of exercise for one day. And, with every passing minute, the exercise of going up and down was becoming more dangerous. The first dense shadows, still shot with glimmers of transparency, were occupying the building.

A shudder ran through Patri's body. Her legs were shaking, but not because of the stairs, or even because of the thickening darkness. She felt dazed. She went down two steps, then sat. There was something she'd been meaning to reflect on, and after sitting for a moment, she was able to give it some serious thought. Except that since she was, as her mother said, "frivolous," she never thought seriously about anything. And in this case her frivolity was exacerbated by the subject of her would-be serious reflections, which was something quintessentially frivolous: a party.

But in a way parties were serious and important too, she thought. They were a way of suspending life, all the serious business of life, in order to do something unimportant:

and wasn't that an important thing to do? We tend to think of time as taking place within time itself, but what about when it's outside? It's the same with life: normal, daily life, which can seem to be the only admissible kind, conceived within the general framework of life itself. And yet there were other possibilities, and one of them was the party: life outside life.

Was it possible to decline an invitation to a party? Patri wondered. Leaving aside the specious argument according to which, if an invitation, like the one she had just received, came from outside life, simply to hear it was to accept, it clearly *was* possible to decline. People did it every day. But how many such invitations could you expect to receive in a lifetime? As well as the vertical stratification of life into layers or doors through which one could "enter" or "exit," there was a "horizontal" or temporal axis, which measured the duration of a life. Invitations to a magic party with ghosts were obviously going to be very rare. There might be another chance, but for Patri that was beside the point. She was wondering how many such invitations there could be in eternity. That was a different question. Repetition in eternity was not a matter of probabilities, no matter how large the numbers. In eternity, as distinct from "in life" or "outside life," this party was an absolutely unique occasion.

All these questions came to her wrapped in another: Why not simply accept? And that was where life came back into the picture, denser than ever. Life had an annoying way of setting dates for everything, using time to hollow things out, until what had been compact became as diffuse as a cloud. For a frivolous girl like her, life should have been a solid block, a chunk of marble. Even thought could take on that quality, if the gaps between the elements of the proposition were eliminated. Frivolity is saying four is four. Seriousness is gradually deduced, fraction by tiny fraction, from such moderately useful statements as "two plus two is four," until one arrives at "Columbus discovered America." Frivolity is the tautological effect, produced by *everything* (because you can't be selectively frivolous: it's an all-or-nothing affair). It's the condition of knowing it all in advance, because everything is repetition of itself, tautology, reflection. To be frivolous, then, is to go sliding over those repetitions, supported by nothing else. What else was there? For Patri, nothing.

And yet she hadn't lied when she had said that she was "thinking it over." Thinking is also opening a gap, but, in her case, it was inevitable; she considered herself almost as an object of thought, someone else's thought, of course, and someone remote at that. The ghosts put her in a position where she had to think, had to attend to thinking.

But not because there was something to think over: as always, the decision had already been taken, automatically. Of course she would go. And they must have known she would, which is why they stuck to the essentials and dispensed with the customary practice of praising the party in advance. She would go. She didn't even feel the need to make a list of all her reasons for going.

The sound of footsteps interrupted her reasoning; she couldn't tell if they were coming from above or below. She lifted her head, but couldn't see much; night had fallen. The voices of her family up on the terrace carried clearly, as if they were within arm's reach. The steps sounded almost like whispers. Finally she realized that someone or something was coming up the flight of stairs immediately below the one on which she was sitting. She got to her feet, but didn't have time to turn around and go up, as she had intended, because a shadow appeared on the landing and began to climb, apparently still unaware of her presence. It was only when that shadow reached the midpoint of the flight of stairs that the light coming in through the hazardous gaps in the flooring around the staircase allowed her to see more clearly. It was a man about thirty years old, and the best-looking man she had ever seen in her life: white T-shirt, white moccasins, cream-colored trousers with well-ironed creases, gold watch and necklace, a ring with a red stone, bulging biceps emerging from his short sleeves, a pony-tail but the rest of his hair trimmed fashionably short, in a South American "pudding bowl" cut, with no sideburns, aerodynamic wrap-around sunglasses, and a cigarette in the corner of his mouth. He smiled at her languidly:

You must be Patri.

She couldn't even open her mouth. She had no idea who this gentleman could be, or how he knew who she was.

I'm Roberto.

Roberto? she asked, as she would squirm to remember later on: it was such an impolite question, almost as bad as saying: What Roberto?

But he wasn't offended. He chuckled, stepped forward, took her by the arm, and up they went. Inés Viñas's boyfriend, he said. Ah, Roberto, cried Patri, blushing so deeply that, if not for the darkness, she would have looked like a tomato—but this individual, with his sunglasses, could probably see in the dark. Am I late? No sir, I don't think dinner has been served yet. He laughed again, and asked her please not to be so formal. Call me Roberto, he said.

It was nine. There were various signs that dinner was imminent, including the smell of roast chicken and its effect on the guests. In the absence of a miracle, it had, predictably, turned out to be one of those oppressively hot Buenos Aires nights, exactly like the day, but without light. The children had restricted the ambit of their games and cries to the lighted area, with occasional escapes and chases into the darkness, from which they soon returned to the center of their fun. This made them more annoying than before, but also gave the whole gathering a more joyful and intimate feel, as if they were all enclosed in a room without walls. In the darkness, the red and blue toy cars looked the same. A bare light globe over the dining-room door was all the lighting they had, and all they needed. A few mosquitoes and moths traced their paths through the zones of light. Raúl Viñas remarked that one advantage of living so high up was that not many flying critters came to visit. There were none of the insects that precede a storm. The conversation continued, fluidly, in grand style. Conversation was paramount. The presence of men changed its nature, not so much because they focused on particular themes; it was more that they altered the form of the exchange, with their emphatic affirmations and deeply misguided ideas about everyday matters. Generally, the women acknowledged this difference, and appreciated it, especially since they had so few opportunities to talk all together: only at family gatherings like this one, or meetings called to resolve a particular issue, but in that case they weren't as free to change the subject. Still, the women went on speaking amongst themselves, under cover of the general conversation, even sending each other subtle signals, which were received with little smiles here and there.

The appearance of Roberto caused a sensation. They all agreed that he wasn't like they had imagined him. Not that he was better or worse: different. But that was just because he had really appeared. Even Carmen and Javier, who already knew him, had imagined him differently. He seemed Argentinean, which could be explained by the fact that he was, partly; although, of course, he was far more Chilean than Argentinean. Inés looked at him with surprise when he arrived: Hadn't he brought anything? The bottles of wine? The ice cream? But weren't you going to bring them? he asked, looking even more surprised. There had been a misunderstanding. After all that discussion about what they should bring to the party! They had made careful, considered decisions, but then they got mixed up about who was to bring it all. Soon everyone was laughing about it. Especially Elisa Vicuña. Roberto was nice and very polite. Raúl Viñas invited him to sit down with them—him and Javier—and they started talking. He took off his dark glasses, revealing small green eyes, the eyes of a good boy. You don't look Chilean! exclaimed Carmen, while her husband expressed the opposite opinion. There are so many kinds of Chileans! said Elisa. That's what I always say, added Roberto.

His arrival allowed Patri's absence to go unnoticed. But not entirely, because when she came into the kitchen, once all the fuss of greeting the boyfriend was over, Inés, who was apologizing again to her sister-in-law for the mix-up, asked: Where have you been, kid? Just around, she replied, without going into details. Her mother glanced across at her. Who knows where she got to, off in some mysterious dream-world of her own, probably. Your boyfriend is so good-looking, Elisa said to Inés Viñas. Do you think? Oh yes!

The table had to be taken out, so the men went to do it, or rather the brothers, since they wouldn't let Roberto help. But the table, as it turned out, didn't want to go through the kitchen door. They couldn't tell if it was because alcohol and nightfall combined had befuddled them, or if there was a geometrical difficulty; in any case it proved to be difficult, indeed apparently impossible. If it went in, said Javier Viñas, it must be possible to get it out. But *did* it go in? asked

Raúl Viñas, joking at first, but then, almost straight away, his mind was thrown into confusion by a panicky doubt, as he wondered whether the table hadn't been put in the dining room before the walls went up. He remembered putting up those walls, but at the time, he could have sworn, they were living on the ground floor. Just then, while he was still in a daze, having got two of the legs out, he tilted the table top slightly, and it came through, to unanimous applause. They put it in what seemed like the best place, neither too far from the door (that is, the light) nor too close. Half-light is always pleasant for dining, but the heat made it even more intimate and mystical. The adults, seven if Patri was included in the count, fitted around it perfectly. They set up a low table for the children, with planks and trestles, as they generally did for more formal meals: a kind of long coffee table, like the one the builders threw together for their lunchtime barbecues downstairs. Seating was the problem. The family's four chairs and four benches were sufficient only for the adults. The solution was to take another leaf from the builders' book: they could go down and fetch the boxes they sat on every day at lunchtime. All three of the men went, none of them wanting to seem less polite, but also because several arms would be required. They set off joyfully, following Raúl Viñas's torch.

Meanwhile, Patri was busy setting the table. First she spread a pretty white table cloth, and the rest happened almost automatically: plates, forks, knives. As for the glasses, which the men had left on the floor, she had a supernatural knack for guessing who they belonged to, and she never made a mistake. In the kitchen, Iñes Viñas and her two sisters-in-law were preparing the salads, and of course chatting. The main topic was Roberto, considered from various points of view, but one in particular. The unspoken question behind all the remarks, which were magically transformed into preemptive replies, was: How did Inés Viñas avoid getting pregnant? She seemed to be wondering too, as if she didn't trust her own thoughts or her life.

Elisa had put a melon into a tureen full of ice cubes, to cool it down. Inés had made an innovative suggestion: wrap it in wet newspaper first, then cover it with ice, so it would cool more quickly. The result was sensational. The green and white rind was frosted. Elisa worked out when the chickens would be done. When it came to timing, she was an expert and she liked the courses to follow one another fairly rapidly; the children were happier that way, and it meant her husband had less idle time for drinking.

Well, now they could begin. Carmen Larraín went out to ask the men if they were ready. Of course they were, ready and waiting! Just one thing: there were no napkins. She came back to the kitchen with the message, and Patri raised a hand to her forehead: how could she have forgotten? She always did. Her mother told her to check on the children once she had put the napkins out. Meanwhile Elisa was serving the melon, with the help of Inés Viñas, placing the slices on a long platter, and covering each one with a sliver of ham. Carmen and Patri went to quiet the children down. Juan

Sebastián, who had been appointed head of the table, was barking despotic orders, mainly at his siblings (he was slightly afraid of his cousins, with their disciplined air).

The melon arrived, and the cook sat down: the meal was beginning. There were two slices each for the grown-ups, and one (cut in two) for the children. It wasn't real sustenance yet, just a treat to whet the appetite. It's important to remember that, for this family, food was not a major concern. They gave it almost no consideration. The melon was perfectly ripe; had they eaten it a day later (or a day earlier), it wouldn't have been the same. The sweetness, with all its exquisite intensity, did not detract from the particular flavor of melon, which was not, in itself, sweet at all. And the ham was perfect too; it had a kind of salty warmth that contrasted aptly with the icy sweetness of the fruit. After the melon came the salads, and then, almost immediately, the chickens: perfectly golden, crisp, and moderately seasoned. To accompany the poultry, Raúl Viñas had put aside some bottles of aged Santa Carolina, which he bought at a good price from his favorite wine store. Chilean wines are so dry! they all said, sipping it, with a touch of nostalgia, which they reined in so as not to spoil the evening. They're so dry, so dry! Paradoxically, that dryness filled their eyes with tears. But overall, the meal was a thoroughly joyful occasion; sometimes, in order for joy to be complete, a discreet trace of sadness is required. In any case, the children were well behaved.

The only one who had a secret thought was Patri. Less

an idea than a feeling: she felt that she still had to do something; that there was some unfinished business. What she really wanted was to stop thinking. She didn't like feeling that she was a mechanism performing a function, but since she had told the ghosts that she "had to think about it," she felt obliged to do so. By nature she was particularly taciturn, but this predicament helped her to see the usefulness of speaking. When you speak, you automatically stop thinking; it's like being released from a contract. Or rather, as she said to herself, it's like those stories in which an especially handsome man appears, to whom the virile protagonist feels inexplicably attracted, which he finds disturbing, understandably, until it is finally revealed that the handsome man is in fact a woman in disguise. Such is the dialectic of thinking and speaking. But having reached this point in her reflections, Patri wondered if she wasn't herself (and this was the secret of all her thought) a woman in disguise, brilliantly disguised . . . as a woman. But she didn't go down those mysterious passageways, preferring to remain on the surface of her frivolity, because there was also a dialectical relation between thought and secrecy. Or, more pertinently in this case, between thought and time. It simply wasn't possible to go on thinking all the time. It would be like a painter who has to delay the completion of a picture for technical reasons, say to allow certain thick layers of color to dry, and meanwhile is assailed by new ideas—a figure, a mountain, an animal, and so on—which go on filling up the painting until the pressure of multiplicity makes it explode.

The children kept escaping from their little table. Stunned by the bliss of the meal, their parents let them be, except when they strayed out of the circle of variably feeble light shed by the globe, because the darkness beyond hid the irrevocable edges of the void, and those of the deep swimming pool, which were dangerous if not so terrible. When they did stray, one of the women would volunteer to go and bring them back, or frighten them into submission with a scolding if that was sufficient. Patri, lost in thought while all the others had gone rounding up the children, was the last to take her turn. There had been a veritable exodus, and some stern words from Elisa had failed to bring them all back to their places, so Patri pushed her chair back and went into the darkness to see what she could see. She walked toward the back of the terrace, to the left of the pool, until she heard the older children running around the right side to get away. But she went all the way to the back anyway, to make sure there were none left. There were no children, and once she was close to the edge, she could see more clearly, because of the light coming up from the houses and the streets. She stopped on the brink, but was not in any danger, because of her pensive mood: she was continually stopping to think, and that moment was no exception. Some ghosts appeared, floating in the air two or three yards away. Night had made them majestic, monumental, perhaps because they were illuminated from below by the glow coming from the Avenida Alberdi on the other side of the block, and they looked like foreshort-

ened figures, barely a few golden lines in the darkness. They
seemed more serious too, but there was no way to be sure.
In Patri's eyes, at any rate, they had entered a spacious domain of seriousness. For her, those volumes swimming in
shadow, those volumes reduced to lines, as if to suggest that
they existed in a dimension of aggravated unreality, seemed
strangely, almost incredibly, solemn. The shadows served a
different function for the ghosts, since they had "nothing
to hide" (because they weren't alive). I accept the invitation, said Patri. A minute before midnight I'll jump off here.
Here? asked one of the ghosts, as if he had not heard. Yes,
here. Ah. It's more practical, said Patri, feeling obliged to
explain. Then they nodded; and that simple movement, in-
dicating that they had heard, made them seem less serious.
One of them said: Thank you for the confirmation, young
lady. Everything is ready for the feast.

When she came back to the table, she noticed that her
mother was looking at her strangely, and wondering briefly
what she was thinking. Over the chicken bones and empty
salad bowls, the diners were speaking of this and that. By
a curious coincidence, all of them, without exception, had
been born in the city of Santiago, the most beautiful city in
the world, as they readily agreed, having already made up
their minds. The way they praised Santiago, they could have
been employed by a travel agency.

It's a pity you can't see the stars in Santiago, because of
the smog, said Roberto. I've seen them, said Raúl Viñas,
leaning forward. Under close observation, some of Raúl

Viñas' mannerisms, such as a certain way of swaying his head, could seem to be typical of a drunkard. But it happened that his brother, who didn't drink, or never to excess, had the same mannerisms. So the observer's judgment had to be revised: they were family traits. Roberto was constantly making this readjustment when he spoke with his future brothers-in-law. I've *seen* them, said Raúl Viñas, leaning forward and exaggerating the swaying movement of his head. Yeah, all right, very clever, replied his sister's boyfriend, I've seen them too, otherwise how would I know they exist? I didn't discover them in Argentina. But I saw them in the old days, when I was a kid. I've seen them just recently, said Raúl Viñas. And his brother Javier repeated his words. Listen Roberto, they said, Listen . . . (Right from the start they had decided to dispense with formalities, since they were going to be brothers-in-law; and the women had done the same. Otherwise Roberto would have felt uncomfortable.) Since they weren't agreeing about what they had seen in Santiago, they moved on to not agreeing about something closer to hand. The same thing happens here, said Inés Viñas, although there's no smog. It's because there's too much street lighting. Some people think you can't have enough, Carmen pointed out. But you can see them here too! said Javier Viñas. Don't you believe it, Roberto replied. Hey kids, let's do a test, cried Elisa, then she asked the children to behave, because it was going to be dark for a while. She went to the kitchen, and switched off the light. They all threw their heads back and looked up. When their pupils dilated, an immense starry sky, the whole Milky Way in its rare magnificence, appeared before them. You can hardly see it, said Raúl Viñas. I can see it clear as anything, said Javier. Yes, it's true. Yes, yes. They all looked up and abandoned the conversation. There are the galaxies! said Javier's children. If only we had a telescope!

While the others were going into raptures about the stars, Patri felt that she could see her family in the sky, her beloved family, and realized that she was bidding them farewell. It wasn't true what they said about the dead being turned into stars for the living to see: it was the other way around. She couldn't say that she was sad to be leaving them for ever, but she saw them scattered over the black sky, each a beautiful, everlasting point of light, and felt a kind of nostalgia, not in anticipation but almost as if she were looking back already. She was telling herself that as long as a sacrifice is worthwhile, it is possible. The thing is, the stars were so far away ... The kids were right: they needed a telescope; but that would have made them look even more distant. She moved her head slightly, and felt that the stars, remote as they were, had entered her. The "state of farewell" implied a certain detachment. That detachment or doubling affected thought as well, and under its influence Patri conceived the following analogy. In the course of his everyday activities, it occurs to a man that in an ideal state of perfect happiness, satisfying all the requirements set out by the philosophers (and some have been extremely particular in these matters, not so much because they were naturally fussy, although they were, because most of them were bachelors, but mainly because they got carried away by their ontological deductions), he would be doing exactly what he is doing now, not something equivalent, but the very same thing, as if in a parallel world. Of course not if his work was really terrible, as so much work is, but these days, thought Patri, quite a few people live without working, so the objects of this man's hypothetical comparisons would be a walk, a session at the gym, a train trip to the suburbs, that sort of thing, and it wouldn't require a great imaginative effort to arrive at the conclusion that there could indeed be a perfect identity between what he is doing in reality, and what he would be doing at the same time, on the same day, in a state of perfect happiness (individual, social and even cosmic happiness, if you like, the end of alienation, etc. etc.). In fact it wouldn't require any imaginative effort at all, because there would be no need to call on the imagination; all he'd have to do would be to modify his gestures, or their form: slightly slower movements, a conceited little smile, the head held slightly higher . . . It's always the way, she thought: you look up at the starry sky, and before you know it you're thinking about other worlds. How idiotic!

Of course, the stars over Santiago, said Javier, are completely different. What do you mean different? he was asked in surprise and bewilderment. They're not the same, he replied. Appalled, Raúl Viñas put his head in his hands. What a dumb thing to say! We're in the same hemisphere! What's that got to do with it? Neither brother knew whether to credit the other's implausible ignorance or assume it was an exercise in mutual leg-pulling. The women laughed. Elisa Vicuña, who was justly reputed for her intelligence, backed up her brother-in-law: But they *are* different. It's true, said Roberto, supporting her. Raúl Viñas had no choice but to yield, mainly because, on that point, he actually was in agreement. Of course they're different, he said, but that doesn't mean they're not the same constellations, the same arrangements, the same stars, if you like. They all looked very carefully at the stars. Was there anything familiar about them? They couldn't say there was, but they couldn't say there wasn't either. What I think, said Patri, is that they're the same but back to front. *Exactly*, said Raúl, Patricita is right. Point of view is everything, said Carmen. And to think we've seen those stars from the other side, said Inés Viñas, poised between melancholy and delight. But their necks had begun to hurt, and since the children had taken advantage of the darkness to escape and tear around like little devils, they switched on the light again. They emerged from that plunge into the starry darkness smiling more broadly, and saw each other with different eyes, which were, of course, logically, the same. They drank a toast: To the stars of Chile. There's a current that carries the stars away! said Raúl Viñas, between mouthfuls.

Soon the fruit was served and they were tasting it. All the family preferred fruit to desserts, which was lucky for the mistress of the household, because it meant less work, although she still had to peel, pit, and remove seeds, especially for the children. When they told Roberto, he couldn't believe it. It turned out that he was exactly the same. His devotion to fruit was matched only by his aversion to desserts; serving them after the finest meal was enough to spoil all the pleasure retrospectively. He was sure that Inés must have mentioned it, that quirk of his, but no, on the contrary, Elisa Vicuña had been worried that he wouldn't be satisfied with plain fruit, served in the primitive style. Even so she hadn't wanted to spoil the rest of the family's pleasure. It was almost telepathic, a coincidence that proved he was meant to be part of the family. And what fruit! Glorious nectarines, so ripe they were violet, mosque-shaped apricots, bunches of green and black grapes, each one sublime, bleeding strawberries, Anjou pears with snow-white flesh, purple cherries, big black plums, all the abundance of nature, civilized to a supreme degree of refinement by grafting and husbandry, to the point where any improvement in flavor would almost have been imperceptible. Nothing less could satisfy this family of insatiable fruit-eaters; luckily fruit was cheap in summer.

Did you know, said Elisa, that we have ghosts on this site? Real ghosts? they asked. Well, they're never real, are they? But you can see them, every day, at siesta time. And other times, added Patri. Yes, other times too. The conversation moved on to ghosts. Everyone could contribute an experience, a memory, or at least something they had heard. It was the ideal subject for storytelling.

Raúl Viñas told the story of the ghost who was walking

along and, distracted by the sight of a plane flying over, fell into a well. In the well there was a hare, and they struck up a conversation. The hare (a male hare, while the ghost, as it happened, was the ghost of a woman) had also fallen in by accident, and had stayed there, not because he couldn't get out (it wasn't a very deep well) but to rest. Were you watching the plane flying over too? asked the ghost. No, said the hare, I was running away. Uh huh? said the ghost, her curiosity piqued. What from? The hare shrugged his shoulders, difficult as that may be to imagine. He went on to explain that in fact he was always running away, from everything, so in the end he didn't really distinguish between reasons for flight. But you should, advised the ghost. Why? said the hare. Why run away more quickly from what seems to be more dangerous, and more slowly from what seems a lesser threat? That would be a grave mistake, because you can always judge wrongly, and even if you don't, the lesser threat could turn out to be fatal. The ghost concurred, and said reflectively that it had been rash of her to offer advice on a subject she knew nothing about. Understandably enough, since her specialty—appearing—was the opposite of flight. The hare sighed, envying his chance companion's lot: how wonderful not to have to worry about preserving your life! Except that you have to start by losing it, the ghost remarked wisely. Ah, but then . . . You see . . . No, sorry, but you're mistaken . . . Allow me to . . . They were so absorbed in their philosophizing that they didn't notice the arrival of a hunter, a bad sport as we shall see, and inept too, who looked over the edge of the well, and seeing a defenseless hare at his feet, cocked his shotgun (that sinister "click" finally brought the hare and the ghost back down to earth, but all they had time to do was freeze), and fired: bang. Since he was a poor shot, he hit the ghost, who of course he hadn't seen. Transparent as air, blood spurted from a wound on the left side of her chest. The hare had no time to pity her, since, like the classic moral at the end of a fable, he had leapt out of the well with a single bound, and was already far away, fleeing as fast as he could.

Javier Viñas told the story of the old watchmaker who could tell what time it was by observing the positions of ghosts, which led him, by association, to depressing reflections on the decline of his trade. All things analog were losing ground, and the tendency seemed to be irreversible. It saddened him to hear people say "Eleven fifty-six, seven thirty-nine, two-o-one" as they walked past his poky little shop. Nobody said "it's just gone twenty to two" because even a child would have replied, "You mean one forty-one? Or one forty-two?" Now his only clients were little old men like himself with some broken-down antique, an Omega, a Vacheron Constantin, or a Girard Perregaux, and he was no longer surprised when one of them decided that it wasn't worth repairing, and walked past the next day with a Japanese watch on his wrist. Soon no one would know that the hour is made up of two halves. Already the ticking of a watch was a thing of the past: the heart was an outmoded organ. Because the ticking of a watch was "like" that of the heart; in other words, they were analogs. And analog watches were the old ones, the ones with hands. It was true that there were also imitation analog watches, with hands, which operated digitally, but that was ostentatious or condescending, and gave the old watchmaker little hope. He spent the day sitting still, feeling depressed, stiller and more depressed each day, staring at the back wall of the shop, where two ghosts showed the time, all day long. They were two child-sized ghosts, so punctual and patient that the watchmaker found it natural for them to be there, showing the time. And the stiller he became, the more natural the slow, sure movement of the ghost-hands seemed. But he shouldn't have been so complacent. Because one afternoon, the ghosts came down from their places and said to him with a mischievous smile: Time passes, you stupid old miser, technology changes, but not human greed, and "backwards" people like you just spread gloom, which has spoilt life for ghosts. Aren't you ashamed? The old watchmaker was so astonished, he couldn't even open his mouth. He felt himself being swept up by an impalpable force, into the air, and carried to that place by the back wall where the ghosts had shown the time. Now he was showing it, his body marking the hour, as on the first clock faces, before the invention of the minute hand. Meanwhile the real ghosts had vanished.

Not to be outdone, the women told ghost stories too. Inés Viñas told the story of a portraitist who abandoned his art as a result of specializing in ghost portraits. The ghosts materialized only to pose and then disappeared again. It was frustrating for the artist not to have any enduring reality with which to compare his work. But that was not the worst thing. The worst thing was that the ghosts rationed their visibility in a rather drastic manner, and didn't even materialize in their entirety; only the feature that the artist was copying at a particular moment appeared, and not even that: just the line, the mere brush-stroke . . . They duplicated his work so perfectly that the exasperated painter broke his brushes, stamped on his palette, kicked the easel over, and bought himself a Leica. Which only made things worse, much worse.

As for Carmen Larraín, she told them about Japanese ghosts. In the Celestial Empire, when an elder died, there was a general reckoning of where he had left the bones on the plate every time he ate fish. If the positions formed a satisfactory circle, he went to Paradise. If not, he became a ghost whose task was to teach the children good table manners. And those who did not succeed in that mission, she concluded, became ikebana instructors.

Finally, instead of telling a story, Roberto made an observation: ghosts, he said, are like dwarves. Thinking about them in abstract terms, you could come to the conclusion that they don't exist, and depending on the kind of life you lead, you can go for months or years without seeing one, but sooner or later, when you least expect it, there they are. That's just a result of life's general conditions, the chances and coincidences that make up existence; for example, it can happen that in a single day, you see two dwarves, or two dozen, and then you don't see any more for the rest of the year. Now looking at it from the other side, from the dwarf's point of view, the situation's very different, because the dwarf is always present to himself, as he is: 44 inches tall, with his big head, and his short, bandy legs. He is the occasion that prompts casual passersby to say, that night: "Today I saw a dwarf." But for him, dwarfhood is constant, continual, and merits no special remark. It's perpetual appearing, occasion transformed into life and destiny.

Isn't Patricita going to tell us a story? they asked, looking at her; it was true that she hadn't said a word. The children had approached the table and were listening to the stories with gaping mouths. Patri thought for a moment before speaking: I remember a story by Oscar Wilde, about a princess who was bored in her palace, bored with her parents, the king and queen, bored with the ministers, the generals, the chamberlains, and the jesters, whose jokes she knew by heart. One day a delegation of ghosts appeared to invite her to a party they were giving on New Year's Eve, and their descriptions of this party, which included the disguises they would wear and the music to be played by the ghost orchestra, were so seductive, and she was so bored, that without a second thought that night she threw herself from the castle's highest tower, so that she could die and go to the party. The others pondered the moral. So the story doesn't say what happened at the party? asked Carmen Larraín. No. That's where it stops. Must have been a bit of a surprise for the girl! said Elisa, giggling. Why? Because ghosts are gay, of course! Raucous guffaws. That Oscar Wilde, he's priceless! said Roberto, choking with laughter. They all thought Elisa Vicuña's reply was a great joke, in the surrealist mode. An inspired one-liner. Patri, however, only laughed so that they wouldn't think she was upset; the idea had shocked and distressed her. At that moment, the children were pointing at the moon, which had been rising in the sky, partly hidden by the neighboring buildings, partly eclipsed by the absorbing conversation. They all looked up. It reminded them that they were dining outdoors. It was a very white full moon, without haloes, the kind of moon you could spend your life watching, except that in life the moon is always changing.

When Elisa got up to prepare the coffee, Patri was quick to follow her into the kitchen, saying "I'll give you a hand." The rest of them went on talking and drinking wine. Raúl Viñas drank four glasses in the time it took the others to finish one. The result was an exquisite inebriation that went unnoticed in social situations, but sent his whole body into orbit, endowing it with a peculiar movement, shifting it to places where no one thought it was. Once they were alone, Patri asked what Elisa had meant by the quip that had gone down so well. But, my girl . . . her mother began, and here the expression "my girl," so common in the familiar speech of Chileans, so normal that even daughters sometimes use it without thinking when addressing their mothers, also took on a broader sense, which neutralized the typically Chilean connotations. The language shifted to its most abstract level, almost as if Elisa were speaking on television: But my girl, we never know what we mean, and even if we did, it wouldn't matter. You're always saying things don't matter, said Patri, in a slightly reproachful tone, which, as always in their conversations, was tempered with affection. But as Elisa put the water on to boil, spooned the coffee into the pot, passed the cups to her daughter so that she could check they were clean and put them on the tray with the saucers and the little spoons, she became very serious. There were things she needed to say to her daughter, things that really did matter. They had spoken so much, half-jokingly, about the "real men" who were destined to make them happy, and they had made light of them so often, that in their respective imaginations, the subject had lost its gravity. She had to restore it, by reasoning if need be, and there was no time like the present, now, before the end of the year. How can I tell you, she said to her daughter, then stopped and thought. Patricita, I'm afraid you're not the most observant member of the family. Come on, tell me, tell me, said her daughter, without a trace of self-pity, maintaining her characteristic reserve.

Listen, said Elisa Vicuña: Chilean men, all Chilean men, speak softly, with a slightly feminine tone of voice, don't they? Whereas Argentinean men are always shouting out loud. I don't know what they've got in their throats, but they're like megaphones. Well, at first you can get the impression that all Argentinean men are super-virile, I mean, *we* can get that impression. But more careful and detailed observation reveals something else, almost the opposite, in fact. Haven't you noticed? Patri shrugged her shoulders. Her mother went on: Think of the architect who designed this building, and the decorators who come with the owners, all the men who came this morning, for example ... Don't tell me you haven't noticed, Patricita: those pink silk cravats, the aftershave, those tank tops, the oohs! and ahs! In spite of everything that was on her mind, Patri couldn't help smiling at her mother's mimicry. Elisa went on:

Now there's another question, and it's closely related: the question of money. Having money is a kind of virility, *the only kind that counts in Argentina.* That's why this country we have come to is so unique and strange. That's why it has cut us off from the rest of the world, to which we belong by right as foreigners, and held us like hostages. It's true that there is, or at least should be, another form of virility, which doesn't depend on money. But where we are now, it's hard to imagine; as if, to understand it, we'd have to go back in time and space, back to Chile and even further, to something before that. What is that other form of virility? *Popular* virility? No, because the popular is subordinate; it's an eminently subordinate form in the hierarchy of virilities. It's the primitive form; that is, virility independent of the state. Although in principle it might seem preferable to the popular form, the primitive form can be dangerous for us too. It could imply that women are condemned to the primitive, to savagery. And wouldn't that be dangerous? Isn't the state, after all, a safeguard, a kind of guarantee, which stops us disappearing altogether, even if it relegates us to the bottom of the ladder? Women, said Patri, will never disappear. That, my girl, replied her mother vigorously, is precisely what's in doubt.

But what has all this got to do with ghosts? Patri asked her again.

Ah, ghosts ... Well, what is a ghost? I've been talking about Argentinean men and Chilean men, but that was just to make it clearer, the way animals are used in fables. Well, so far it's not all that clear, said Patri. Come on, a smart girl like you ... You see, for us there are always ghosts. Subtract a Chilean man from an Argentinean, or vice versa. Or add them up. You can actually do whatever you like. The result will always be the same: a ghost.

OK, but why do they have to be gay?

Even at that critical moment, when, as she was intuitively aware, her beloved daughter's life hung in the balance, Elisa Vicuña could not bring herself to answer with anything more than a mysterious smile, the "serious smile."

Since the coffee was ready, and a fragrant plume of steam was rising from the spout of the pot, they went back out. Patri put the tray on the table, and Inés Viñas took charge of filling each cup. The coffee was so well brewed, so aromatic, that hardly anyone felt the need to sweeten it. Patri took a sip, and waited for it to cool. She was thinking about the conversation with her mother just before: they hadn't come to any kind of conclusion; in fact, her doubts had multiplied. And yet the conversation had produced effects, and that was what she was thinking about as she drank her coffee. The danger, she thought, was not so much that the ghosts who were waiting for her would turn out to be a complete flop as far their virility was concerned, but that none of them would deign to talk to her, and give her the explanations she needed so badly. On second thought, however, the conversation had produced the opposite effect, since it was all about entering a state where she would no longer need anyone to look after her, or provide explanations, or even give her what her mom gave as abundantly as anyone could: love. And as she proceeded from this conclusion to a third stage in her reflections, the question of the ghosts' real virility recovered its importance. It might seem odd that this relatively uneducated young woman, who hadn't even finished secondary school, should entertain such elaborate thoughts. But it's not as strange as it seems. A person might never have thought at all, might have lived as a quivering bundle of futile, momentary passions, and yet at any moment, just like that, ideas as subtle as any that have ever occurred to the greatest philosophers might dawn on him or her. This seems utterly paradoxical, but in fact it happens every day. Thought is absorbed from others, who don't think either, but find their thoughts ready-made, and so on. This might seem to be a system spinning in a void, but not entirely; it is grounded, although it's hard to say just how. An example might clarify the point, though only in an analogical mode: imagine one of those people who don't think, a man whose only activity is reading novels, which for him is a purely pleasurable activity, and requires not the slightest intellectual effort; it's simply a matter of letting the pleasure of reading carry him along. Suddenly, some gesture or sentence, not to speak of a "thought," reveals that he is a philosopher in spite of himself. Where did he get that knowledge? From pleasure? From novels? An absurd supposition, given his reading material (if he read Thomas Mann, at least, it might be a different story). Knowledge comes *through* the novels, of course, but not really *from* them. They are not the ground; you couldn't expect them to be. They're suspended in the void, like everything else. But there they are, they exist: you can't say that it's a complete void. (With television, the argument would be harder to sustain.)

The guests were cracking jokes and laughing heartily as they drank their coffee and smoked cigarettes. They all gulped their cups down and asked if there was more. If I'd known you were going to like it so much I would have made a bigger pot, said Elisa Vicuña. Still, there was enough left to give a few people a smaller second cup. The children had started to agitate about the rockets, and since Javier, who was in charge of all the pyrotechnic gear, had told them to wait for the grown-ups, not even letting them have the lighter, they kept begging the adults to finish their coffee and come and help. All right, all right. The moon bathed them all in a marvelous whiteness, which even crept into the light globe's yellow glow. An atmosphere of carefree triviality reigned: keeping an eye on the time to see how many minutes were left, that sort of thing. The "real men" thought Patri, in her philosophical reverie, were none other than the men she could see before her now. And that was how it had to be, given everything her mother had been telling her for years. Elisa Vicuña's thoughts had not come out of nowhere, arbitrarily. They had come out of men, and gone in a circle, from men back to men, and that route made them "real" whether or not they really were. It was almost like getting used to something, anything, even this after-dinner banality. She started to think more carefully about the problem or the choice she was facing; she tried to put her thoughts in order.

Finally the parents agreed to oversee the lighting of the fireworks. Although it would have seemed impossible only a minute before, the level of excitement among the children rose abruptly. Roberto, who according to his girl-friend was a child at heart, was the keenest to join in, and to the amusement of all present, he even reached into his pocket and produced a sizeable supply of rockets, which he had brought "just in case." So they started with rockets, as well as jumping jacks and firecrackers. The explosions were lots of fun. They tried throwing a cracker into the pool, and the explosion resonated like a building collapsing. More! Come on! They wanted to make a much bigger din. But Javier suggested they fire off some tubes. They used an empty bottle as a launcher. Instead of choosing a dis-tant constellation, they aimed straight at the moon. I think it'll make it, said Ernesto. Roberto had an excellent silver lighter, which allowed him to adjust the flame's intensity as well as its length. Raúl Viñas called it a blowtorch. They lit the first tube's fuse and waited. Miraculously, or because it was well made (a rarity in recent times), it shot straight up into the sky leaving a golden wake. This time they all looked. It exploded way up high in a burst of very white phosphorescence. The same thing happened with the second tube, except that the explosion was red, a dark, metallic red. They had some very big, powerful fireworks, but they were keeping them for later. The smaller children, Ernesto and Jacqueline, were twirling sparklers.

The only one who wasn't taking part in the fun, or not directly, was Patri, because she was busy thinking. It had occurred to her that she didn't really have to wait to find out, she could make a deductive leap: by deducing correctly it was possible to tell what would happen. She couldn't base her deductions on the ghosts, because she didn't know anything about them. But she could use facial expressions instead. She did her very best, calling on her imagination, her unschooled—some might say naïve—creative gifts, but she kept coming to the same conclusion: the mysterious smile on the lips of the ghosts. It was inevitable, given her skeptical nature: ending with a mysterious smile, like an impenetrable barrier.

And what was the meaning of the mysterious smile? She could deduce that too, but in reverse, since any of the people here, the women sitting, the men crouching with the children and playing with the rockets, any of the things they might say or do, could provoke the mysterious smile.

It was within everyone's reach. So life in its entirety, with its infinite conclusions, was, it turned out, the deduction, the genealogy, of the mysterious smile.

While Raúl Viñas had gone off to refill his glass and drink it (which meant he would have to fill it again, but that was his business), Roberto and Javier put one of the really big rockets in a bottle to fire it off, and decided that in spite of the sparks, they would have to hold the bottle, using a napkin if need be to protect against burns, because it was so big and top-heavy it might fall over before take-off. So that was what they did; they brought Roberto's aerodynamic lighter up to the fuse, and shouted to get everyone's attention. Magnificently, triumphantly, trailing a dense wake or jet of sparks, the rocket shot up into the starry sky, crowded now with fireworks from every quarter of the city. As it went past the big parabolic dish, the glow lit up two ghosts floating in the night air, one perfectly vertical, the other at a slight angle, his head behind the head of his companion. That was the time: five to midnight, more or less. At midnight, they would be lined up perfectly, one behind the other, stuck together. Javier and Roberto smiled and whispered obscene remarks about that position; then almost immediately, prompted by the same association of ideas, they both looked at Patri, who was sitting very stiffly, staring into space, white as a sheet, cadaverous, so thin and haggard she could have been mistaken for a lifelike tailor's dummy.

Around her, the women were talking about New Year's resolutions, promises and hopes, which were sometimes indistinguishable. For Inés, it would be the pivotal year of her life, she said: the year of her marriage. The others agreed: afterward they would say "a year ago . . . two years ago . . . ten years ago"; it would be the milepost. And for Carmen, of course, the year would be marked by an event that was no less important for being repeated: the birth of a child. The years, they said, rolled on, and the children were the years, springing from the earth like capricious little butterflies, blown about by the breezes, by the days and weeks and months . . .

Suddenly the sirens blared. Midnight was imminent. The men rushed to light a string of rockets, which began to explode like joyous machine-gun fire. Before the volley was over, Patri got up and headed for the back of the terrace. Her step grew steadily quicker, although she didn't break into a run. All at once the others realized what she was intending to do; and far from being paralyzed by surprise, they got up in turn and went to stop her: the women, the men and the children, shouting out as rockets exploded near and far, and thousands of fireworks flowered in the sky. They didn't catch up with her, of course, although they came close. Patri leaped into the void. And that was it. The whole family came to a halt on the brink, right on the brink, and stood there speechless, as if their hearts, carried on by the momentum of the chase, had leaped as well. As she fell, Patri's thick glasses came off and went on falling separately, beside her. A ghost, appearing suddenly from somewhere, caught them safely before they hit the ground, and rose as if lifted by a gentle spring to the edge of the terrace, where he came to rest, in front of the family, who were stunned by the tragedy. He held the glasses out to Raúl Viñas, who reached out and took them. Man and ghost stared at each other.

13th of February 1987

AN EPISODE
IN THE LIFE
OF A
LANDSCAPE PAINTER

WESTERN ART can boast few documentary painters of true distinction. Of those whose lives and work we know in detail, the finest was Rugendas, who made two visits to Argentina. The second, in 1847, gave him an opportunity to record the landscapes and physical types of the Río de la Plata—in such abundance that an estimated two hundred paintings remained in the hands of local collectors—and to refute his friend and admirer Humboldt, or rather a simplistic interpretation of Humboldt's theory, according to which the painter's talent should have been exercised solely in the more topographically and botanically exuberant regions of the New World. But the refutation had in fact been foreshadowed ten years earlier, during Rugendas's brief and dramatic first visit, which was cut short by a strange episode that would mark a turning point in his life.

Johann Moritz Rugendas was born in the imperial city of Augsburg on the 29th of March 1802. His father, grandfather and great-grandfather were all well-known genre painters; one of his ancestors, Georg Philip Rugendas, was famous for his battle scenes. The Rugendas family (although Flemish in origin) had emigrated from Catalonia in 1608 and settled in Augsburg, hoping to find a social environment more hospitable to its Protestant faith. The first German Rugendas was a master clockmaker; all the rest were painters. Johann Moritz confirmed his vocation at the age of four. A gifted draftsman, he was an outstanding student at the studio of Albrecht Adam and then at the Munich Art Academy. When he was nineteen, an opportunity arose to join the expedition to America led by Baron Langsdorff and financed by the Czar of Russia. His mission was one that, a hundred years later, would have fallen to a photographer: to keep a graphic record of all the discoveries they would make and the landscapes through which they would pass.

At this point, to get a clearer idea of the work upon which the young artist was embarking, it is necessary to go back in time. It was Johan Moritz's great-grandfather, Georg Philip Rugendas (1666–1742) who founded the dynasty of painters. And he did so as a result of losing his right hand as a young man. The mutilation rendered him unfit for the family trade of clockmaking, in which he had been trained since childhood. He had to learn to use his left hand, and to manipulate pencil and brush. He specialized in the depiction of battles, with excellent results, due to the preternatural precision of his draftsmanship, which was due in turn to his training as a clockmaker and the use of his left hand, which, not being his spontaneous choice, obliged him to work with methodical deliberation. An exquisite contrast between the petrified intricacy of the form and the violent turmoil of the subject matter made him unique. His protector and principal patron was Charles XII of Sweden, the warrior king, whose battles he painted, following the armies from the hyperborean snows to sun-scorched Turkey. In later years he became a prosperous printer and publisher of engravings—a natural extension of his skills in military documentation. His three sons, Georg Philip, Johan and Jeremy, inherited both the business and the skills. Christian (1775–1826), the son of Georg Philip junior, was the father of our Rugendas, who brought the cycle to a close by painting the battles of another warrior king, Napoleon.

Napoleon's fall ushered in a "century of peace" in Europe, so inevitably the branch of the profession in which the family had specialized went into decline. Young Johan Moritz, an adolescent at the time of Waterloo, was obliged to execute a swift change of direction. Initially apprenticed to Adam, a battle painter, he began taking classes in nature painting at the Munich Academy. The "nature" favored by buyers of paintings and prints was exotic and remote, so he would have to follow his artistic calling abroad, and the direction his travels would take was soon determined by the opportunity to participate in the voyage mentioned above. On the threshold of his twentieth year, the world that opened before him was roughly mapped out yet still unexplored, much as it was, at around the same time, for the young Charles Darwin. The German painter's Fitzroy was Baron Georg Heinrich von Langsdorff, who, during the crossing of the Atlantic turned out to be so "obdurate and harebrained" that when the boat arrived in Brazil, Rugendas parted company with the expedition, and was replaced by another talented documentary painter, Taunay. By this decision he spared himself a good deal of grief, for the voyage was ill-starred: Taunay drowned in the Guaporé River and in the middle of the jungle Langsdorff lost what few wits he had. Rugendas, meanwhile, after four years of travel and work in the provinces of Rio de Janeiro, Minas Gerais, Mato Grosso, Espiritu Santo and Bahia, returned to Europe and published an exquisite illustrated book entitled *A Picturesque Voyage through Brazil* (the text was written by Victor Aimé Huber using the painter's notes), which made him famous and put him in touch with the eminent naturalist Alexander von Humboldt, with whom he was to collaborate on a number of publications.

Rugendas's second and final voyage to America lasted seventeen years, from 1831 to 1847. His industrious journeying took him to Mexico, Chile, Peru, Brazil again and Argentina, and resulted in hundreds, indeed thousands of paintings. (An incomplete catalogue, including oil paintings, watercolors and drawings, numbers 3353 works.) Although the Mexican phase is the best represented, and tropical jungles and mountain scenes constitute his most characteristic subject matter, the secret aim of this long voyage, which consumed his youth, was Argentina: the mysterious emptiness to be found on the endless plains at a point equidistant from the horizons. Only there, he thought, would he be able to discover the other side of his art ... This dangerous illusion pursued him throughout his life. Twice he crossed the threshold: in 1837, he came over the Andes from Chile, and in 1847, he approached from the east, via the Rio de la Plata. The second expedition was the more productive, but did not take him beyond the environs of Buenos Aires; on his first journey, however, he ventured towards the dreamed-of center and in fact reached it momentarily, although, as we shall see, the price he had to pay was exorbitant.

Rugendas was a genre painter. His genre was the physiognomy of nature, based on a procedure invented by Humboldt. The great naturalist was the father of a discipline that virtually died with him: *Erdtheorie* or *La Physique du monde*, a kind of artistic geography, an aesthetic understanding of the world, a science of landscape. Alexander von Humboldt (1769–1859) was an all-embracing scholar, perhaps the last of his kind: his aim was to apprehend the world in its totality; and the way to do this, he believed, in conformity with a long tradition, was through vision. Yet his approach was new in that, rather than isolating images and treating them as "emblems" of knowledge, his aim was to accumulate and coordinate them within a broad framework, for which landscape provided the model. The artistic geographer had to capture the "physiognomy" of the landscape (Humboldt had borrowed this concept from Lavater) by picking out its characteristic "physiognomic" traits, which his scholarly studies in natural science would enable him to recognize. The precise arrangement of physiognomic elements in the picture would speak volumes to the observer's sensibility, conveying information not in the form of isolated features but features systematically interrelated so as to be intuitively grasped: climate, history, customs, economy, race, fauna, flora, rainfall, prevailing winds ... The key to it all was "natural growth," which is why the vegetable element occupied the foreground, and why, in search of physiognomic landscapes, Humboldt went to the tropics, which were incomparably superior to Europe in terms of plant variety and rates of growth. He lived for many years in tropical regions of Asia and America, and encouraged the artists who had adopted his approach to do likewise. Thus he established a circuit, stimulating curiosity in Europe about regions that were still little known and creating a market for the works of the traveling painters.

Humboldt had the highest admiration for the young Rugendas, whom he dubbed the "founding father of the art of pictorial presentation of the physiognomy of nature," a description that could well have applied to himself. He played an advisory role in the painter's second great voyage, and the only point on which they disagreed was the decision to include Argentina in the itinerary. Humboldt did not want his disciple to waste his efforts south of the tropical zone, and in his letters he was generous with recommendations such as the following: "Do not squander your talent, which is suited above all to the depiction of that which is truly exceptional in landscape, such as snowy mountain peaks, bamboo, tropical jungle flora, groups composed of a single plant species at different ages; *filiceae*, *Lataniae*, feathery-fronded palms, bamboo, cylindrical cactuses, red-flowered mimosas, the inga tree with its long branches and broad leaves, shrub-sized malvaceous plants with digitate leaves, particularly the Mexican hand plant (*Cheirantodendron*) in Toluca; the famous ahuehuete of Atlisco (the thousand-year-old *Cupressus disticha*) in the environs of Mexico City; the species of orchids that flower beautifully on the rounded, moss-covered protuberances of tree trunks, surrounded in turn by mossy bulbs of *Dendrobium*; the forms of fallen mahogany branches covered with orchids, *Banisteriae* and climbing plants; gramineous species from the bamboo family reaching heights of twenty to thirty feet, Bignoniaceae and the varieties of *foliis distichis*; studies of *Pothos* and *Dracontium*; a trunk of *Crescentia cujete* laden with calabashes; a flowering *Teobroma cacao* with flowers springing up from the roots; the external roots of *Cupressus disticha*, up to four feet tall, shaped like stakes or planks; studies of a rock covered with fucus; blue water lilies in water; *Guastavia* (pirigara) and flowering lecitis; a tropical jungle viewed from a vantage point high on a mountain, showing only the broad crowns of flowering trees, from which the bare trunks of the palms rise like a colonnade, another jungle on top of the jungle; the differing material physiognomies of pisang and heliconium ..."

The excess of primary forms required to characterize a landscape could only be found in the tropics. In so far as vegetation was concerned, Humboldt had reduced these forms to nineteen: nineteen physiognomic types that had nothing to do with Linnean classification, which is based on the abstraction and isolation of minimal differences. The Humboldtian naturalist was not a botanist but a landscape artist sensitive to the processes of growth operative in all forms of life. This system provided the basis for the "genre" of painting in which Rugendas specialized.

After a brief stay in Haiti, Rugendas spent three years in Mexico, from 1831 to 1834. Then he went to Chile, where he was to live for eight years, with the exception of his truncated voyage to Argentina, which lasted roughly five months. The original aim had been to travel right across the country to Buenos Aires, and from there to head north to Tucumán, Bolivia and so on. But it was not to be.

He set out at the end of December 1837 from San Felipe de Aconcagua (Chile), accompanied by the German painter Robert Krause, with a small team of horses and mules and two Chilean guides. The plan was to take advantage of the fine summer weather to cross the picturesque passes of the Cordillera at a leisurely pace, stopping to take notes and paint whenever an interesting subject presented itself. And that was what they did.

In a few days—not counting the many spent painting—they were well into the Cordillera. When it rained they could at least make headway, with their papers carefully rolled up in waxed cloth. It was not really rain so much as a benign drizzle, enveloping the landscape in gentle tides of humidity all afternoon. The clouds came down so low they almost landed, but the slightest breeze would whisk them away ... and produce others from bewildering corridors which seemed to give the sky access to the center of the earth. In the midst of these magical alternations, the artists were briefly granted dreamlike visions, each more sweeping than the last. Although their journey traced a zigzag on the map, they were heading straight as an arrow towards openness. Each day was larger and more distant. As the mountains took on weight, the air became lighter and more changeable in its meteoric content, a sheer optics of superposed heights and depths.

They kept barometric records; they estimated wind speed with a sock of light cloth and used two glass capillary tubes containing liquid graphite as an altimeter. The pink-tinted mercury of their thermometer, suspended with bells from a tall pole, preceded them like Diogenes' daylight lamp. The regular hoofbeats of the horses and mules made a distant-seeming sound; though barely audible, it too was a part of the universal pattern of echoes.

Suddenly, at midnight, explosions, rockets, flares, resonating on and on among the immensities of rock and bringing quick splashes of vivid color to those vast austerities: it was the start of 1838, and the two Germans had brought a provision of fireworks for their own private celebration. They opened a bottle of French wine and drank to the new year with the guides. After which they lay down to sleep under the starry sky, waiting for the moon, which emerged in due course from behind the silhouette of a phosphorescent peak, putting a stop to their drowsy listing of resolutions and launching them into true sleep.

Rugendas and Krause got on well and had plenty to talk about, although both were rather quiet. They had traveled together in Chile a number of times, always in perfect harmony. The only thing that secretly bothered Rugendas was the irremediable mediocrity of Krause's painting, which he was not able to praise in all sincerity, as he would have liked. He tried telling himself that genre painting did not require talent, since it was all a matter of following the procedure, but it was no use: the pictures were worthless. He could, however, appreciate his friend's technical accomplishment and above all his good nature. Krause was very young and still had time to choose another path in life. Meanwhile he could enjoy these excursions; they would certainly do him no harm. Krause, for his part, was in awe of Rugendas, and the pleasure they took in each other's company was due in no small measure to the disciple's devotion. The difference in age and talent was not obvious, because Rugendas, at thirty-five, was timid, effeminate and gawky as an adolescent, while Krause's aplomb, aristocratic manners and considerate nature narrowed the gap.

On the fifteenth day they crossed the watershed and began the descent, advancing more rapidly. There was a risk of the mountains becoming a habit, as they obviously were for the guides, who charged by the day. The Germans would be protected against this danger by the exercise of their art, but only in the long term; in the short term, as they acquainted themselves with the surroundings and their representation, the effect was reversed. Riding on slowly or stopping to rest, they passed the time discussing questions of a technical nature. Each novel sight set their tongues in motion as they sought to account for the difference. It should be remembered that the bulk of the work they were doing was preliminary: sketches, notes, jottings. In their papers, drawing and writing were blended; the exploitation of these data in paintings and engravings was reserved for a later stage. Engravings were the key to circulation, and their potentially infinite reproduction had to be considered in detail. The cycle was completed by surrounding the engravings with a text and inserting them into a book.

Krause was not alone in his appreciation of Rugendas's work. It was obvious how well he painted, primarily because of the simplicity he had attained. Everything in his pictures was bathed in simplicity, which gave them a pearly sheen, filled them with the light of a spring day. They were eminently comprehensible, in conformity with the physiognomic principles. And comprehension led to reproduction; not only had his one published book been a commercial success throughout Europe, the engravings illustrating his *Picturesque Voyage through Brazil* had been printed on wallpaper and even used to decorate Sèvres china.

Krause would often refer, half jokingly, to this extraordinary triumph, and in the solitude of the Cordillera, with no one else there to see, Rugendas would smile and accept the compliment, which was accompanied but not undercut by gentle, affectionate mockery. This was the spirit in which he considered the suggestion that a drawing of Aconcagua be used to decorate a coffee cup: the greatest and smallest of things conjoined by the daily labor of a skilled pencil.

Yet it was not so simple to capture the form of Aconcagua, or any given mountain, in a drawing. If the mountain is imagined as a kind of cone endowed with artistic irregularities, it will be rendered unrecognizable by the slightest shift in perspective, because its profile will change completely.

In the course of the crossing they were constantly making thematic discoveries. Themes were important in genre painting. The two artists documented the landscape artistically and geographically, each in accordance with his capacities. And while they could comprehend the vertical, that is the temporal or geological, dimension unaided, since they knew how to recognize schist and slate, carboniferous dendrites and columnar basalts, plants, mosses and mushrooms, when it came to the horizontal or topographical dimension they had to rely on the Chilean guides, who turned out to be an inexhaustible source of names. "Aconcagua" was only one of many.

The landscape's structuring grid of horizontal and vertical lines was overlaid by man-made traces, which were gridlike in turn. The guides responded to reality without preconceptions. The varying weather and the whims of their German clients, whom they regarded with a combination of respect and disdain so reasonable it could hardly offend, made the changeless world they knew by heart resonate with mystery. The Germans, after all, represented the meeting of science and art on equal terms, as well as the convergence, but not the confusion, of two quite distinct degrees of talent.

Travel and painting were entwined like fibers in a rope. One by one, the dangers and difficulties of a route that was tortuous and terrifying at the best of times were transformed and left behind. And it was truly terrifying: it was hard to believe that this was a route used virtually throughout the year by travelers, mule drivers and merchants. Anyone in their right mind would have regarded it as a means of suicide. Near the watershed, at an altitude of two thousand meters, amid peaks disappearing into the clouds, rather than a way of getting from point A to point B, the path seemed to have become quite simply a way of departing from all points at once. Jagged lines, impossible angles, trees growing downwards from ceilings of rock, sheer slopes plunging into mantles of snow under a scorching sun. And shafts of rain thrust into little yellow clouds, agates enveloped in moss, pink hawthorn. The puma, the hare and the snake made up a mountain aristocracy. The horses panted, began to stumble, and it was time to stop for a rest; the mules were perpetually grumpy.

Peaks of mica kept watch over their long marches. How could these panoramas be rendered credible? There were too many sides; the cube had extra faces. The company of volcanos gave the sky interiors. Dawn and dusk were vast optical explosions, drawn out by the silence. Slingshots and gunshots of sunlight rebounded into every recess. Grey expanses hung out to dry forever in colossal silence; airshafts voluminous as oceans. One morning Krause said that he had had nightmares, so their conversations that day and the next turned on moral mechanics and methods of regaining composure. They wondered if one day cities would be built in those mountains. How might that be? Perhaps if there were wars, when they ended, leaving the stone fortresses empty, with their terraced fields, their border posts and mining villages, a hardworking frontier community composed of Chileans and Argentineans could settle there, converting the buildings and the infrastructure. That was Rugendas's idea, probably influenced by the military painting of his ancestors. Krause, on the other hand, in spite of his worldly outlook, was in favor of mystical colonization. A chain of affiliated monasteries perched in the most remote attics of stone could spread new strains of Buddhism deep into the inaccessible realms, and the braying of the long horns would awaken giants and dwarves of Andean industry. We should draw it, they said. But who would believe it?

Rain, sun, two whole days of impenetrable fog, night winds whistling, winds far and near, nights of blue crystal, crystals of ozone. The graph of temperature against the hours of the day was sinuous, but not unpredictable. Nor, in fact, were their visions. The mountains filed so slowly past that the mind amused itself devising constructivist games to replace them.

A series of studies in vertigo occupied them for the best part of a week. They encountered all sorts of mule drivers, and had the most curious conversations with Chileans and Argentineans from Mendoza. They even came across priests, and Europeans, and the guides' uncles and brothers-in-law. But their solitude was soon restored, and the sight of the others receding into the distance was a source of inspiration.

For some years, Rugendas had been experimenting with a new technique: the oil sketch. This was an innovation and has been recognized as such by art history. It was to be exploited systematically by the Impressionists only fifty years later; but the young German artist's only precursors were a handful of English eccentrics, followers of Turner. It was generally thought that the procedure could only produce shoddy work. And in a sense this was true, but ultimately it would lead to a transvaluation of painting. The effect on Rugendas's daily practice was to punctuate the constant flow of preparatory sketches for serial works (engravings or oil paintings) with one-off pieces. Krause did not follow his example; he was content to witness the frenetic production of these pasty little daubs with their clashing acid colors.

Eventually it became clear that they were leaving the mountain landscapes behind. Would they recognize them if they passed that way again? (Not that they had any plans to do so). They had folders full to bursting with souvenirs. "I can still see it in my mind's eye . . ." ran the stock phrase. But why the mind's *eye* in particular? They could still feel it on their faces, in their arms, their shoulders, their hair and heels . . . throughout their nervous systems. In the glorious evening light of the 20th of January, they wondered at the assembly of silences and air. A drove of mules the size of ants appeared in silhouette on a ridgetop path, moving at a star's pace. The mules were driven by human intelligence and commercial interests, expertise in breeding and bloodlines. Everything was human; the farthest wilderness was steeped with sociability, and the sketches they had made, in so far as they had any value, stood as records of this permeation. The infinite orography of the Cordillera was a laboratory of forms and colors. In the meditative mind of the traveling painter, Argentina opened before them.

But looking back one last time, the grandeur of the Andes reared, wild and enigmatic, excessively wild and enigmatic. For a few days now, descending steadily, they had felt an exhausting heat closing around them. While his soul dreamt on, contemplating that universe of rock from the last lookout, Rugendas's body was bathed in sweat. A wind at high altitude stripped tufts of snow from the peaks and flung them towards the toiling painters, like a devoted servant bringing cones of vanilla ice cream to refresh them.

The landscape revealed by this backward glance revived old doubts and crucial quandaries. Rugendas wondered if he would be able to make his way in the world, if his work, that is, his art, would support him, if he would be able to manage like everyone else ... So far he had, and comfortably, but that was due in part to the energy of youth and the momentum he had acquired through his training at the Academy and elsewhere. Not to mention good luck. He was almost sure that he would not be able to keep it up. What did he have to fall back on? His profession, and practically nothing else. And what if painting failed him? He had no house, no money in the bank, and no talent for business. His father was dead, and for years he had been wandering through foreign lands. This had given him a peculiar perspective on the argument that begins "If other people can do it ..." All the people he came across, in cities or villages, in the jungle or the mountains, had indeed managed to keep going one way or another, but they were in their own environments; they knew what to expect, while he was at the mercy of fickle chance. How could he be sure that the physiognomic representation of nature would not go out of fashion, leaving him helpless and stranded in the midst of a useless, hostile beauty? His youth was almost over in any case, and still he was a stranger to love. He had ensconced himself in a world of fables and fairy tales, which had taught him nothing of practical use, at least he had learnt that the story always goes on, presenting the hero with new and ever more unpredictable choices. Poverty and destitution would simply be another episode. He might end up begging for alms at the door of a South American church. No fear was unreasonable, given his situation.

These reflections occupied pages and pages of a letter to his sister Luise in Augsburg, the first letter he wrote from Mendoza.

For suddenly there they were in Mendoza, a pretty town with treelined streets, the mountains within arm's reach and skies so immutably blue they were boring. It was midsummer; the locals, stunned by the heat, extended their siestas until six in the evening. Luckily the vegetation provided plenty of shade; the foliage filled the air with oxygen, so breathing, when possible, was very restorative.

Armed with letters of introduction from Chilean friends, the travelers stayed at the house of the attentive and hospitable Godoy de Villanueva family. A large house overshadowed by trees, with an orchard and various little gardens.

Three generations inhabited the ancestral home in harmony, and the smaller children rode around on tricycles, which Rugendas duly sketched in his notebooks; he had never seen them before. Those were his first Argentinean sketches, portents of an interest in vehicles that would soon develop unexpectedly.

They spent a delightful month in and around Mendoza and its environs. The locals bent over backwards to welcome the distinguished visitor, who, invariably accompanied by Krause, made the obligatory excursions to the ranges (which were no doubt more interesting for travelers who had come from the other direction), toured the neighboring estates and generally began to soak up the spirit of Argentina, so similar to Chile in that town near the border, and yet, even there, so different. Mendoza was, in effect, the starting point for the long eastward voyage across the pampas to the fabled Buenos Aires, and that gave it a special, unique character. Another notable feature was that all the buildings in the town and the surrounding country looked new; and so they were, since earthquakes ensured that all man-made structures were replaced approximately every five years. Rebuilding stimulated the local economy. Comfortably riding the seismic activity, the ranches supplied the Chilean markets, exploiting the early maturation of the cattle, speeded by the dangers emanating from the underworld. Rugendas would have liked to depict an earthquake, but he was told that it was not a propitious time according to the planetary clock.

Nevertheless, throughout his stay in the region, he kept secretly hoping he might witness a quake, though he was too tactful to say so. In this respect, and in others, his desires were frustrated. Prosaic Mendoza held promises that, for one reason or another, were not fulfilled and which, in the end, prompted their departure.

His other cherished dream was to witness an Indian raid. In that area, they were veritable human typhoons, but, by their nature, refractory to calendars and oracles. It was impossible to predict them: there might be one in an hour's time or none until next year (and it was only January). Rugendas would have paid to paint one. Every morning of that month, he woke up secretly hoping the great day had come. As in the case of the earthquake, it would have been in poor taste to mention this desire. Dissimulation made him hypersensitive to detail. He was not so sure that there was no forewarning. He questioned his hosts at length, supposedly for professional reasons, about the premonitory signs of seismic activity. It seemed they appeared only hours or minutes before the quake: dogs spat, chickens pecked at their own eggs, ants swarmed, plants flowered, etc. But there was no time to do anything. The painter was convinced that an Indian raid would be anticipated by equally abrupt and gratuitous changes in the cultural domain. But he did not have the opportunity to confirm this intuition.

Despite all the delays they allowed themselves, and their habit of letting nature encourage and justify their lingering, it was time to move on. Not only for practical reasons in this case, but also because, over the years, the painter had gradually constructed a personal myth of Argentina, and after a month spent on the threshold, the pull of the interior was stronger than ever.

A few days before their departure, Emilio Godoy organized an excursion to a large cattle ranch ten leagues south of the town. Among the picturesque sites they visited on the trip was a hilltop from which they had a panoramic view of forests and ranges stretching away to the south. According to their host, it was from those wooded corridors that the Indians usually emerged. They came from that direction, and in pursuit of them, on a punitive expedition after a raid, the ranchers of Mendoza had glimpsed astonishing scenes: mountains of ice, lakes, rivers, impenetrable forests. "That's what you should be painting ..." It was not the first time he had heard this sentence. People had been repeating it for decades, wherever he went. He had learnt to be wary of such advice. How did they know what he should paint? At this point in his career, within reach of the vast emptiness of the pampas, the art most authentically his own was, he felt, drawing him in the opposite direction. In spite of which, Godoy's descriptions set him dreaming. In his imagination, the Indians' realm of ice was more beautiful and mysterious than any picture he was capable of painting.

Meanwhile, what he was capable of painting took a new and rather unexpected, form. In the process of hiring a guide, he came into contact with a supremely fascinating object: the large carts used for journeys across the pampas.

These were contraptions of monstrous size, as if built to give the impression that no natural force could make them budge. The first time he saw one, he gazed at it intently for a long time. Here, at last, in the cart's vast size, he saw the magic of the great plains embodied and the mechanics of flat surfaces finally put to use. He returned to the loading station the next day and the day after, armed with paper and charcoal. Drawing the carts was at once easy and difficult. He watched them setting off on their long voyages. Their caterpillar's pace, which could only be measured in the distance covered per day or per week, provoked a flurry of quick sketches, and perhaps this was not such a paradox in the work of a painter known for his watercolors of hummingbirds, since extremes of movement, slow as well as quick, have a dissolving effect. He set aside the problem of the moving carts—there would be plenty of opportunities to observe them in action during the journey—and concentrated on the unhitched ones.

Because they had only two wheels (that was their peculiarity), they tipped back when unloaded and their shafts pointed up at the sky, at an angle of forty-five degrees. The ends of the shafts seemed to disappear among the clouds; their length can be deduced from the fact that they could be used to hitch ten teams of oxen. The sturdy planks were reinforced to bear immense loads; whole houses, on occasion, complete with furniture and inhabitants. The wheels were like fairground Ferris wheels, made entirely of carob wood, with spokes as thick as roof beams and bronze hubs at the center, laden with pints of grease. To give an idea of the carts' real dimensions, Rugendas had to draw small human figures beside them, and, having eliminated the numerous maintenance workers, he chose the drivers as models: imposing characters, equal to their task, they were the aristocracy of the carting business. Those hypervehicles were under their control for very considerable periods of time, not to mention the cargoes, which sometimes comprised all the goods and chattels of a magnate. Surely it would take a lifetime at least to travel in a straight line from Mendoza to Buenos Aires at a rate of two hundred meters per day. The cart drivers were transgenerational men; their gaze and manner were living records of the sublime patience exercised by their predecessors. Turning to more practical matters, it seemed that the key variables were weight (the cargo to be transported) and speed: the less the weight, the greater the speed and vice versa. Obviously the long-haul carters, given the flatness of the pampas, had opted to maximize weight.

And one day, suddenly, the carts set off . . . A week later, they were still a stone's throw away, but sinking inexorably below the horizon. Rugendas, as he informed his friend, was possessed by an urgent, almost infantile desire to depart in their wake. He felt it would be like traveling in time: proceeding rapidly on horseback along the same route, they would catch up with carts that had set off in other geological eras, perhaps even before the inconceivable beginning of the universe (he was exaggerating), overtaking them all on their journey towards the truly unknown.

They set off on that trail. Following that line. A straight line leading all the way to Buenos Aires. What mattered to Rugendas, however, was not at the end of the line but at its impossible midpoint. Where something would, he thought, finally emerge to defy his pencil and force him to invent a new procedure.

The Godoys bid him farewell most affectionately. Would he come back one day? they asked. Not according to his itinerary: from Buenos Aires he would proceed to Tucumán, and from there he would head north to Bolivia and Peru, before eventually returning to Europe, after a voyage of several years ... But perhaps one day he would retrace his South American journey in reverse (a poetic idea that came to him on the spur of the moment): once again he would see all that he was seeing now, speak all the words he was speaking, encounter the smiling faces before him, identical, not a day younger or older ... His artist's imagination figured this second voyage as the other wing of a vast, mirrored butterfly.

They took an old guide, a boy to cook for them, five horses and two little mares (they had finally managed to get rid of the grumpy mules). The weather, still hot, became drier. In a week of unhurried progress, they left behind trees, rivers and birds, as well as the foothills of the Andes. A ruse against

Orphic disobedience: obliterate all that lies behind. There was no point turning around any more. On the plains, space became small and intimate, almost mental. To give their procedure time to adjust, they abstained from painting. Instead they engaged in almost abstract calculations of the distance covered. Every now and then they overtook a cart, and psychologically it was as if they had leapt months ahead.

They adapted to the new routine. A series of slight bumps indicated their way across the flat immensity. They began to hunt systematically. The guide entertained them with stories at night. He was a mine of information about the region's history. For some reason (no doubt because they were not practicing their art), Rugendas and Krause, in their daily conversations on horseback, hit upon a relation between painting and history. It was a subject they had discussed on many previous occasions. But now they felt they were on the point of tying up all the loose ends of their reasoning.

One thing they had agreed about was the usefulness of history for understanding how things were made. A natural or cultural scene, however detailed, gave no indication of how it had come into being, the order in which its components had appeared or the causal chains that had led to that particular configuration. And this was precisely why man surrounded himself with a plethora of stories: they satisfied the need to know how things had been made. Now, taking this as his starting point, Rugendas went one step further and arrived at a rather paradoxical conclusion. He suggested, hypothetically, that, were all the storytellers to fall silent, nothing would be lost, since the present generation, or those of the future, could experience the events of the past without needing to be told about them, simply by recombining or yielding to the available facts, although, in either case, such action could only be born of a deliberate resolution. And it was even possible that the repetition would be more authentic in the absence of stories. The purpose of storytelling could be better fulfilled by handing down, instead, a set of "tools," which would enable mankind to reinvent what had happened in the past, with the innocent spontaneity of action. Humanity's finest accomplishments, everything that deserved to happen again. And the tools would be stylistic. According to this theory, then, art was more useful than discourse.

A bird flashed across the empty sky. A cart immobile on the horizon, like a midday star. How could a plain like this be remade? Yet someone would, no doubt, attempt to repeat their journey, sooner or later. This thought made them feel they should be at once very careful and very daring: careful not to make a mistake that would render the repetition impossible; daring, so that the journey would be worth repeating, like an adventure.

It was a delicate balance, like their artistic procedure. Once again Rugendas regretted not having seen the Indians in action. Perhaps they should have waited a few more days ... He felt a vague, inexplicable nostalgia for what had not happened, and the lessons it might have taught him. Did that mean the Indians were part of the procedure? The repetition of their raids was a concentrated form of history.

Rugendas kept delaying the beginning of his task, until one day he discovered that he had more reasons for doing so than he had realized. A casual remark made beside the campfire provoked a rectification from the old guide: No, they were not yet in the renowned Argentinean pampas, although the country they were crossing was very similar. The real pampas began at San Luis. The guide thought they had simply misunderstood the word. And in a sense, they must have, the German reflected, but the thing itself was involved as well; it had to be. He questioned the guide carefully, testing his own linguistic resources. Were the "pampas," perhaps, flatter than the land they were crossing? He doubted it; what could be flatter than a horizontal plane? And yet the old guide assured him that it was so, with a satisfied smile rarely to be seen among the members of his grave company. Rugendas discussed this point at length with Krause later on, as they smoked their cigars under the starry sky. After all, he had no good reason to doubt the guide. If the pampas existed (and there was no good reason to doubt that either), they lay some distance ahead. After three weeks of assimilating a vast, featureless plain, to be told of a more radical flatness was a challenge to the imagination. It seemed, from what they could understand of the old hand's scornful phrases, that, for him, the current leg of the

journey was rather "mountainous." For them, it was like a
well-polished table, a calm lake, a sheet of earth stretched
tight. But with a little mental effort, now that they had
been alerted, they saw that it might not be so. How odd,
and how interesting! Needless to say their arrival in San
Luis, which was imminent according to the expert, became
the object of eager anticipation. For the two days following
the revelation they pressed on steadily. They started seeing
hills everywhere, as if produced by a conjurer's trick: the
ranges of El Monigote and Agua Hedionda. On the third
day they came to expanses resonant with emptiness. The
sinister nature of the surroundings made an impression on
the Germans, and, to their surprise, on the Gauchos too.
The old man and the boy talked in whispers, and the man
dismounted on a number of occasions to feel the soil. They
noticed that there was no grass, not the least blade, and the
thistles had no leaves: they looked like coral. Clearly the
region was drought stricken. The earth crumbled at a touch,
yet a layer of dust did not seem to have formed, although
they could not be sure, because the wind had dropped to
nothing. In the mortal stillness of the air, the sounds of the
horses' hooves, their own words and even their breathing
were accompanied by menacing echoes. From time to time
they noticed that the old guide was straining anxiously to
hear something. It was contagious; they started listening too.
They could hear nothing, except perhaps the faint hint of
a buzzing that must have been mental. The guide clearly

suspected something, but a vague fear prevented them from questioning him.

For a day and a half they advanced through that terrifying void. Not a bird to be seen in the sky, no guinea pigs or rheas or hares or ants on the ground. The planet's peeling crust seemed to be made of dried amber. When they finally came to a river where they could take on water, the guide's suspicions were confirmed. He solved the enigma, which was especially perplexing there on the river banks: not only were they devoid of the least living cell of vegetation, the numerous trees, mainly willows, had been stripped of all their leaves, as if a sudden winter had plucked them bare for a joke. It was an impressive spectacle: livid skeletons, as far as the eye could see, not even trembling. And it was not that their leaves had fallen, for the ground was pure silica.

Locusts. The biblical plague had passed that way. That was the solution, revealed to them at last by the guide. If he had delayed doing so, it was only because he wanted to be sure. He had recognized the signs by hearsay, never having seen them with his own eyes. He had also been told about the sight of the swarm in action, but preferred not to talk about that, because it sounded fanciful, though, considering the results, fancy could hardly have outstripped the facts. Alluding to his friend's disappointment at having missed the Indians, Krause asked if he did not regret having arrived too late on this occasion too. Rugendas imagined it. A green field, suddenly smothered by a buzzing cloud, and, a moment later, nothing. Could a painting capture that? No. An action painting, perhaps.

They proceeded on their way, wasting no time. It was idle to wonder which direction the swarm had taken, because the area affected was too large. They had to concentrate on getting to San Luis, and try to enjoy themselves in the meantime, if they could. It was all experience, even if they had missed out by minutes. The residual vibration in the atmosphere had an apocalyptic resonance.

As it turned out, a number of practical problems made it hard for the painters to enjoy themselves. That afternoon, after two days of involuntary fasting, the horses reached the limits of their endurance. They became uncontrollable, and there was no choice but to stop. To make things worse, the temperature had continued to rise, and must have been near one hundred and twenty two degrees. Not an atom of air was moving. The barometric pressure had plummeted. A heavy ceiling of grey clouds hung over their heads, but without affording any relief from the glare, which went on blinding them. What could they do? The young cook was frightened, and kept clear of the horses as if they would bite him. The old man would not raise his eyes, ashamed of his failure as a guide. There were attenuating circumstances: this was the first time he had crossed an area stricken by a plague of locusts. The Germans conferred in whispers. They were in a lunar ocean, rimmed around with hills. Krause was in favor of grinding up some biscuits, mixing them with water and milk, patiently feeding the horses with this paste, waiting a few hours for them to calm down and setting off again in the cool of the evening. For Rugendas, this plan was so absurd it did not even merit discussion. He proposed something a little more sensible: heading off at a gallop to see what was on the other side of the hills. Accustomed to reckoning distance in paintings, they misjudged the remoteness of those little mountains; in fact they were almost among them already. So the vegetation on their slopes had probably not been spared by the mobile feast. They consulted the guide, but could not get a word out of him. All the same, it was reasonable to suppose that the hills had served as a screen to deflect the swarm, so if they went around to the other side they would find a field with its full complement of clover leaves. Rugendas already had a plan: he would ride south to the hills, while his friend would ride north. Krause disagreed. Given the state of the horses, he thought it reckless to make a dash. Not to mention the storm that was brewing. He categorically refused. Tired of arguing, Rugendas set off on his own, announcing that he would be back in two hours. He spurred his horse to a gallop and it responded with an explosion of nervous energy; horse and rider were drenched with sweat, as if they had just emerged from the sea. The drops evaporated before they hit the ground, leaving a wake of salty vapor. The grey cones of the hills, on which Rugendas fixed his gaze, kept shifting as he rode on in a straight line; without becoming noticeably bigger, they multiplied and began to spread apart; one slipped around behind him surreptitiously. He was already inside the formation (why was it called El Monigote: The Puppet?). The ground was still bare and there was no indication that there would be grass ahead, or in any direction. The heat and the stillness of the air had intensified, if that was possible. He pulled up and looked around. He was in a vast amphitheater of interlayered clay and limestone. He could feel the horse's extreme nervousness; there was a tightness in his chest, and his perception was becoming abnormally acute. The air had turned a lead-grey color. He had never seen such light. It was a see-through darkness. The clouds had descended further still, and now he could hear the intimate rumbling of the thunder. "At least it will cool off," he said to himself, and those trivial words marked the end of a phase in his life; with them he formulated the last coherent thought of his youth.

What happened next bypassed his senses and went straight into his nervous system. In other words, it was over very quickly; it was pure action, a wild concatenation of events. The storm broke suddenly with a spectacular lightning bolt that traced a zigzag arc clear across the sky. It came so close that Rugendas's upturned face, frozen in an expression of idiotic stupor, was completely bathed in white light. He thought he could feel its sinister heat on his skin, and his pupils contracted to pinpoints. The thunder crashing down impossibly enveloped him in millions of vibrations. The horse began to turn beneath him. It was still turning when a lightning bolt struck him on the head. Like a nickel statue, man and beast were lit up with electricity. For one horrific moment, regrettably to be repeated, Rugendas witnessed the spectacle of his body shining. The horse's mane was standing on end, like the dorsal fin of a swordfish. From that moment on, like all victims of personalized catastrophes, he saw himself as if from outside, wondering, Why did it have to happen to me? The sensation of having electrified blood was horrible but very brief. Evidently the charge flowed out as fast as it had flowed into his body. Even so, it cannot have been good for his health.

The horse had fallen to its knees. The rider was kicking it like a madman, raising his legs till they were almost vertical, then closing them with a scissor-like clicking action. The charge was flowing out of the animal too, igniting a kind of phosphorescent golden tray all around it, with undulating edges. As soon as the discharge was complete, in a matter of seconds, the horse got to its feet and tried to walk. The full battery of thunder exploded overhead. In a midnight darkness, broad and fine blazes interlocked. Balls of white fire the size of rooms rolled down the hillsides, the lightning bolts serving as cues in a game of meteoric billiards. The horse was turning. Completely numb, Rugendas tugged at the reins haphazardly, until they slipped from his hands. The plain had become immense, with everywhere and nowhere to run, and so busy with electrical activity it was hard to get one's bearings. With each lightning strike the ground vibrated like a bell. The horse began to walk with supernatural prudence, lifting its hooves high, prancing slowly.

The second bolt of lightning struck him less than fifteen seconds after the first. It was much more powerful and had a more devastating effect. Horse and rider were thrown about twenty meters, glowing and crackling like a cold bonfire. The fall was not fatal, no doubt because of exceptional alterations to atomic and molecular structure, which had the effect of cushioning their impact. They bounced. Not only that, the horse's magnetized coat held Rugendas in place as they flew through the air. But once on the ground the attraction diminished and the man found himself lying on the dry earth, looking up at the sky. The tangle of lightning in the clouds made and unmade nightmarish figures. Among them, for a fraction of a second, he thought he saw a horrible face. The Puppet! The sounds all around him were deafening: crash on crash, thunderclap on thunderclap. The circumstances were abnormal in the extreme. The horse was spinning around on its side like a crab, cells of fire exploding around it in thousands, forming a sort of full-body halo, which moved with the animal and did not seem to be affecting it. Did they cry out, the man and his horse? The shock had probably struck them dumb; in any case their cries would have been inaudible. The fallen horseman reached for the ground with his hands, trying to prop himself up. But there was too much static for him to touch anything. He was relieved to see the horse getting up. Instinctively he knew this was a good thing: better the solitude of a temporary separation than the risk of a third lightning strike.

The horse did indeed rise to its feet, bristling and monumental, obscuring half the mesh of lightning, his giraffe-like legs contorted by wayward steps; he turned his head, hearing the call of madness ... and took off ...

But Rugendas went with him! He could not understand, nor did he want to—it was too monstrous. He could feel himself being pulled, stretching (the electricity had made him elastic), almost levitating, like a satellite in thrall to a dangerous star. The pace quickened, and off he went in tow, bouncing, bewildered ...

What he did not realize was that his foot was caught in the stirrup, a classic riding accident, which still occurs now and then, even after so many repetitions. The generation of electricity ceased as suddenly as it had begun, which was a pity, because a well-aimed lightning bolt, stopping the creature in its flight, might have spared the painter no end of trouble. But the current withdrew into the clouds, the wind began to blow, rain fell ...

It was never known how far the horse galloped, nor did it really matter. Whatever the distance, short or long, the disaster had occurred. It was not until the morning of the following day that Krause and the old guide discovered them. The horse had found his clover, and was grazing sleepily, with a bloody bundle trailing from one stirrup. After a whole night spent looking for his friend, poor Krause, at his wits' end, had more or less given him up for dead. Finding him was not entirely a relief: there he was, at last, but prone and motionless. They hurried on and, as they approached, saw him move yet remain face down, as if kissing the earth; the flicker of hope this aroused was quenched when they realized that he was not moving himself, but being dragged by the horse's blithe little browsing steps. They dismounted, took his foot from the stirrup and turned him over ... The horror struck them dumb. Rugendas's face was a swollen, bloody mass; the bone of his forehead was exposed and strips of skin hung over his eyes. The distinctive aquiline form of his Augsburg nose was unrecognizable, and his lips, split and spread apart, revealed his teeth, all miraculously intact.

The first thing was to see if he was breathing. He was. This gave an edge of urgency to what followed. They put him on the horse's back and set off. The guide, who had recovered his guiding skills, remembered some ranches nearby and pointed the way. They arrived half way through the morning, bearing a gift that could not have been more disconcerting for the poor, isolated farmers who lived there. It was, at least, an opportunity to give Rugendas some simple treatment and take stock of the situation. They washed his face and tried to put it back together, manipulating the pieces with their fingertips; they applied witch hazel dressings to speed the healing and checked that there were no broken bones. His clothing was torn, but except for minor cuts and a few abrasions to his chest, elbow and knees, his body was intact; the major damage was limited to his head, as if it were the bearing he had rolled on. Was it the revenge of the Puppet? Who knows. The body is a strange thing, and when it is caught up in an accident involving nonhuman forces, there is no predicting the result.

He regained consciousness that afternoon, too soon for it to be in any way advantageous. He woke to pain such as he had never felt before, and against which he was defenseless. The first twenty-four hours were one long howl of pain. All the remedies they tried were useless, although there was not much they could try, apart from compresses and good will. Krause wrung his hands; like his friend, he neither slept nor ate. They had sent for the doctor from San Luis, who arrived the following night in the pouring rain on a horse flogged half to death. They spent the next day transporting the patient to the provincial capital, in a carriage sent by His Excellency the governor. The doctor's diagnosis was cautious. In his opinion the acute pain was caused by the exposure of a nerve ending, which would be encapsulated sooner or later. Then the patient would recover his powers of speech and be able to communicate, which would make the situation less distressing. The wounds would be stitched up at the hospital and the extent of the scarring would depend on the responsiveness of the tissue. The rest was in God's hands. He had brought morphine and administered a generous dose, so Rugendas fell asleep in the carriage and was spared the uncertainties of a night journey through quagmires. He woke in the hospital, just as they were stitching him up, and had to be given a double dose to keep him quiet.

A week went by. They took the stitches out and the healing proceeded rapidly. They were able to remove the bandages and the patient began to eat solids. Krause never left his side. The San Luis hospital was a ranch on the outskirts of the city, inhabited by half a dozen monsters, half man, half animal, the results of cumulative genetic accidents. There was no way to cure them. The hospital was their home. It was an unforgettable fortnight for Rugendas. The sensations impinging on the raw, pink flesh of his head were recorded indelibly. As soon as he could stand and go out for a walk on Krause's arm, he refused to go back in. The governor, who had surrounded the great artist with attentions, offered his hospitality. Two days later Rugendas began to ride again and write letters (the first was to his sister in Augsburg, presenting his misfortunes in an almost idyllic light; by contrast, the picture he painted for his friends in Chile was resolutely grim). They decided to leave without delay. But not to follow their original route: the unknown immensity separating them from Buenos Aires was a challenge they would have to postpone. They would return to Santiago, the nearest place where Rugendas could receive proper medical treatment.

For his recovery, though miraculous, was far from complete. He had hoisted himself out of the deep pit of death with the vigor of a titan, but the ascent had taken its toll.

Leaving aside the state of his face for the moment, the exposed nerve, which had caused the unbearable suffering of the first days, had been encapsulated, but although this meant the end of the acute phase, the nerve ending had reconnected, more or less at random, to a node in the frontal lobe, from which it emitted prodigious migraines. They came on suddenly, several times a day; everything went flat, then began to fold like a screen. The sensation grew and grew, overpowering him; he began to cry out in pain and often fell over. There was a high-pitched squealing in his ears. He would never have imagined that his nervous system could produce so much pain; it was a revelation of what his body could do. He had to take massive doses of morphine and the attacks left him fragile, as if perched on stilts, his hands and feet very far away. Little by little he began to reconstruct the accident, and was able to tell Krause about it. The horse had survived, and was still useful; in fact, it was the one he usually chose to ride. He renamed it Flash. Sitting on its back he thought he could feel the ebbing rush of the universal plasma. Far from holding a grudge against the horse, he had grown fond of it. They were fellow survivors of electricity. As the analgesic took effect, he resumed his drawing: he did not have to learn again, for he had lost none of his skill. It was another proof of art's indifference; his life might have been broken in two, but painting was still the "bridge of dreams." He was not like his ancestor, who had to start over with his left hand. If only he had been so lucky!

What bilateral symmetry could he resort to, when the nerve was pricking at the very center of his being?

He would not have survived without the drug. It took him some time to metabolize it. He told Krause about the hallucinations it had caused during the first few days. As clearly as he was seeing his friend now, he had seen demonic animals all around him, sleeping and eating and relieving themselves (and even conversing in grunts and bleats!) ... Krause undeceived him: that part was real. Those monsters were the poor wretches interned for life in the San Luis hospital. Rugendas was stunned by this, until the onset of the next migraine. What an amazing coincidence! Or correspondence: it suggested that all nightmares, even the most absurd, were somehow connected with reality. He had another memory to recount, different in nature, although related. When they took the stitches out of his face, he was vividly aware of each thread coming loose. And in his addled, semiconscious state, he felt as if they were removing all the threads that had controlled the puppets of his feelings, or the expressions that manifested them, which came to the same thing. Averting his gaze, Krause made no comment and hastened to change the subject. Which was not so easy: changing the subject is one of the most difficult arts to master, the key to almost all the others. And in this case, change was a key part of the subject.

For Rugendas's face had been seriously damaged. A large scar descended from the middle of his forehead to a piglet's nose, with one nostril higher than the other, and a net of red streaks spread all the way to his ears. His mouth had contracted to a rosebud puckered with furrows and folds. His chin had been shifted to the right, and transformed into one big dimple, like a soupspoon. This devastation seemed to be irreversible, for the most part. Krause shuddered to think how fragile a face was. One blow and it was broken forever, like a porcelain vase. A character was more robust. A psychological disposition seemed eternal by comparison.

Even so, he might have grown accustomed to that mask, talking to it, waiting for replies, even predicting them. But the worst thing was that the muscles, as Rugendas himself had intuited in his fantasy about the threads, no longer responded to his commands; each one moved autonomously. And they moved much more than normal. It must have been because of the damage to the nervous system. By chance, or perhaps by miracle, this damage was limited to Rugendas's face, but the contrast with his calm trunk and limbs made it all the more striking. The twitching would begin with a slight quiver, a trembling, then spread suddenly and within seconds his whole face was jerking in an uncontrollable St. Vitus's dance. It also changed color, or colors, becoming iridescent, full of violets, pinks and ochres, shifting constantly as in a kaleidoscope.

Viewed from that protean rubber, the world must have looked different, thought Krause. Hallucinations colored not only Rugendas's recent memories but also the scenes of his daily life. On this subject, however, he remained discreet;

he must have been still getting used to the symptoms. And no doubt he did not have time to follow a line of thought through to its conclusion, because of the attacks, which occurred once every three hours, on average. When the pain came on, he was possessed, swept away by an inner wind. He hardly needed to explain what was happening: it was all too visible, although he did say that in the grip of an attack he felt amorphous.

A curious verbal coincidence: amorphous, morphine. The drug went on accumulating in his brain. With its help he began to practice his art again, and organized his routine around spells of pain relief and drawing. In this way he recovered a certain degree of normality. The physiognomic procedure sustained his undiminished skill. The charmingly intimate landscapes of San Luis provided ideal subjects for his convalescent exercises. Nature, in its nineteen vegetal phases, adapted itself to his perception, enveloped with Edenic light: a morphine landscape.

An artist always learns something from the practice of his art, even in the most constraining circumstances, and in this case Rugendas discovered an aspect of the physiognomic procedure that had so far escaped his notice. Namely that it was based on repetition: fragments were reproduced identically, barely changing their location in the picture. If this was not immediately obvious, not even to the artist, it was because the size of the fragments varied enormously, from a single point to a panoramic view (which could greatly exceed the dimensions of the picture). In addition, the fragment's outline could be affected by perspective. As small and as large as the Taoist dragon.

Like so many discoveries, this one seemed at first to be purely gratuitous. But perhaps one day it would have a practical application.

After all, art was his secret. He had conquered it, although at an exorbitant price. He had paid with everything else in his life, so why not the accident and the subsequent transformation? In the game of repetitions and permutations, he could conceal himself even in his new state, and function unseen like any other avatar of the artist. Repetitions: in other words, the history of art.

Why this obsession with being the best? Why did he have to assume that only quality could legitimize his work? In fact, he could hardly even begin to think about it except in terms of quality. But what if he was making a mistake? Or indulging in an unhealthy fantasy? Why couldn't he be like everyone else (like Krause, for example), simply painting as well as he could and giving more weight to other things? That kind of modesty could have considerable effects; for a start it would allow him to practice other arts, should he wish . . . or all of them. His medium could become life itself. The absolutist ambition came from Humboldt, who had designed the procedure as a universal knowledge machine. But that pedantic automaton could be dismantled without giving up the array of styles, each of which was a kind of action.

Within ten days they were back in Mendoza (a journey of one hundred and fifty miles): they rode the same horses along the same route and passed the same carts, accompanied by the same guide and the same cook. The only thing that had changed was Rugendas's face. And the direction. They were slightly delayed by the rain, the wind and the way things looked the same. The Godoy family, notified of the ghastly incident weeks before, renewed their hospitality, but this time they tactfully provided a separate room, where the painter would have more peace and quiet, while still enjoying all the benefits of being in the family's care. His room was perched on the roof; it had once been a lookout, before the trees around the house blocked the view. They could offer him the use of it now because the heat was easing off (it was mid-March); in midsummer, it was a kiln.

Solitude was good for him: he was beginning to cope on his own, and it was a relief to do without Krause for a whole day at a time—not that he was in any way annoyed by the presence of his faithful friend, who was an ideal companion, but because he wanted to leave him in peace, to let him go out and amuse himself in Mendoza after his bedside vigils. He abhorred the thought of being a burden. Secluded in his dovecote, he began to regain his self-esteem, in so far as it was possible.

Those were days of introspection and soul-searching. He had to assimilate what had happened and try to find a viable way forward. He played out internal debates in his correspondence, to which he devoted a great deal of time. He filled pages and pages with his small, compact handwriting. Throughout his life he was a prolific letter writer: clear, organized, explicit, precise. Nothing escaped him. As his letters have been preserved, there is no shortage of documentary material for his biographers, and although none of them has tried, it would be perfectly possible to reconstruct his travels day by day, almost hour by hour, following every movement of his spirit, every reaction, every scruple. The treasure trove of his letters reveals a life without secrets, yet somehow still mysterious.

There were two reasons for his feverish activity during those first days in Mendoza. He was behind in his correspondence, since all he had sent from San Luis were a few brief, faltering notes in a shaky hand, containing a bare minimum of information and making promises to elaborate later, which it was now time to fulfill. But he also needed to clarify things for himself and come to terms with the gravity of his situation, and the only means of doing so at his disposal was the familiar practice of letter writing. That is why there is so much information directly or indirectly related to this episode, concerning not only the events themselves but also their intimate repercussions. The artist's mastery of documentation had carried over to the rest of his life, becoming second nature to the man.

His first and principal correspondent was his sister Luise, back in his hometown of Augsburg. With her he was touchingly sincere. He had never hidden anything from her and could not see why he should do so now. Yet at this juncture he discovered that Luise could not take in the whole range of possible documentation. Or, rather: although she could (because there were no secrets between them), certain things would be left out. This was one of those situations in which the whole is not enough. Perhaps because there were other "wholes," or because the "whole" made up by the speaker and his personal world rotates like a planet, and the combined effect of rotation and orbital movement is to keep certain sides of certain planets permanently hidden. To use a modern term, which does not appear in the letters, we might call this a problem of "discursive form." As if he had been aware of it from the start, Rugendas had prudently built up a range of correspondents scattered around the globe. So now he resumed the task of writing to other addresses; among his interlocutors he counted physiognomic painters and naturalists, ranchers, farmers, journalists, housewives, rich collectors, ascetics and even national heroes. Each set the tone for a different version, but all the versions were his. The variations revolved around a curious impossibility: how could he communicate the proposition "I am a monster"? It was easy enough to set it down on paper. But transmitting its significance was far more difficult. In the case of his Chilean friends the problem was pressing, and he took particular care over his letters to them, especially the Guttikers, who had already written inviting him to stay at their house in Santiago, as he had before setting out on his journey a few months before. Since they would be seeing him shortly, he felt he had to warn them. The obvious thing to do in this case would have been to exaggerate, in order to diminish the surprise. But it was not easy to exaggerate, given the state of his face. He ran the risk of falling short, especially if they were allowing for obvious exaggeration. Which would make the surprise even worse.

In any case, he certainly did not shut himself away. His body's natural regimen required a good deal of fresh air and exercise. And even in his semi-invalid state, in spite of the frequent migraines, the nervous attacks and the constant medication, it became imperative for him to dedicate the hours of good daylight to riding and painting the natural world. The faithful Krause never left his side, because the attacks could occur far from the house, in which case he would hoist Rugendas onto his own horse and gallop back, undaunted by the cries of pain. Those spectacular crises were not, however, the most remarkable aspect of their outings. Rugendas attracted a great deal of attention even when he was behaving with perfect calm and propriety. People gathered to look at him, and in half-civilized places like the picturesque environs of Mendoza, one could hardly expect discretion to be the rule. The children were not the worst, because the adults behaved like children too. They watched him intently drawing the large hydraulic devices used for irrigation (his latest enthusiasm), and they were consumed by the desire to see his papers. What did they imagine? As for Rugendas, each time he took up his pencil he had to resist the temptation to sketch himself.

At summer's end the weather had attained ultimate perfection. The landscapes took on an infinite plasticity; the shifting light of the Cordillera enveloped them hour by hour, made them transparent, endless cascades of detail. The afternoon light, filtered by the imposing stone ramparts of the Andes, was a ghost of its morning self, an optics of the mind, inhabited by the untimely pinks of midafternoon. Twilight went on for ten or twelve hours. And during the friends' night walks, gusts of wind rearranged stars and mountains. If it was true, as the Buddhists said, that everything, even a stone, a dead leaf or a blowfly, had already existed and would exist again, that everything was part of a great cycle of rebirths, then everything was a man, a single man on the scale of time. Any man, Buddha or a beggar, a god or a slave. Given sufficient time, all the elements of the universe would combine to form a man. This had major consequences for the procedure: for a start, it could not operate automatically like a transcendent mechanics, with each fragment being slotted into its predetermined place; each fragment could become any other, and the transformation would be accomplished not in the dimension of time but in that of meaning. This idea could give rise to a totally different conception of reality. In his work, Rugendas had come to the conclusion that the lines of a drawing should not represent corresponding lines in visible reality, in a one-to-one equivalence. On the contrary, the line's function was constructive. That was why the practice of drawing remained irreducible to thought, and why, although he had completely incorporated the procedure, he could continue to draw.

The Godoys had still not grown accustomed to his new appearance. This was an interesting sign of things to come. People can get used to any deformity, even the most frightful, but when it is accompanied by an uncontrollable movement of the features, a fluid, senseless movement, habit has no stable base on which to build. Perception remains correspondingly fluid. Although sociable and talkative by nature, Rugendas began to retire shortly after dinner and spend the evenings on his own. This he could do without awkwardness, since he had a legitimate excuse: struck down by superhuman migraines, he was at first incapable of anything but writhing on the bed of his attic room ... and not only the bed, on the floor too, and the walls, and the ceiling ... when the medication took effect, he returned to his letters.

In his writing he tried to be absolutely sincere. He reasoned as follows: in principle, telling the truth and lying require the same amount of effort, so why not tell the truth, without omissions or ambiguities? If only as an experiment. But this was easier to say than to do, especially since in this case the doing was a kind of saying.

Perhaps the morphine would never be metabolized. Perhaps he was entering a second or a third phase. Or was the combination of the opiate, the migraines and the nervous meltdown of a physiognomic landscape painter producing an unprecedented result? In any case the concept of truth took on monstrous proportions in his imagination, and rent his nights in the little rooftop room.

The letters from this period are much concerned with an apparently extraneous matter, to which Rugendas returns obsessively, like a monomaniac. His book *A Picturesque Voyage through Brazil*, the basis of his considerable fame throughout Europe, had in fact been written by someone else, the French journalist and art critic Victor Aimé Huber (1800–1869), using Rugendas's manuscript notes. Although this had not struck him as irregular at the time, it now seemed very odd indeed, and he wondered how he could have consented to such a scheme. Surely it was fraudulent to publish a book under the signature of X when it had in fact been written by Y? He had been so distracted by the whole process of the publication, which was absurdly complicated because of the nature of the book, that he had agreed without thinking. There were so many tasks involved, from financing the project to the coloring of the plates; the writing of the text seemed a mere detail. The lithographs were the book's main attraction: a hundred of them, executed by French artists, except for three, which Rugendas had done himself. Although the lithographers, Engelmann & Co., had a well-deserved reputation as the finest in Europe, he still had to supervise the preparation of the lithographs in person and in minute detail; the process consisted of various stages and was beset with pitfalls. He had thought of the text as an accompaniment to the images; but what he had not seen at the time, and was now beginning to realize, was that by considering it an accompaniment or a complement he was separating the text from the "graphic" content. And the truth, he now saw, was that both were part of the same thing. Which meant that the ghostwriter, the "nègre," had infiltrated the very essence of the work, under the pretext of carrying out a purely technical task: making coherent sentences out of the disjointed scraps of oral documentation. But everything was documentation! That was where it all began and where it ended too. Where it began especially (because the end was far off down the misty ways of science and art history). Nature itself, preformed by the procedure, was already documentation. There were no pure, isolated data. An order was implicit in the phenomenal revelation of the world; the order of discourse shaped things themselves. And since his current mental state was part of that order, he would have to examine it and find rational explanations for what seemed to be a visionary or maniacal chaos. It should be added here that Rugendas was not medicating himself with pure morphine—which could not be synthesized at the time—but with a tincture of opium in a bromide solution. This combined the benefits of the best analgesic and those of the best antidepressant. His face twitched like a second hand timing an eternity of Buddhist reincarnations. It was one way to cure the "publishing pains" resulting from his past errors of judgment.

Although in their letters the Guttikers kept urging him to return to Chile, the journey across the mountains was repeatedly postponed. He was engrossed in the work of letter writing and still apprehensive about confronting acquaintances with his new face, while the need for medical attention had become less urgent, partly because his torments had settled into a more or less stable pattern and partly because he was beginning to accept the futility of any treatment. But the preponderant reason for the delay was that conditions in Mendoza at that time of year were ideal for painting. And this, in turn, encouraged the two friends to extend their excursions, in so far as Rugendas's health permitted, always venturing southwards, towards the forests and lakes, where, despite the cold, a mysterious tropical zone of blue light and endless foliage seemed to begin. They would spend the night in San Rafael, a little village ten leagues south of the provincial capital, or at one of the ranches in the area belonging to friends or relatives of the Godoys, and then set off, sometimes for whole days at a time, up winding valleys, in search of views, which they captured in increasingly strange watercolors. After a few such exquisite outings, they could not bear to give them up. The vagueness of the letters Rugendas wrote during those weeks has allowed a legend to spring up, according to which he journeyed far into the south, to regions unexplored by white men, perhaps all the way to the fabled glaciers, shifting mountains of ice, impregnable portals of another world. The field sketches dating from that time lend credence to the myth. They have an air of impossible distance about them. For the legend to be true, Rugendas would have had to fly through the air, like an Immortal, from the known to the unknown. Which is what he was doing all the time, mentally. But for him it was a normal, everyday activity, a mere background for incredible events, anecdotes or episodes.

Whatever the truth of the matter, the Germans found themselves in natural surroundings that were excitingly unfamiliar, so unfamiliar that Rugendas required confirmation from his friend that what he was seeing existed objectively and was not a product of his altered state. Urgent, impertinent birds flung outlandish cries in the tangled vegetation, guinea fowl and hairy rats scampered away before them, powerful yellow pumas kept watch from rock ledges. And the condor soared pensively over the abysses. There were abysses within abysses and trees rose like towers from the deep underground levels. They saw gaudy flowers open, large and small, some with paws, others with rounded kidneys of apple flesh. In the streams there were siren-like molluscs and, at the bottom, always swimming against the current, legions of pink salmon the size of lambs. The deep green of the auraucaria trees thickened to a velvety black or parted to reveal floating landscapes that always seemed upside down. Around the lakes, forests of delicate myrtle, with trunks like tubes of yellow rubber, smooth to the touch and cold as ice. Moss plumped up to form wilderness sofas;

the airy lacework of fern fronds quivered nervously.

And then one day they remembered: when the Indians mounted their deadly, lightning raids, it was from those zones that they emerged. It would not have surprised them to learn that they appeared from thin air. But obviously they came from a place on earth, somewhere further away, who knows where, and the forests flanking the Cordillera provided them with handy passages for making quick incursions into civilization and equally quick getaways. They were reminded of these events, which had greatly exercised Rugendas's imagination before the accident, not by an association of ideas, but by reality itself, in the most abrupt manner. They had spent the night at a ranch near San Rafael, after three days of camping at high altitude amid Edenic greenery. During the descent they had decided to go straight back to Mendoza, but then they stopped to paint and had to spend the night at the ranch house, whose owner was coming to the end of his summer stay on the property and preparing to return to town, where his children went to school. Rugendas, who was going through a particularly critical phase, had attacks of vertigo and cerebral short-circuiting all night; he could only withstand them by taking an excessive dose of morphine, and dawn found him sleepwalking, covered in sweat, his face a jig of lightning tics, his pupils shrunk to pinpoints as if he were at the center of the sun.

And when the sun rose the yard began to resound with shouts and the noise of horses.

Indians! Indians!

What?

Indians! Indians!

The household swung into action in an instant; it sounded as if all its occupants were hurling themselves against the walls like raving lunatics. The two friends came to the door of their room, which opened onto a gallery around the yard. Krause intended to find out what was happening, how serious the disturbance was and if there was any possibility of setting out for Mendoza, while his friend went back to bed; but Rugendas came out after him, half-dressed and staggering. Krause could have stood on his authority and sent him back, but it was not worth the trouble: in the confusion, no one would pay any attention to the monster's somnolent bumbling, and besides there was no time to lose. So he let him reel freely.

The men were organizing the defense. It was not the first time they had taken up arms to drive the Indians back, nor would it be the last, and their manner was relaxed. It was simply part of the job. But the customary nature of the occurrence had not led to improved organization; how could the response be organized when the raids were so erratic and unpredictable? With a bare minimum of information they improvised a counterattack, as swift as possible, and combined, as best they could, with an emergency roundup, because the main aim was to limit the losses of livestock.

According to a messenger, the attack had begun at dawn with a massacre at the post office, and spread from there as the Indians went rustling cattle all around the area. They could not have advanced much further and mounted parties were already setting out in pursuit from the surrounding ranches. The number of Indians was estimated at one thousand; it was a medium-to-large raid.

A contingent of farmhands would remain at the ranch house to defend the women and children; the house, as the owner told Krause, could be transformed into a fort using simple panels, which were already being put into place. He asked what the Germans were intending to do; they could be useful either way, going along or staying behind.

This conversation, interrupted by shouts and orders (and energetic gestures), took place in the middle of the yard, where the men were already gathering with their guns. Krause, still half asleep, was of two minds, and went back to see if his friend had returned to the room ... but no, there he was, using a hat to cover his face, still as a tree. He gave a violent start when Krause took him by the arm. Asked if he had heard the news, he mumbled indistinctly in reply ... No, he had clearly neither heard nor understood what was happening. Krause decided immediately to put him back to bed and stay to help with the defense of the house, if it came to that. He could not help feeling a twinge of regret: they had cherished the dream of seeing the Indians in action, and now their chance had come, but they would have to miss it. While the ranch owner and his men made a noisy exit through the gates, Krause took his friend's arm and started leading him back to the house. To stop him falling in the other direction, he had to guide him from behind, gripping both arms and holding him up. Rugendas walked stiffly but all the parts of his body seemed to be working loose. He went on mumbling, and since Krause was ignoring him, raised his voice to a shout. They were already back in the gallery. Krause came around to face him, and, rather embarrassed, asked what he was saying. It was something about a mantilla. Krause opened the door of the room and Rugendas darted in, went straight to his painting kit, and pointed to his friend's. Krause could not believe his eyes, but he had to bow to the evidence: in spite of the state he was in, the great Rugendas wanted to go and sketch the Indian raid. Krause sat down on the bed disconsolately. It's impossible, impossible, he said. Rugendas paid no attention. He had realized he was barefoot and begun the laborious business of putting on his boots. He looked up at Krause: The horses, he said. Krause tried a dissuasive argument that had just occurred to him: they could sleep for a couple of hours and leave around midday. The action was bound to continue into the afternoon. But Rugendas was not listening; he was in another dimension. His movements had transformed the room into a mad scientist's laboratory where some transformation of the world was being hatched. The nocturnal half-light gave the interior a Flemish touch. Like a purple-faced lion he fumbled with his boots, on all fours. Krause rushed out, heading for the stables, pursued by the stammering of his half-shod friend: Man! Manti! Mantilla! They would take only Flash and the bay horse, Dash. It would not have to be more than an outing, after all, a painter's picnic; and perhaps the ride and the activity would help to clear Rugendas's mind. He had probably overexerted himself during the previous days, because of the abundance of beauty they had encountered. The raid had come at a bad time, and yet it could still serve a purpose: to exhaust the painter's energy, or rather, to complete that process; given his current state the only hope of improvement lay in plumbing the depths.

Rugendas was waiting for him in the yard with his little box of charcoal sticks and his hat pulled down over his face. He kept talking about a mantilla, and Krause finally understood what he meant. It was a good idea; he should have thought of it himself, but he could hardly be blamed, what with everything else he had to think of. I'll go and see, he said, and tell our hostess what we are planning to do. Rugendas went with him, and when they found the lady of the house, in the kitchen, it was the invalid who summoned all his ebbing strength to make the unusual request for a lace mantilla, of the kind worn at mass, black, naturally, it went without saying. South American ladies were well supplied with such Catholic accessories. He did not explain in detail why he needed it, and she must have supposed it was to hide the hideous disfigurement of his face and his ghastly nervous tics. In which case, she can only have been surprised that he had taken so long to equip himself with that charitable disguise. For inhabitants of Mendoza (as for Chileans), the idea of a man wearing a mantilla was not so strange, because there was a long and venerable tradition of "masked men" in the region. In any case, it was a situation in which people kept making peremptory demands for the most incongruous objects without a word of explanation. She sent someone to fetch the mantilla, and while they were waiting, gave them some indication of where the fighting was taking place and how the sides were maneuvering. The idea of going out to paint the action struck her as splendid; she was sure they would capture some interesting images. But they had to remember to take precautions, and not get too close. Were they armed? Both had revolvers. No, there was no need to worry about her; the house was safe. It was not the first time she had been through this exercise and it no longer scared her. They even exchanged jokes; the hardy pioneers made light of the absurdity of the age. Their scale of values accommodated the most outrageous nuisances. For them, the Indians were simply part of reality. So the foreigner wanted to paint them? They could see nothing strange in that.

The mantilla arrived; it was made of fine black lace. Rugendas took it reverently, and the first thing he did was to gauge its transparence, which was, it seemed, to his satisfaction. He took his leave without further ado, promising to return the mantilla intact that evening. By then, said the lady with a heroic laugh, I may be Madame Pehuenche. God forbid! exclaimed Krause, bowing to kiss her outstretched hand.

So they set off. A farmhand held the yard gate open; it would be barred behind them. Rugendas was waving the mantilla like a madman, and he bumped into one of the pillars of the gallery. Up they leapt onto their horses. But Rugendas landed facing backwards, looking at the tail. The animals took off; he covered his face with the mantilla, put his hat on top of it, and knotted it around his neck ... But when he came to look for the reins of course he could not find them. The horse was headless! That was when he realized he was sitting backwards, and turning around was a nightmare circus trick. By the time he had pulled it off (Krause, embarrassed, had gone ahead), they were already out of the yard, and the enormous grilles shut behind them with a *clang* to which the birds replied.

The beautiful San Rafael morning greeted them with songs of freedom. The sun was rising behind the trees. They rode side by side. Rested and docile, Flash and Dash stepped evenly, their faces inexpressive. Is everything all right? asked Krause. Yes! Are you all right? Yes! And it was true: he looked absolutely fine, with the mantilla covering his face. It hid the damage. Although, of course, that was not why he had chosen to wear it. He had wanted something to filter the light. Direct sunlight tormented his poor addled head and his shattered nervous system. His pinpoint pupils could not contract any further; the drug had deactivated the adaptive reflex and even moderate illumination soon became too much for him. It was as if he had taken another step into the world of his paintings. By virtue of a curious phenomenon of conditioning, Krause kept guessing at the absurd grimaces hidden by the black lace.

The morning was truly glorious, perfect for a raid. There was not a cloud in the sky; the air had a lyrical resonance; birds were combing the trees. The lid had been taken off the world specifically to reveal the conflict, the clash of civilizations, as at the dawn of history. They came to a vast prairie, heard shots in the distance and set off at a gallop.

Krause did not write letters, or if he did, no one bothered to keep them. So his thoughts can only be reconstructed in an indirect or speculative manner. Rugendas remarked repeatedly that he seemed to be preoccupied (describing his own state in the letters, he tended to use Krause as a rhetorical device, a supplementary "color": the feelings attributed to his friend, or, in some instances, invented for him, served to express what tact or shame prevented Rugendas from saying about himself, for example, "K. thinks that the quality of my sketches has not declined"). While continuing to fulfill his self-imposed duties, if anything with greater vigilance, Krause withdrew into a melancholy abstraction. As they rode out that day he was assailed by gloomy thoughts about the state of his friend's health. He felt guilty about going along with his mad plan, and not just because it was mad: agreeing to it was like saying "What the hell," like granting a dying man his last wish. All his reactions were colored by the idea that death had come between them and struck a blow, whether fatal or a mere foretaste was immaterial for the moment. In the course of a journey one encounters so many people, such a mass of humanity, that to be singled out seemed unjust. Yet since it was so natural not to ask of another "Why him?," the question "Why me?" seemed scandalous and impossible. Of course in Krause's case it was not "Why me?" but "Why him?" Nevertheless the close bond between the two men gave the question a new twist, producing its most disturbing form: "Why not me?" This made Krause think of himself as a survivor, an inheritor, a vessel for his friend's whole life, dragged along by an immense force of time. If, as he had often felt, simplifying intuitively, he and Rugendas made up all of humanity, each of them was equally likely to be struck down. And whichever it was, the balance would be maintained. After all, this splendid raiding day might be remembered as "the day Krause died." That was why they stayed together, in spite of everything that could have driven them apart. Having a partner was a way of outliving oneself, in life and in death. And although, regrettably, this led to feelings of guilt and nostalgia, the resulting melancholy had a role to play in the general system of euphoria: only melancholy generated good ideas about the dead, and those ideas could contribute to the procedure.

Indian fever was catching. Where where they? Rugendas and Krause rode off into the radiant dawn in search of them, as in an illustration. By chance they came across a path, which must have led to the post office, so they followed it at a dash, hearing shots closer and closer at hand, then shouts. It was the first time they had heard Indians.

They passed through a series of parallel windbreaks and the action came into view, the first action of that memorable day. In the distance, the white post office, tiny like a die. Closer, a party of ranchers on horseback, shooting into the air, and the Indians, on horseback too, galloping around and shouting. Everything was moving very quickly, including them, as they rushed down into the little valley at full tilt. The engagement, like all the others they were to witness, operated as follows: the savages were equipped only with cutting and stabbing weapons, pikes, lances and knives; the white men had shotguns, but they used them to fire warning shots into the air, thus keeping the enemy far enough away to render their weapons ineffective. And so they skirmished back and forth. This balance could only be maintained at high velocity: both sides kept accelerating, and as the other side had to keep up, they reached their physical limits almost immediately. The scene was very fluid, very distant, a mere optical play of appearances . . .

They could not let this pass; they had to draw it. And they did, without dismounting, resting the paper on portable drawing boards. When they looked up again, there was no one left. Krause glanced across at his friend's sketch. It was strange and disturbing to see him sketching with his head hidden in that black cocoon. He asked if Rugendas could see properly.

He had never seen better in his life. In the depths of that mantled night the pinpricks of his pupils woke him to the bright day's panorama. And powdered poppy extract, a concentrated form of the analgesic, provided sleep enough for ten reawakenings per second.

They put their papers into the saddlebags and spurred the horses on, for this scene had been a mere appetizer. And as they came out of the valley (beginner's luck!) they saw a hundred or so Indians veering off to the north, no doubt heading for one of the undefended ranches in the area. This provided subjects for more sketching; Rugendas filled five sheets before the group disappeared from view. As they were setting off again, they encountered a band of ranchers, whom they were able to inform of the Indians' movements. They could be useful, even while keeping out of the mêlée.

On their own again, they headed southwards at walking pace, exchanging their first impressions. Luckily both of them had good eyesight. It seemed they would have to re-sign themselves to seeing the Indians in miniature, like lead soldiers. Yet the details were all there, violently impressed on their retinas, magnified on the paper. In fact, if they wanted to, they could draw isolated details. The detail that fascinated them was the brevity of it all, the way organization emerged from chance, the speed of the organization. The procedure of the combat between Indians and white men mirrored that of the painters: it was a matter of exploiting the balance between proximity and distance.

Coming over a rise they saw more action: this time the Indians were beating a hasty retreat up a rocky slope, the horses scrambling like goats, leaving behind dozens of rustled bull calves, while the ranchers fired through the gaps in the herd. The scene was picturesque in the extreme. The stick of charcoal began to fly across the paper. The mountain, lit by perpendicular sunlight, offered the racing figures a fan of escape routes, like a peacock's open tail. The artists had to be careful not to exaggerate in their depiction, for the Indian horsemen in their ascent could easily become so many variations on Pegasus. Yet realism was guaranteed as long as they kept sketching naturally, and in that sense having to draw quickly and work out the perspective as they went was a help.

When the Indians had disappeared, they galloped over to the ranchers to see what they were doing. The shots had taken their toll on the herd. Some of the bull calves had been killed; others were still standing, stunned. The men were arguing about brands, which were all mixed up, and nonexistent on some of the recently weaned animals. The Germans were surprised to discover that brands could be objects of dispute; they had always thought of them as signs designed to be read unequivocally. They learnt that troops from the fort were engaged in hand-to-hand combat in the stockyards at El Tambo, two leagues away. Thanking the ranchers for this information, they set off.

But halfway there they had to stop again, for the fourth

time, to sketch a scrap at a stream crossing. They were starting to feel that there were Indians everywhere. As is often
the case with collectors, the problem was not a lack but an
excess of specimens. The devils were obviously using disper-
sion as an added weapon.

It was like wandering from room to room at a party, from
the living room to the dining room, from the bedroom to
the library, from the laundry to the balcony, all full of noisy,
happy, more or less drunk guests, looking for a place to cuddle or trying to find the host to ask him for more beer. Except
that it was a house without doors or windows or walls, made
of air and distance and echoes, of colors and landforms.

This stream could have been the bathroom. The Indians
wanted to charge but they were retreating; the white men
wanted to retreat, but in order to do so they had to charge (in
order to scare the enemy more effectively with their bangs).
This ambivalence was driving the horses crazy; they plunged
into the water, splashed about, or simply stopped to drink,
very calmly, while their riders yelled themselves hoarse in
simultaneous flight and pursuit. The skirmish had an infinite
(or at least algebraic) plasticity, and since Rugendas was observing it at closer range this time, his flying pencil traced details of tense and lax muscles, wet hair clinging to supremely
expressive shoulders. . . Everything sketched in this explosive
present was material for future compositions, but although
it was all provisional, a constraint came into play. It was as if
each volume captured in two dimensions on the paper would

have to be joined up with the others, in the calm of the studio, edge to edge, like a puzzle, without leaving any gaps. And that was indeed how it would be, for the magic of drawing turns everything into a volume, even air. Except that for Rugendas the "calm of the studio" was a thing of the past; now there was only torment, drugs and hallucinations.

The savages scattered in all directions, and four or five came climbing up the knoll where the painters had stationed themselves. Krause drew his revolver and fired twice into the air; Rugendas was so absorbed that his only reaction was to write BANG BANG on his sheet of paper. The sight of his head wrapped in black lace must have frightened the Indians, for they veered away immediately and made off across the hillside. The painters went down to the stream, where their horses drank. They had come a long way, and what with one thing and another, the morning was already half gone. They struck up a conversation with the men who had remained by the crossing. They were soldiers from the fort; they had ridden from El Tambo in pursuit of the Indians, and were about to return. They could go all together.

Krause was intrigued by the fact that neither these men nor those they had met earlier seemed in the least taken aback by the mask covering Rugendas's face. Yet their lack of surprise was logical enough, since in such difficult situations, adapting any object to any purpose was the norm. In everyday life there were explanations for everything, and in abnormal circumstances, there were explanations for the explanations.

Apparently there was a regular battle underway at El Tambo; the soldiers wanted to leave immediately. Krause suggested that he and Rugendas rest for an hour or so on the shady banks of the stream; he was worried about his friend's state of overexcitement and the effect it might have on his system. But Rugendas would not listen: he had not even begun; there was so much to do, right now! And from his point of view, he was right: he had not begun, and he never would.

Off they went, with the young soldiers, who joked and bragged about their comical exploits. It all seemed fairly innocuous. So this was an Indian raid? This series of tableaux vivants? There was still a possibility that it could live up to the popular image, turning ugly and barbaric. But if not, what did it matter?

They did not reach El Tambo. Halfway there, Rugendas had an attack, a severe one. The soldiers were alarmed by his cries and the way he writhed on the saddle. Krause had to tell them to continue on their way, he would take care of it. There was a little hill close by and as the artists struck out in that direction, Rugendas pulled off his hat and flung it away, punching at his temples. What had really shaken the soldiers was not being able to see the origin of the cries, hidden inside the black mantilla. They could not link them to a subjective expression. Oddly, it was the same for Krause. After hours of riding and drawing together without seeing his friend's face, the cries made him realize that he could no longer reconstruct its appearance.

They dismounted in the shade. Between convulsions, Rugendas took all his remedies at once, without measuring the doses, and fell asleep. He woke up half an hour later, free of acute pain but in a delirious daze. The only thread attaching him to reality was an urgent desire to follow the events at close hand. By this stage, of course, the raid seemed to be simply one more hallucination. He was still wearing the mantilla, and must have needed it more than ever now. Krause did not dare ask him to remove it for a moment so he could see his face. He was beginning to speculate wildly about what might be hidden behind the lace. He tried to stop thinking about it, but could not help himself. Lifting Rugendas back into the saddle, he was amazed by the coldness of his body.

In terms of the physiognomy of combat, the best was still to come, at El Tambo. They sketched the battle from various points of view, for hours, until after midday. It was an uninterrupted parade of Indians, compensating for the brevity of their appearances by repeating them. Rugendas found himself making pluralist sketches. But wasn't that what he always did? Even when he drew one of the nineteen types of vegetation identified by the procedure, he was taking its reproduction into account, seeing it as part of a multitudinous species, which would go on making nature. Continually reappearing from the wings, the Indians were, in their way, making history.

The postures they adopted on horseback were beyond belief. This exhibitionism was part of a system for inspiring fear at a distance. There was something circus-like about it, with shooting instead of applause. They didn't care about the laws of gravity, or even whether the full value of their performance was being appreciated; the postures, it is true, had no value in themselves. Rugendas would have to rectify them on paper, to make them plausible in the context of a static composition. But in his sketches the rectification was incomplete, so traces of their real strangeness remained, archeological traces in a sense, because they were overlaid and obscured by speed.

Mounted squads emerged periodically from El Tambo—a complex of low buildings adjoined by extensive corrals—with all their firearms blazing, momentarily breaking the rings of savages, which reformed within seconds. The dairy cows had lain down; they looked like dark lumps. The dances of the Indian horsemen attained extremes of fantasy when it came to displaying their captives. This was a distinctive feature of the raids, almost a defining trait. Stealing women, as well as livestock, was what made it all worthwhile. In fact, it was an extremely rare occurrence, and functioned more as excuse and propitiatory myth. Unsuccessful as usual, the Indians at El Tambo displayed the captives they had not been able to take, with defiant and, again, extremely graphic gestures.

They came around the hill by the stream, a little group of them, lances raised, yelling: Huinca! Kill! Arrghh! The loudest, in the middle of the group, was triumphantly holding a "captive," perched sideways on the neck of his horse. Naturally this was not a captive at all, but another Indian, disguised as a woman; he was making effeminate gestures, but no one could have fallen for such a crude trick, and even the Indians seemed to be treating it as a joke.

Whether for fun or to make a symbolic point, they took it further. An Indian rode past comically cuddling a "captive" which was in fact a white calf. The soldiers intensified their fire, as if the taunts had enraged them, but perhaps that was not the reason. The next display took extravagance to the limit: the "captive" was an enormous salmon, pink and still wet from the river, slung across the horse's neck, clasped by a muscular Indian, who was shouting and laughing as if to say: "I'm taking this one for reproduction."

All these scenes were much more like pictures than reality. In pictures, the scenes can be thought out, invented, which means that they can surpass themselves in terms of strangeness, incoherence and madness. In reality, by contrast, they simply happen, without preliminary invention. There at El Tambo, they were happening, and yet it was as if they were inventing themselves, as if they were flowing from the udders of the black cows.

Had the artists been close to the action, it would have been impossible to transfer it to paper, even using some kind of shorthand. But distance made a picture of it all, by including everything: the Indians, the path by the stream, El Tambo, the soldiers, the cart track, the shots, the cries and the broader view of the valley, the mountains and the sky. They had to shrink everything down to a dot, and be ready to reduce it further still.

Within each circle there was a transitive, transparent cascade, from which the picture recomposed itself, as art. Tiny figures running around the landscape, in the sun. Of course, in the picture, they could be seen close up, although they were no bigger than grains of sand; the viewer could come as near as he liked, subject them to a microscopic scrutiny. And that would bring out the hidden strangeness: what would be called "surrealism" a hundred years later but was known, at the time, as "the physiognomy of nature"; in other words, the procedure.

The parade continued, at varying speeds. It seemed the riders would never tire. Suddenly all the soldiers came out at once and the Indians scattered, heading for the mountains. Taking advantage of the informal truce that ensued, our friends entered El Tambo, where a wake was being held. One of the dairy farmers had been killed by the Indians early that morning. The women had put his body back together. So there had been one casualty at least. The two Germans respectfully asked permission to draw the corpse. They reflected that it would not be easy to find the culprit, were anyone to try. Then they visited the labyrinthine stock-yards and accepted an invitation to lunch. There was roast meat and nothing else, not even bread. "Roast Indian," said the soldier turning the spit, with a guffaw. But it was veal, very tender and cooked to perfection. They drank water, because there was a busy afternoon ahead. Since everyone else was retiring for the siesta, Krause was able to persuade Rugendas to rest for a while. They went and lay down on the banks of the stream.

Krause was intrigued. He had not expected his friend to bear up under the strain, yet he seemed willing to keep going, although not to show his face. He had eaten very little, barely lifting the hem of his lace mask away from his chin, and when his friend had diffidently asked if it was not awkward to eat like that, he had replied that the midday light would wound his eyes like a knife. It was the first time Krause had seen him so cautious, even on days of very bright light and after having ingested large quantities of analgesics. No doubt the circumstances were exceptional. Still it was odd for someone so fastidious to persist in wearing a grease-spattered mantilla.

Rugendas took some more powdered poppy extract, but remained awake behind the opaque black lace. As Krause was not sleepy either, they looked over their drawings and discussed them. There was certainly no shortage of material, but they were not so sure about its quality and the subsequent reconstruction. Both of them had been making these discrete sketches with the sole aim of composing stories, or scenes from stories. The scenes would be part of the larger story of the raid, which in turn was a very minor episode in the ongoing clash of civilizations. There is an analogy that, although far from perfect, may shed some light on this process of reconstruction. Imagine a brilliant police detective summarizing his investigations for the husband of the victim, the widower. Thanks to his subtle deductions he has been able to "reconstruct" how the murder was committed; he does not know the identity of the murderer, but he has managed to work out everything else with an almost magical precision, as if he had seen it happen. And his interlocutor, the widower, who is, in fact, the murderer, has to admit that the detective is a genius, because it really did happen exactly as he says; yet at the same time, although of course he actually saw it happen and is the only living eyewitness as well as the culprit, he cannot match what happened with what the policeman is telling him, not because there are errors, large or small, in the account, or details out of place, but because the match is inconceivable, there is such an abyss between one story and the other, or between a story and the lack of a story, between the lived experience and the reconstruction (even when the reconstruction has been executed to perfection) that widower simply cannot see a relation between them; which leads him to conclude that he is innocent, that he did not kill his wife.

Something else the Germans had to take into account, as they remarked in their conversation, was that the Indian was an Indian through and through, right down to minimal fragments, such as a toe, from which the whole Indian could be reconstructed, although they had a different example in mind: not a toe or a cell, but the pencil stroke on paper tracing the outline of a toe or a cell.

All this led Krause to a conclusion that was almost as be-wildering as the story of the innocent assassin: compensation was alien to the Indians. In fact this conclusion derived from a thought that had often crossed his mind (and not only his): every physical defect, however minor or inevitable, even the gradual, imperceptible wear and tear of aging, requires a compensation, in the form of intelligence, wisdom, talent, practical or social skills, power, money, etc. This was why Krause the dandy attached so much importance to his physical appearance, his elegance and his youth: they allowed him to dispense with everything else. And yet, as a civilized man, he could not escape from the compensatory system. Painting, his art of choice, was a way of complying with its minimal requirements. Requirements which, until that day, he had considered absolute; without a minimum of com-pensation it would be impossible to go on living. But that was before he had seen the Indians, and now he had to admit that they did not respect the minimum—on the contrary, as objects of painting, they made fun of it. The Indians had no need of compensation, and they could allow themselves to be perfectly coarse and unpleasant without feeling any obligation to be well dressed and elegant to make up for it. What a revelation it was for him!

But no sooner had he said this than he remembered the state of his poor friend's face (hidden though it was behind the mantilla) and began to worry about how Rugendas might interpret his disquisition.

Needless scruples, for his friend was plunged in the deepest of hallucinations: the non-interpretive kind. In a sense, Rugendas was the one who had taken non-compensation to the limit. But he did not know this, nor did it matter to him.

The proof of this achievement was that while conversing silently with his own altered state (of appearance and mind), he continued to see things and, whatever those things were, they seemed to be endowed with "being." He was like a drunk at the bar of a squalid dive, fixing his gaze on a peeling wall, an empty bottle, the edge of a window frame, and seeing each object or detail emerge from the nothingness into which it had been plunged by his inner calm. Who cares *what* they are? asks the aesthete in a flight of paradox. What matters is *that* they are.

Some might say these altered states are not representative of the true self. So what? The thing was to make the most of them! At that moment, he was happy. Any drunk, to pursue the comparison, can vouch for that. But, for some reason, in order to be happier still (or unhappier still, which comes to the same thing, more or less) one has to do certain things that can only be done in a sober state. Such as making money (which more than any other activity requires a clear head) so as to go on purchasing elation. This is contradictory, paradoxical, intriguing, and may prove that the logic of compensation is not as straightforward as it seems.

Reality itself can reach a "non-compensatory" stage. Here it should be recalled that Mendoza is not in the tropics, not even by a stretch of the imagination. And Humboldt had developed his procedure in places like Maiquetía and Macuto ... in the midst of that peculiarly tropical sadness: night falling suddenly, without twilight, the sea washing back over Macuto again and again, futile and monotonous, the children always diving from the same rock ... And what for? What were they living for? So they could grow up to become ignorant primitives and, worse, deplorable human ruins by the time they reached maturity.

In the afternoon everything became stranger still. The action had shifted away from El Tambo, so the two Germans set off in search of more views, guided by noises and hearsay. If the San Rafael valley was a crystal palace, and the tributary valleys its wings and courtyards, the Indians were coming out of the closets, like poorly kept secrets. The scenes followed one another in a certain order, but their traces on paper suggested other orders, which, in turn, affected the original scenes. As for the landscape, it remained indifferent. The catastrophe simply came in on one side and went out on the other, changing nothing in between.

The Germans continued with their work. New impressions of the raid replaced the old ones. Over the course of the day, there was a progression—though it remained incomplete—towards unmediated knowledge. It is important to remember that their point of departure was a particularly laborious kind of mediation. Humboldt's procedure was, in fact, a system of mediations: physiognomic representation came between the artist and nature. Direct perception was eliminated by definition. And yet, at some point, the mediation had to give way, not so much by breaking down as by building up to the point where it became a world of its own, in whose signs it was possible to apprehend the world itself, in its primal nakedness. This is something that happens in everyday life, after all. When we strike up a conversation, we are often trying to work out what our interlocutor is thinking. And it seems impossible to ascertain those thoughts except by a long series of inferences. What could be more closed off and mediated than someone else's mental activity? And yet this activity is expressed in language, words resounding in the air, simply waiting to be heard. We come up against the words, and before we know it, we are already emerging on the other side, grappling with the thought of another mind. *Mutatis mutandis*, the same thing happens with a painter and the visible world. It was happening to Rugendas. What the world was saying was the world.

And now, as if to provide an objective complement, the world had suddenly given birth to the Indians. The non-compensatory mediators. Reality was becoming immediate, like a novel. The only thing missing was the notion of a consciousness aware not only of itself but of everything in the universe. Yet nothing was missing, for the paroxysm had begun.

The afternoon was not a repetition of the morning, not even in reverse. Repetition is always a matter of waiting, rather than the repeated event itself. But in the grip of the paroxysm, there was no waiting for anything. Things simply happened, and the afternoon turned out to be different from the morning, with its own adventures, discoveries and creations.

In the end, Rugendas collapsed, slumping onto the paper, struck down by a terrible cerebral seizure. Faint moans could be heard emerging from the balloon of black lace, inflated and deflated by his labored breathing. He slipped over Flash's neck, his stick of charcoal still pirouetting in the air, and fell to the ground. Krause got down to help him. Off in the distance, against a superb background of pinks and greens, the Indians were scattering, so tiny they could have been mounted on mosquitoes.

Like a Mater Dolorosa, Krause held the unconscious body of his friend and master, under crowns of foliage multiplied to infinity. The trills of a sky-blue cephalonica encircled the silence. Night was falling. It had been falling for some time.

In the last, miraculously drawn-out light, soldiers and ranchers gathered at the fort to debrief. The horses were exhausted. The riders hung their heads, speaking in mournful grunts; all were grimy, their faced powdered with dust, some were falling asleep in the saddle. Krause joined one of the parties, with Rugendas slung over the back of his horse, sleeping off a dose of powdered poppy extract, his head hanging level with the stirrup, which gave it a ding like a bell's clapper at every step. The mantilla, however, had remained in place. Night had fallen by the time they reached the fort, and they reached it none too soon, for the darkness was absolute.

Rugendas woke at two, in a dreadful state. Swinging back and forth between sickness and health throughout the course of that incredible day had left him a wreck. Yet he resumed his work without a moment's delay. And the strangest thing was that he did not remove his mantilla, simply because he had forgotten that he was wearing it. He and Krause were in the situation room at the fort, feebly lit by a pair of candles; a murky gloom reigned in that vast space. The poor painter could see nothing through the veil, but did not realize. His vision had been so perturbed during the day, that not being able to see made no difference to him now. Thrashing about blindly, he was an outlandish sight, and his shuffling of the papers attracted the other men's attention. He had taken it into his head to classify the scenes, and since he could not see them, he got so mixed up that the contortions of his body, understandably limited by his shattered nerves, seemed to be mimicking the postures of the Indians. Krause could not bear to see him make a spectacle of himself and slipped out discreetly, as if he were going to relieve himself. Less tactful, the soldiers and ranchers gazed in wonder at the puppet with the wrapped-up head. The obvious solution would have been to tear the rag off, but this did not occur to Rugendas because he was so used to it, while, for precisely the opposite reason, the others were too stunned to act; there was only one person who, being in between these extremes, might have done the sensible thing, but he was not present.

At that moment, Krause was experiencing a revelation of his own. Depressed and preoccupied, he had gone out into the blackest of nights. He could sense the forests and mountains as pure afterimages, black forms plunged in an ocean of black. After an uncertain lapse of time spent in melancholy rumination, he suddenly realized he could see everything: the mountains, the trees, the paths, the panoramas with their slightly dreamy perspectives ... Was he seeing or remembering? He marveled at the faculty of sight, its prodigious, ultra-physiognomic capacities, the dilation of the pupil, the brain's interpretations. In fact, the moon had come out, that was all. And yet he had not been mistaken.

Back inside, the men had been waiting for the moonlight so they could return to their respective homes. They put on their hats and went out. That was when Rugendas, who had not been entirely oblivious to their conversations, noticed the owner of the ranch where he had stayed the previous night, and by association, remembered his wife and what she had lent him, at which point he finally raised his hands to his face, felt the lace, realized he was still wearing the mantilla and pulled it off without bothering to untie the knots. In spite of the fact that it was now a filthy, malodorous rag, soiled with grease, sweat and dust, he held it out, trying to make his numb tongue articulate words of thanks intended for the rancher's wife. All eyes were fixed on him, in wonder as much as in fright. When the rancher was finally able to respond, he mumbled a no, still mesmerized by Rugendas. What he meant to say was that the painter could return the mantilla himself and thank his wife in person, since he would presumably be returning to the ranch with them to spend the night. But when the monster insisted, he took the rag, and as there was nothing more to say, let the conversation lapse and stood there staring. What an ugly sight! The reason he had initially refused the filthy shroud was that, unconsciously, he had wanted to say: Keep it on.

They all came out together, and when Krause saw them, he went to fetch the horses; he too was assuming that they would return to the ranch from which they had set out that morning. As he approached the group, leading the two beasts, it took him a moment to realize that Rugendas had removed his mask. He had grown used to it too, from the other side. His friend's face, fully illuminated by the moonlight, seemed larger now and more frightful. He froze for a moment. The men were beginning to mount and ride off. Krause had thought they would have to carry Rugendas, but there he was, standing, steady enough, except for his face. His face occupied the compartments of the night. Was the moon illuminating his face or was it the other way around?

Be that as it may, Rugendas had made other plans. To Krause's astonishment, he had plans for the rest of the night. Incredible as it seemed, he wanted to go on working. What did it matter if he was ill, since the remedies he had taken allowed him to begin again with undiminished energy? And what could be more common than the act of beginning again? It was being repeated all the time. What else could really be repeated? In the beginning was Repetition, and only there. It was Krause, not Rugendas, who by virtue of his health, was moving along an unbroken line, a continuum, without beginning or end.

Krause did not understand what Rugendas had said to him. The painter's face overpowered everything else, even speech. Besides, there was no time to talk, since they were already riding, just the two of them, not towards the ranch but into the forest, drawn into the twisting funnels and bottlenecks, the horses clattering like bronze octopuses, southwards, towards the unknown, guided by the painter's facial compass. Tall, slender silhouettes, as if they were riding giraffes, all in black yet visible, they sped on, sucked towards another and a further slice of space, slipping in among the black's grey shades. The sound of the galloping hooves preceded them and bounced back, warning of obstacles. In that sense they were like bats. Like the bats that abound in those mountains and come streaming out of their caves at that time of night. And they could feel them brushing past! It is extremely uncommon to feel the touch of a bat, because those little creatures are equipped with infallible anti-crash devices. But a touch is not a crash, and occasionally sheer speed makes a touch unavoidable. Which is what happened to Rugendas on this occasion. A bat coming in the opposite direction brushed gently against his forehead. The contact lasted barely a hundredth of a second; it was hardly distinguishable from a breeze or the chance stimulation of a cell. But in the world of nature, there is always an explanation for delicacy. And this delicacy was supreme, incomparable, not only because of the mechanism that produced the contact, but also because of the material that sensed it: a forehead in which all the nerves had been torn loose. What could possibly be gentler or subtler?

This last part of the episode is even more inexplicable than the rest. Yet we cannot doubt that the events really took place, since the artist recorded them in his subsequent correspondence. In his letters he apologizes to family and friends, and principally to his sister, for what he calls his "daring"—though "recklessness" might have been more apt—in going to observe the Indians at close quarters, so he could complete the day's sketches, filling in the foregrounds. There is, of course, a certain irony in his words. After all, what could have happened? They might have killed him. A minor detail. In any case, by the time his correspondents saw the resulting pictures, that is by the time his work reached European galleries or museums, he would certainly be dead. The artist, as artist, could always be already dead. There was something absurd about trying to preserve his life. An accident, big or small, could kill a man, or a thousand, or a thousand million men at once. If night were lethal, we would all die shortly after sunset. Rugendas might have thought, as people often do: "I have lived long enough," especially after what had happened to him. Since art is eternal, nothing is lost.

He was in the lead. He had heard the soldiers at the fort say that, after a battle, the Indians usually camped close by. Weary of the distances that had given form to the raid, they could not wait to have done with them and stopped a stone's throw away.

For that reason, or perhaps because the Germans had been riding so quickly, they arrived almost at once. Beside a waterfall, on a broad platform of pink schist, the Indians were dining. They had built fires and were sitting in circles around them. Not a thousand of them. That had been an exaggeration. A hundred. The stolen cattle were in a small field nearby, surrounded by the horses to stop them from wandering. The Indians had butchered twenty for ribs and sirloins to roast, and had already begun to eat. To say that they were astonished to see the monstrous painter break into the circle of light would be an understatement. They did not believe their eyes. They could not. It was an all-male gathering: no women or children were present. Had they wanted to, whatever they might have said, the Indians could have taken the plunder back to their tents, a few hours' ride away. But they had decided to make a night of it: using the raid as an excuse, they had left their women waiting, worried and famished. Not that they needed to get away from the women to get drunk and go wild; they were capping off the foray with a binge, just to please themselves and to hell with the others. The drinking had begun with an aperitif, in the local manner. They swigged from the bottles they had managed to steal. Drunkenness and guilt fused into terror when they saw that moonlit face, that man who had become all face. They did not even notice what he was doing: all they could see was him. They would never have been able to guess why he was there. How could they know that there was such a thing as a procedure for the physiognomic representation of nature, a market hungry for exotic engravings, and so on? They did not even know that there was an art of painting, and although they possessed that art in some different, equivalent form, they could not establish the equivalence.

So Rugendas was able to enter the circle of firelight undisturbed, open his pad of good canson paper and go to work with charcoal and red chalk. Now he really was at close range and every detail was visible: big mouths with lips like squashed sausages, Chinese eyes, figure-eight noses, locks matted with grease, bull necks. He drew them in the blink of an eye. The paradoxical effect of the morphine had made him extra quick in his application of the procedure. He went from one face to another, one sheet to the next, like a lightning bolt striking a field. And the resulting psychic activity ... A brief aside is apposite here: psychic activity is normally translated into facial expressions. In the case of Rugendas, whose facial nerves had been lacerated, the "representation commands" from the brain did not reach their destination; or rather they did, unfortunately, but scrambled by dozens of synaptic confusions. His face expressed things he did not mean to express, but no one realized, not even Rugendas, because he could not see himself. He could only see the faces of the Indians, which to him were horrible too, but all in the same way. His face was not like any other. It was like the things that no one ever sees, like the reproductive organs viewed from inside. Not exactly as they are—in that case they would be recognizable—but badly drawn.

The tongues of flame flickered higher, splashing the Indians with golden light, illuminating a detail here, another there, or plunging everything into a sudden wave of darkness, animating the absent gesture, endowing mindless stupor with a continuous activity. They had begun to eat, because they couldn't resist, but everything they did led them back to the center of the fable, where drunkenness was mounting. Following their foray, a painter had emerged from the night to reveal the delirious truth of the day's events. Owls began to moan deep in the woods and the terrified Indians were captured in swirls of blood and optical effects. In the dancing firelight, their features drifted free. And although they were gradually beginning to relax and crack rowdy jokes, their gazes kept converging on Rugendas: the heart, the face. He was the focal point of that waking nightmare, the realization of the terrifying possibility that had haunted the raid in its various manifestations over the years: physical contact, face to face. As for the painter, he was so absorbed in his work that he remained oblivious to the rest. In the depths of that savage night, intoxicated by drawing and opium, he was establishing contact as if it were simply another reflex. The procedure went on operating through him. Standing behind him, hidden in the shadows, the faithful Krause kept watch.

24th of November, 1995

THE
LITERARY
CONFERENCE

PART I

The Macuto Line

ON A RECENT trip to Venezuela I had the opportunity to admire the famous "Hilo de Macuto" or "The Macuto Line," one of the wonders of the New World—a legacy left by anonymous pirates, a tourist attraction, and an unsolved enigma. A strange monument to human ingenuity that remained a mystery for centuries and, in the process, became an integral part of a Nature that at those latitudes is as rich as all the innovations to which She gives rise. Macuto itself is one of several coastal towns spread out at the foot of Caracas and adjacent to Maiquetía, where the airport I landed in is situated. They put me up temporarily at Las Quince Letras, the modern hotel built on the beach in front of the bar and restaurant of the same name. My room faced the sea, the enormous yet intimate Caribbean Sea, blue and brilliant. The "Line" passed a hundred yards in front of the hotel; I caught a glimpse of it from my window, then went out to take a closer look.

Throughout my childhood, I, like every child of the Americas, indulged in vain speculations about the Macuto Line, a living relic through which the fictional world of pirates became real and tangible. Encyclopedias—mine was *A Childhood Treasury,* which didn't deserve its name except in those pages—contained diagrams and photographs, which I reproduced in my notebooks. And in my games I would untie the knot, reveal the secret ... Much later, I watched documentaries about the Line on television; I bought books on the subject and came across it many times during my studies of Venezuelan and Caribbean literature, where it appears as a leitmotif. I also followed, along with everyone else (though without any special interest), newspaper articles about new theories, new attempts to solve the enigma ... The fact that new ones were continually cropping up was a clear indication that the previous ones had failed.

According to the age-old legend, the Line was devised to recover a treasure from the deep sea, a haul of immense value placed there by pirates. One of the pirates (none of the chronicles and archives used in the research identified him by name) must have been an artistic-scientific genius of the first order, a shipboard Leonardo, to have invented such a marvelous instrument that could both hide and recover the loot.

The apparatus was ingeniously simple. It was, as the name states, a line, a single line, in reality, a rope made of natural fibers stretched about three yards above the surface of the water over a marine basin off the Macuto coast. One end of the rope disappeared into the basin, then reappeared when it passed through a naturally occurring stone sheave in a rock that rose above the surface of the water about two hundred yards from shore; from there it returned to shore, where it made a somersault of slipknots through an "obelisk"—also natural—then rose to the peaks of two mountains in the coastal range, whence it returned to the obelisk, thereby forming a triangle. The contraption had remained intact for centuries—without needing restoration or any specialized maintenance; on the contrary, always impervious to gross and even brutal mishandling by treasure hunters (everybody, that is), predators, the merely curious, and legions of tourists.

I was just one more ... The last, as we shall see. I was quite excited to find myself face to face with it. It doesn't matter what you know about a famous object—being in its presence is altogether a different story. You must find that sensation of reality, peel back the veil of dreams—which is the substance of reality—and rise to the occasion of the moment, the Everest of the moment. Needless to say, I am not capable of such a feat, I, less than anybody. In any case, there it was ... gorgeous in its invincible, tense, and lean fragility, capturing the ancient light of navigators and adventurers. I was also able to ascertain the truth of its reputation: it was never completely silent. On stormy nights the wind made it sing, and those who heard it during a hurricane became obsessed for the rest of their lives with its cosmic howls. Sea breezes of all kinds had strummed this lyre with a single chord: memory's handmaiden, the wind. But even that afternoon, when the air was utterly still (if a bird had dropped a feather, it would have fallen to the ground in a straight line), its murmurings were thunderous. They were solemn and sharp microtones, deep within the silence.

My presence there, in front of the monument, had enormous consequences: objective, historical consequences;

not only for me but for the entire world. My discreet, un-assuming, fleeting presence, almost like that of any other tourist ... Because that afternoon I solved the enigma, activated the slumbering device, and recovered the treasure from the depth of the sea.

It is not that I am a genius or exceptionally gifted, not by any means. Quite the contrary. What happened (I shall try to explain it) is that every mind is shaped by its own experiences and memories and knowledge, and what makes it unique is the grand total and extremely personal nature of the collection of all the data that have made it what it is. Each person possesses a mind with powers that are, whether great or small, always unique, powers that belong to them and to them alone. This renders them capable of carrying out a feat, whether grandiose or banal, that only they could have carried out. In this case, all others had failed because they had counted on the simple quantitative progression of intelligence and ingenuity, when what was required was an unspecified quantity, but of the appropriate quality, of both. My own intelligence is quite minimal, a fact I have ascertained at great cost to myself. It has been just barely adequate to keep me afloat in the tempestuous waters of life. Yet, its quality is unique; not because I decided it would be, but rather because that is how it must be.

This is and always has been the case in just this way with all people, at all times, everywhere. A single example taken from the world of culture (and what other world should we take it from?) might help clarify this point. An intellectual's uniqueness can be established by examining their combined readings. How many people can there be in the world who have read these two books: *The Philosophy of Life Experience* by A. Bogdanov, and *Faust* by Estanislao del Campo? Let us put aside, for the moment, any reflections these books might have provoked, how they resonated or were assimilated, all of which would necessarily be personal and nontransferable. Let us instead turn to the raw fact of the two books themselves. The concurrence of both in one reader is improbable, insofar as they belong to two distinct cultural environments and neither belongs to the canon of universal classics. Even so, it is possible that one or two dozen intellectuals across a wide swathe of time and space might have taken in this twin nourishment. As soon as we add a third book, however, let us say *La Poussière de soleil* by Raymond Roussel, that number becomes drastically reduced. If it is not "one" (that is, I), it will come very close. Perhaps it is "two," and I would have good reason to call the other "mon semblable, mon frère." One more book, a fourth, and I could be absolutely certain of my solitude. But I have not read four books; chance and curiosity have placed thousands in my hands. And besides books, and without departing from the realm of culture, there are records, paintings, movies ...

All of that, as well as the texture of my days and nights since the day I was born, gave me a mental configuration different from all others. And it just so happened to be precisely the one required to solve the problem of the Macuto Line; to solve it with the greatest of ease, effortlessly, like adding two plus two. To solve it, I said, not explain it; by no means am I suggesting that the anonymous pirate who devised it was my intellectual twin. I have no twin, which is why I was able to come upon the key that unlocked the enigma, which hundreds of scholars and thousands of treasure hunters had sought in vain for four centuries—and in more recent years with access to a much broader range of resources, including deep-sea divers, sonar, computers, and teams of multidisciplinary experts. I was the only one; in a certain sense, I was the appointed one.

Though, I must warn you, not unique in the literal sense. Anybody who'd had the same experiences as I'd had (all of them, that is, because it is impossible to determine a priori which are relevant) could also have done it. And they don't even have to be literally the "same" experiences, because experiences can have equivalents.

So, I do not feel much like boasting. All the credit goes to the happenstance that placed me, precisely me, in the right place—at Las Quince Letras Hotel—one November afternoon with several hours and nothing to do (I had missed my connecting flight and had to wait until the next day). On my way there I wasn't thinking about the Macuto Line, I hadn't even remembered its existence. I was surprised to find it, a few steps away from the hotel, like a souvenir from my childhood love for books about pirates.

It just so happened, and in keeping with the rule of the law of explanations, another related enigma got solved, which was the discovery of how the rope (the "line," in question) had withstood the elements intact for such a long time. Synthetic fibers could have, but there was nothing synthetic about the Macuto Line, as exhaustive laboratory analyses had shown, analyses conducted on miniscule strands extracted with diamond-pointed tweezers: the material consisted of nothing but pine and liana fibers around a hemp core.

The solution to the main problem did not occur to me immediately. For two or three hours I was not even aware that my brain was working on it while I was taking a walk, going up to my room to write for a while, watching the sea from my window, and going out again, all in the tedium of waiting. During that interlude I had time to observe the antics of some children who were diving off some rocks into the sea some sixty feet from shore. This already constitutes part of the "short story" and, as a matter of fact, holds interest only for me. But out of such ineffable and microscopic pieces the puzzle is made. Because there is, in fact, no such thing as "in the meantime." For example, I was thinking absentmindedly about the children's game as a humble artifact construed from natural elements, one of which was the recognition of the kinetic pleasure of the plunge, the muscular contractions, the swimming-respiration … How did they avoid those rocky ridges scattered haphazardly among the waves? How did they manage to land only inches away from a rock that would have killed them with its rigid Medusa-like caress? Habit. They probably did the same thing every afternoon. Which gave the game the weight necessary to become a legend. Those children themselves were a habit of the Macuto coast, but a legend is also a habit. And that time of day, that precise hour, twilight in the tropics, which arrives so early and at the same time is so belated, so majestic in its harmonies, that hour was part of this habit...

Suddenly, everything fell into place. I, who only understand anything through sheer exhaustion and resignation, suddenly understood everything. I thought I'd make a note for a short novel, but why not do it for once rather than write about it? I quickly went to the platform where the Line's triangle had its vertex ... I just barely touched the bundle of knots with the tips of my fingers, turning it over without attempting to untie anything ... A humming could be heard for miles around, and the Line began to run over itself at a cosmic velocity. The mountain it was attached to seemed to shudder, surely an illusion created by the sliding of the cord, which soon spread to the section that sank into the sea. The onlookers who had been watching my actions and those who came to the windows of the nearby buildings were all looking out toward the high seas ...

And there, with a prodigious crack and a burst of foam, the treasure chest at the sunken end of the Line leapt so forcefully out of the sea that it rose about two hundred feet in the air, hung there for an instant, then shot down in a straight line, while the Line retracted, pulling back, until the treasure fell intact onto the stone platform, about three feet from where I was standing, waiting for it.

I won't go into the whole explanation here, because it would take many pages, and I have imposed upon myself a strict length limit for this text (of which this is only a prologue) out of respect for the reader's time.

What I would like to point out is that I did not limit myself to solving the enigma speculatively but also did so in practice. That is to say: after understanding what I had to do, I went and did it. And the object responded. The Line, a taut bow for centuries, finally shot its arrow, bringing to my feet the sunken treasure and instantaneously making me a wealthy man. Which was quite practical, because I have always been poor, lately more so than usual.

I had just spent a year in financial despair and, to tell the truth, had been wondering how I was going to get out of a situation that was deteriorating by the day. My literary activities, cloaked in terms of unassailable artistic purity, never rendered me much material gain. The same held true for my scientific labors, in large part due to the secrecy with which I have carried them out and about which I will speak more later. From an early age I have earned my living as a translator. With time I have perfected my professional skills and achieved a certain amount of prestige; during the last several years I enjoyed some stability though never abundance, which never bothered me as my lifestyle is quite austere. But now, the economic crisis has seriously affected the publishing business, which is paying for its previous years of euphoria. The euphoria led to oversupply, the bookstores were filled with locally produced books, and when the public needed to tighten its belt, the purchase of books was the first thing to go. Publishers, then, found themselves with huge inventories they couldn't sell, their only remaining recourse being to cut production. They cut it so much that I spent the whole year unemployed, sorrowfully spending my savings and eyeing the future with increasing anxiety. One can, thus, see how opportune this incident was for me.

Here is an additional cause for astonishment: to wonder how wealth from four hundred years ago could have retained some value, and how this value could be so enormous. Above all taking into account the speed of currency devaluations in our countries, the changes in the denomination of our currencies, and economic policies of all kinds. But I'm not going to go into that subject. On the other hand, wealth always has something inexplicable about it, more so than poverty. As of that moment, I was wealthy, and that's all there is to it. If I hadn't had to leave the next day for Mérida to fulfill a commitment I couldn't (and didn't wish to) break, I would have gone to Paris or New York to show off my newly acquired opulence.

So it was that the next morning, with my pockets full and preceded by a clamor of fame that filled all the newspapers of the world, I boarded an airplane that carried me to the beautiful Andean city where the literary conference, the subject of this story, was being held.

PART II

The Conference

I

IN ORDER TO MAKE myself understood, the following will need to be very clear and very detailed, even at the expense of literary elegance. Though not too profuse with details, for such an accretion can obfuscate the comprehension of the whole; moreover, and as I previously stated, I must monitor the length. In part due to the requisites of clarity (poetic fog horrifies me), and in part to my natural preference for an orderly exposition of the material, I deem it most appropriate to begin at the beginning. Not, however, at the beginning of this story but rather at the beginning of the previous one, the beginning that made it possible for there to be a story at all. Which in turn requires me to switch levels and begin with the Fable that provides the tale's logic. I will then have to do a "translation," which, if carried out in full, would take more pages than I have assigned as the maximum number for this book; thus I will "translate" only when necessary; all other fragments of the Fable will remain in the original language; and though I am aware that this might affect its credibility, I believe it to be the preferred solution. By way of supplemental warning, I would like to add that the Fable in question takes its logic from a prior Fable, on yet another level of discourse; similarly on the other end, the story provides the immanent logic to another story, thus ad infinitum. And (in conclusion) I have filled these plots with contents that have between them a relationship of only approximate equivalencies, not meanings.

So, once upon a time … an Argentinean scientist conducted experiments in the cloning of cells, organs, and limbs, and achieved the ability to reproduce, at will, whole individuals in indefinite quantities. First, he worked with insects, then higher animals, and finally human beings. His success did not vary, though as he approached human beings the nature of the clones subtly changed; they became non-similar clones. He overcame his disappointment with this variation by telling himself that in the final analysis the perception of similarity is quite subjective and always questionable. He had no doubt, however, that his clones were genuine, legions of Ones whose numbers he could multiply as often as he wished.

At this point he reached an impasse and found himself unable to proceed toward his final goal, which was nothing less than world domination. In this respect he was the typical Mad Scientist of the comic books. He was incapable of setting a more modest goal for himself; at his level, it simply wouldn't have been worth his while. He then discovered that to achieve this final goal, his armies of clones (virtual, in the meantime, because for practical reasons he had created only a few samples) were utterly useless.

In a certain sense he had become a prisoner of his own success, according to the classic depiction of the Mad Scientist, who, in the course of the adventure itself, in the politics of the action, always ends up defeated, no matter how great his previous achievements in the field of science have been. Fortunately for him, he was not truly mad—his thirst for power had not blinded him; around the edges he retained enough lucidity to change the direction of his experiments. This was possible due to the material conditions under which he carried them out: the precarious conditions of a do-it-yourself amateur, making do with cardboard boxes and bottles, with recycled toys and bargain basement made-in-China retorts. He had set up his laboratory in the tiny servant's room in his old apartment; as he had no morgue, he let his human clones roam the streets of the neighborhood. Poverty, which had caused him so much frustration, revealed its positive aspect when he saw that he could only achieve his goals by radically transforming his methods, something he could do without any adverse effect on his investments or installations, which either didn't exist or were worth nothing at all.

The problem, and the solution, were the following: he could create a human being from a single cell, a being that was identical in body and soul to the specimen from which the cell was taken. One or many, as many as he wished. Up to this point, everything was okay. The only difficulty, paradoxical if you wish, is that these creatures had to be at his mercy. He could not be at their mercy. They could obey him, but he couldn't obey them; he saw no reason to do so: they were beings with no prestige, no ideas, no originality. This circumstance thwarted all further action, for he still had to carry the burden of the initiative. And what could he do, even as the general in charge of countless legions, to achieve his ultimate goal of world domination? Declare war? Launch an assault against those in power? It would be his to lose. He didn't even have weapons, nor did he know how to acquire them; weapons could not be reproduced through cloning; cloning worked only on living organic material; thus, life was the only element he could count on. And the mere multiplication of life cannot be considered a weapon, at least not under his conditions, through cloning. The miracle of the spontaneous creation of an additional nervous system was cancelled out by stripping it, from the outset, of the ability to give orders, and with that, to create.

It was on this point that our Mad Scientist most differed from the stereotype of the Mad Scientist, who would typically dig in his heels with self-destructive resolve in order to maintain the central role of his own intellect. Ours reached the conclusion that he could only manage to take a "leap forward" from his current stage if he found a way to get out from the middle, if his intellect could be placed at the service of another intellect, his power at the service of another greater power ... if his will deteriorated within a system of external gravitations. Therein lay his unparalleled originality (as far as Mad Scientists go): in recognizing that "another" idea is always more efficient than "an" idea, by the mere virtue of being an-other. And an idea does not get enriched through expansion or multiplication (clones) but rather by passing through another brain.

So, what to do? The obvious solution was to clone a superior man ... Though choosing which one was not a simple matter. Superiority is a relative condition and eminently subject to disagreement. Above all, it is not easy to decide from one's own point of view, which is the only point of view at one's disposition. And the adoption of objective criteria can be deceptive; be that as it may, he had no choice but to adopt some kind of objective criteria, which he would then need to refine. In the first instance, he had to disregard statistical appearances, such as would predominate in a survey, which would skew the sample toward those at the top of the visible pyramid of power: heads of state, business magnates, generals ... No. Just thinking about this put a smile on his lips, the same smile he could well imagine appearing on the lips of those who wielded true power upon hearing those words. Because life experience had taught him that, say what you will, real power—which makes one smile with disdain at apparent power—resided in a different kind of person whose central and defining acquisition was high culture: Philosophy, History, Literature, the Classics. The self-proclaimed stand-ins from popular culture and advanced technology, and those who had accumulated enormous fortunes through financial manipulation, were ineffectual shams. In fact, high culture's disguise as something old fashioned and out-of-date was the perfect strategy to disorient the unsuspecting masses. This is why high culture continued to be the almost exclusive privilege of the upper classes. But the Mad Scientist wasn't even thinking of cloning a member of that class. Precisely because they were so fully guaranteed the exercise of definitive and ultimate power, and because this guarantee lasted throughout all successive generations, they didn't suit his purposes. Then he thought of resorting to a great criminal, but this was a romantic notion, compelling only for its Nietzschean resonance, and at its core, absurd.

Finally, he decided on what was simplest and most effective: a Celebrity. A recognized and celebrated Genius. To clone a genius! This was the decisive step. This would set him firmly on the road to world domination (because, among other reasons, he'd already covered half of it). He felt the excitement of a momentous moment. Beyond this decision, he had no need to make plans or harbor hopes, for everything would be placed, "invested," in the Great Man, who would take charge because he was superior. As for the scientist, he would remain free from all responsibility—other than his role as the bootlicker, the heinous clown—and his own incompetence, his poverty and his blunders, would no longer matter; on the contrary, they would become his trump cards.

He chose his genius carefully, or better said, he didn't need to choose him because fate placed him in his path, within reach: the most unassailable and undisputed genius there could ever be; his level of respectability touched on the transcendent. This was his natural target, and he set to work without further delay.

To say that he had him "within reach" is an exaggeration; in our celebrity culture, celebrities live isolated behind impregnable walls of privacy and move around inside invisible fortresses nobody can breach. But the same opportunity that had called him to his attention also brought him more or less close by ... He didn't need to be too close. All he needed was one cell from his body, any cell, for each one contains the information necessary to clone the entire individual. Unwilling to trust fate to afford him the opportunity to obtain a hair or a nail trimming or a flake of skin, he employed one of his most trusted creatures, a small wasp reduced to the size of a period and loaded from birth with the identifying data of the aforementioned Genius; he sent her on her secret mission at noon under conditions of certain proximity (the wasp has a very short flight range). He trusted her blindly for he knew her to be at the mercy of the infallible force of instinct, of never-erring Nature. And she did not disappoint him: ten minutes later she returned, carrying the cell on her feet ... He immediately placed it on the slide of his pocket microscope and became ecstatic. The strength of his strategy was confirmed: it was a gorgeous cell, deep, filled with languages, iridescent, a limpid blue with transparent highlights. He'd never seen such a cell, it almost didn't seem human. He placed it in the portable cloning machine he had brought with him, called a taxi, told the driver to take him to the highest plateau in the vicinity, continued from there on foot for a few hours, and when he had reached windswept heights where he was gasping for breath, he looked around for a remote spot to leave the machine. Incubation on a mountain peak was not a poetic detail: the specific conditions of pressure and temperature at these altitudes were what the process required: to reproduce them artificially he would need to be in his modest laboratory, from which he was separated by thousands of miles, and he feared the cell would not survive the rigors of the journey, or would lose its vitality. He left it there and climbed down. Now all he could do was wait …

Here I must attempt a first and partial translation. The "Mad Scientist" is, of course, me. The identification of the Genius may end up being more problematic, but it's not worth wasting time with conjectures: it is Carlos Fuentes. If I agreed to go to that conference in Mérida it was only after I had confirmation that he would attend; I needed to get close enough so that my cloned wasp could take a cell from him. It was a unique opportunity to gain access to him for my scientific manipulations. They served him to me on a platter, and I didn't even have to spend money on an airplane ticket, which I wouldn't have been able to afford, given how bad things had been lately. Or how they had been before the Macuto Line episode. I had had a terrible year, without work, a result of the seriousness of the economic crisis, which especially affected publishing. In spite of this, I had not interrupted my experiments, because at the level on which I was working, I didn't need money. In addition to suiting to a tee the pursuit of my secret goals, this invitation to the conference gave me the opportunity to spend a week in the tropics and take a vacation; rest, recuperate, and refresh myself after a year of constant worries.

Upon my return to the hotel, the excitement of the past few hours reached its anticlimax. The first part of the operation, the most demanding part for me, was over: I had obtained a cell from Carlos Fuentes, I had placed it inside the cloning machine, and I had left the machine to operate under optimum conditions. If you add to this the fact that the previous day I had solved the secular enigma of the Macuto Line, I could feel momentarily satisfied and think about other things. I had a few days to do just that. Cloning a living being is not like blowing glass. It happens on its own, but it takes time. Even though the process is prodigiously accelerated, it requires almost a week, according to the human calendar, for it must reconstruct on a small scale the entire geology of the evolution of life.

All I could do was wait. In the meantime, I had to figure out how to spend my time. As I had no intention of attending the tedious sessions of the conference, I bought a bathing suit and, beginning the following day, I spent mornings and afternoons at the swimming pool.

II

At the swimming pool, I focused all my efforts on one goal: to reduce my mental hyperactivity. To let myself be, naked under the sun. To create internal silence. I have pursued this goal through all of life's twists and turns, almost like an idée fixe. This is the small and alarming idea that stands out in the midst of all other ideas and raises the volume of psychic noise, which is already quite considerable. Hyperactivity has become my brain's normal way of being. It's always been like that, to tell the truth, at least since my adolescence, and I've learned about the more normal way most other people are—hesitant and half-empty—through reading, observation, deduction, and conjecture. And because, on a few occasions, for a few seconds, I have had that experience. My readings in Eastern psychic techniques, and even those stupid articles about "meditation" that often appear in women's magazines, have taught me that there is one further step: an empty mind, the complete or almost complete lack of electrical activity in the cerebral cortex, a blackout, rest. And if at one time, with my characteristic ambitiousness,

I, too, wished to achieve that, and practiced all the recommended exercises with innocent trust, I finally grew convinced that I was wasting my time. It wasn't for me. First, I would have to descend from my peaks of frenzy, take hold of the reins, and mollify the runaway beast of my thoughts, force it to slow to a normal pace; only then would I have a chance to glimpse those Eastern worlds of spiritual serenity.

I have often asked myself how I got into this situation, what happened during my formative years that increased the speed of my mental flow so excessively and made it stick there. I have also asked myself (what haven't I asked myself?) what the exact measure of that speed is, for the very concept of "mental hyperactivity" is approximate and must contain gradations.

To the first question, regarding the history of my malady, I have responded for better or for worse with a small and private "creation myth," whose modulations have been all the novels I have written. I would be hard put to spell this out in the abstract because the myths' variations are not specific "examples" of a general form, in the same way that specific thoughts that are always flashing through my head like lightning are not case studies or examples of a type of thought.

That myth of the ideal myriads, that little drama without characters or plot, would be shaped like a valve. Or, in less technical terms, it would have the characteristic Baudelaire called "irreversibility." A formulated thought does not pass back through the same Caudine forks of its birth, does not return to the nothingness from which it came. Which explains not only the fierce overcrowding but also a quite visible feature of my personality: my bewilderment, my imprudence, my frivolity. The withdrawal of an idea to the conditions of its production is the necessary condition for its seriousness.

In my case, nothing returns, everything races forward, savagely being pushed from behind by what keeps coming through that accursed valve. This image, brought to its peak of maturation in my vertiginous reflections, revealed to me the path to the solution, which I forcefully put into practice whenever I have time and feel like it. The solution is none other than the greatly overused (by me) "escape forward." Since turning back is off limits: Forward! To the bitter end! Running, flying, gliding, using up all the possibilities, the conquest of tranquility through the din of the battlefield. The vehicle is language. What else? Because the valve is language. Therein lay the root of the problem. Which doesn't mean that once in a while, such as during those sessions at the pool, I didn't attempt a more conventional method, by relaxing, by trying to forget everything, by taking a short vacation.

But I have no illusions: there's something phony about this effort because I don't believe I'll ever renounce my old and beloved cerebral hyperactivity, which, in the end, is what I am. Despite all our plans to change, we never voluntarily do so at the core, in our essence, which is usually where we find the knot of our worst defects. I could change it—and I surely would have already—if it were a visible defect, like a limp or acne; but it isn't. The rest of the world has no inkling of the mental whirlwinds swirling under my impassive facade, except, perhaps, through the amplification of that impassivity, or through certain digressions I engage in and abandon without warning. Or perhaps, for a superhuman literary critic, through my relationship with language. My cerebral hyperactivity makes itself manifest inside me (and language is my bridge to the exterior) with rhetorical or quasi-rhetorical mechanisms. These then get distorted in a very peculiar fashion. Take metaphor, for example: everything is a metaphor in the hyperkinetic microscope of my psyche, everything is instead of something else... But you cannot extract yourself unscathed from the whole: the whole creates a system of pressures that distorts the metaphors, moving their parts around between metaphors, thereby establishing a continuum.

"Rising above" this situation requires an enormous effort of art-science in the face of which I have not, of course, recoiled. But I engage in this effort on my own terms. Heisenberg's principle also comes into play here: observation modifies the object of observation and increases its velocity. Under my interior magnifying glass, or inside it, each thought takes on the figure of a clone in its rhetorical anamorphosis: an overdetermined identity.

Which reminds me of the answer to the question I left hanging: how to measure the velocity of my thoughts.

César Aira

I am trying a method of my own invention: I shoot a perfectly empty thought through all the others, and because it has no content of its own, it reveals the furtive outlines—which are stable in the empty one—of the contents of the others. That retrograde cloned mini-man, the Speedometer, is my companion on solitary walks and the only one who knows all my secrets.

III

Just as I am total thought, I am total body. This is not a contradiction. All the totals get superimposed upon each other ... The concept of "totals" is fairly slippery; only a subject in motion can confront it, and the moment that subject is able to enunciate it, it becomes a truth. It was the truth within the restricted Universe of those days of rest I allowed myself under the tropical sun in the swimming pool of a luxury hotel on the outskirts of the city while my operation was underway. I regretted it would last for only the few days of a single week; the pleasure of such delicious passivity could only make me wish that life in its totalness was like that, the total world, the total of totals. It was natural for me to slip into totals. My body accepted it, swelled up with it, radiated it. To top it off, the weather was perfect. Few people went to the pool: several youngsters, male and female, some children with their mothers, one or another loner like me ... Some mornings nobody was there. The caretaker swam melancholically, lap after lap, dozed in his chair, and amused himself trying to catch drowned mosquitoes floating just under the surface of the water using a net with a very fine mesh. The water was as clear as well-washed crystal: you could have read a newspaper floating on the bottom. My hosts at the conference told me it was logical so few people went … In fact, they couldn't believe it when I told them I was not the only one there. Who would ever think, they exclaimed, of going swimming in the middle of winter? It's true, it was winter, but being so close to the equator, it made no difference to me; as far as I was concerned it was still summer, and it continued to be a totality of summer, and life.

One curious thing I noticed and wish to make note of in this report is that all of us who went to the pool those few days, without knowing each other or having planned anything at all among us, were perfect specimens of the human race. What I mean is, we all looked human, with all our members and corresponding muscles and nerves in their proper places and proportions. Physical perfection in the human is rare by definition, for the slightest defect nullifies it. If you look at people in the street, scarcely one in a hundred passes the test. All the rest are monsters. But, to my languid surprise, those of us who came to the pool (different ones every day, except me) constituted a gathering of that one percent. I wonder if it isn't always like that, in every unplanned encounter. Be that as it may, what with the swimmers wearing only bathing suits, their bodies exposed to the sun, there was no room for denial. The spectacle soothed my eyes and my mind. I didn't look for defects, because there were none; in a certain sense, there couldn't be any. Deviations from the physical canon produce monsters; all kinds of monsters, even imperceptible ones. One toe slightly wider or longer than it should be is enough to create some sort of monster. One cell, a spelling mistake within a cell ... For some reason, monsters manage to escape from the net that brings humans to the surface. They remain floating like Cartesian devils in the half-light of unreality. I know a lot about such things because this is the branch of science I practice.

Perfections, on the contrary, are all different: perfection in itself is the perfection or full expression of difference. This is why cultivating perfection means collaborating with what a young disciple once defined as the task we should dedicate our lives to: giving birth to the individual.

My daydreams left me paralyzed. For hours I would lie cataleptic in my lounge chair. The art of perfecting the body could only be practiced during an eternal summer, or an eternal day, or an endless life ... But, like the seasons in the tropics, like this anachronistic autumnal summer, such eternities must be silhouetted against an alien psyche, and be invisible to all.

Wasn't this method more practical than cloning? Was there anything stopping me from adopting it? Now that I was rich, thanks to the Macuto Line (it had happened so recently I still wasn't used to the idea), I could settle in under that sky and live naked under the sun without worrying about anything. I wouldn't even have to change my field. Literature, cloning ... transformations ... I have become convinced of what I consider to be the basic premise of everything I will ever do in my life: all transformations occur *without the least expenditure of energy.* This is fundamental. If effort were required, even the most minimal amount—and given that in a transformation the point of departure and arrival are identical, i.e. the "transformed"—energy would be left over and would, in turn, inflate one end or the other of the universe, creating a bulge and returning us to the realm of the monstrous.

But no. I was roused from these fantasies when I remembered the work at hand. I dove into the water one last time, swam for a while in the now-deserted pool, then walked around the edge, letting the setting sun and the gentle breeze from the highlands dry me off. All around me I could see the mountains and their snow-covered peaks. Up there, in some inaccessible spot, the cloning machine, the hidden heart of the heights, was carrying out its secret task.

My shadow stretched out in front of me, a human shadow, but also alien, irreconcilable. I stretched out my arms, and the arms of the shadow did the same; I lifted a leg, bent at the waist, turned my head, and the shadow imitated me. Would it do the same if I stretched out the fingers on one of my hands? I tried it. I abandoned myself to a dance of recognition … The other bathers watched me out of the corners of their eyes, discreetly … When you are traveling the thought that nobody knows you gives you a certain feeling of impunity. That wasn't the case with me. The breeze carried snippets of their conversations, and I realized they were talking about me: "famous writer … Macuto Line … he was in the newspapers …"

Impunity: it's always impunity that gets you dancing. What did I care about being ridiculous? I was on my way to earning a superior kind of impunity, and nobody knew it.

IV

The only interruption to this rash of days of repose and swimming was on Wednesday night, when I felt obliged to perform a very private ceremony. That afternoon, the wasp had died.

Two days earlier, I returned her to the cage I had carried her in from Buenos Aires after she had brought me a cell from Carlos Fuentes. When I decided to bring her, I knew that for her it would be a one-way trip. Those insects have very short lives, and by the time she was five days old, hers, in fact, had already been a long one. Once she had completed her mission, I didn't need her anymore and could have destroyed her, as well as her little cage, and thereby left no trace of my activities. Traveling with her brought with it a touch of risk, so I kept her hidden. Despite there being no law regarding the international transport of cloned materials, the custom agents' sensitivities to the transport of drugs, genetic mutations, and bacterial weapons could have created problems. I had no choice but to bring her, so I took the chance. Luckily nothing happened.

Nor did I want anybody at the hotel to know of her existence: my scientific activities are secret; giving explanations would have put me on the spot, especially if it became known that I was experimenting with a renowned Mexican author. All things considered, disposing of the wasp the moment I no longer needed her would have been the most prudent thing to do; and I needn't have felt any scruples for she would anyway have soon died a natural death. But my loyalty to my little creature won the day. I preferred to wait for her to perish on her own, complete her own life cycle, as if Nature were mediating between her and me according to Her own sacrosanct laws.

Even though I didn't trust the hotel maids, with their curiosity and brutality, I left her in the room. I could have carried her in my pocket wherever I went, but I trusted the maids more than my own absentmindedness: I'm always losing things, or leaving them somewhere, anywhere. So, I left her in the room for whole days at a time during my interminable sessions at the pool. Under lock and key, of course. Fortunately, I had no occasion for regret. Upon returning to my room, I'd take her out and place the little cage on my bedside table while I read lying down or napped. In addition to my sense of loyalty, there must have been an element of sentimentality or loneliness: after all, she was company, a reminder of my life at home and in my laboratory, a minuscule Argentinean spark.

To speak of "wasp" or "insect" as I have is an abusive oversimplification; they are words I use, as I do repeatedly in this book, only to make myself understood. To create my "wasp," I used wasp DNA, that's true, because I needed certain wasp traits, but I used them only as a "mannequin" (I resort to specialized jargon) for other traits my mission required and that I extracted from my gene catalogue. If I chose the wasp mannequin over that of, say, the dragonfly or the bee, it was because of its greater ability to bond with foreign genes. But the resulting critter had little in common with a wasp: for starters, it was the size of a speck of dust. Under the microscope, she looked more like a golden sea horse with strong mothlike wings shaped like fans, and something between a rhinoceros horn and a crab claw—though articulated—sprouted from her head: this was the cell punch. All of these—and more—exist in zoology. She was a prototype, a unique specimen, a nice little monster that would never be repeated.

As I was saying, I found her dead upon my return from the pool on Wednesday afternoon. Her life had been consummated in less than one week: it began in Argentina and ended in Venezuela, several thousand miles to the north. I contemplated her briefly and felt sad without knowing why. Her cadaver, which had become translucent and acquired a touch of an amber hue, was nothing more than a spot on the floor of her little house that nobody else would ever inhabit because I had built it for her. When earlier I spoke of "cage," I did so, once again, to simplify things; it was, in fact, a cubicle the size of a thimble made of cellophane, which on a whim I fashioned into the shape of a Swiss chalet, with a pressurized chamber made of lamprey eel genes. I'm such a perfectionist that if there were a gene for furnishings, I would have made her a beautiful trousseau.

Night came. I went down to eat, then killed some time in the bar until eleven o'clock. Uncustomarily, I drank a cup of coffee. I never do so at that time of day, because then I cannot sleep, and I am terrified of insomnia. But that night I would stay up, because I had already devised a plan of action. Moreover, considering that overdetermination I know so well, how it gets set in motion and proliferates as soon as an action begins, I would need one of the coffee implements: the spoon, which I stole. It was a beautiful silver spoon with a clown engraved on the handle.

A short while later, after telling my bar companions that I was going to sleep, I left the hotel. The city was deserted. I went in the opposite direction from downtown; the road climbed steeply until it reached the highway that encircles the city; once past that, I found myself in open country in the foothills of the mountains. I continued walking for several hundred yards, until I could no longer hear the automobiles. The only light was the light of the stars, but they were so bright, so captivating, so close, that I could see everything, far and near: the blunt masses of the rocks, the deep recesses of the valley, the river flowing under the bridges.

The precise spot didn't matter, and the one I was in was as good as any other, so I reached my hand into my pocket and took out the tiny corpse. At that moment I observed some movement among the dark masses around my feet, which I had assumed were rocks. I looked more carefully and saw that they were all moving with the slowness and regularity of zombies. They were turkey vultures, those black buzzards who spent their days hovering over the valley. Seeing them perched like that for the first time, I thought they looked like small, gloomy hunchbacked chickens. It appears I had happened upon one of their mountainside bedrooms. The walking around I was witnessing may have been due to having woken them up with my intrusion, or perhaps they really were zombies. They seemed the perfect funeral cortege for my wasp's burial. I set to work.

With my spoon I dug a round hole about two inches wide and almost eight deep, at the bottom of which I carved out a nearly circular burial chamber; there I placed the tiny cellophane Swiss chalet with its eternal resident. I sealed the entrance with a coin and filled the vertical tunnel with dirt that I pressed down with my thumb. I placed a triangular-shaped pebble on top for a gravestone.

I stood up and dedicated a final thought to my wasp. Goodbye little friend! Goodbye…! We would never see each other again, but I would never forget her … I would never be able to forget her, even if I wanted to. Because nothing could replace her. Excitement mixed with melancholy. The Mad Scientist (and I, myself, on another level of this story's meaning) could boast about the unprecedented luxury of having made the entire evolutionary process serve a unique and determined—as well as subsidiary—purpose, almost like going to buy a newspaper … I needed somebody to get me a cell belonging to

Carlos Fuentes, and for that reason, and no other, I created a being within which converged millions of years
and many more millions of fine points of selection, ad-
aptation, and evolution … to carry out a unique service
and thereby complete its purpose; a throw-away creature,
as if the miracle that is man had been created one afternoon just so he could walk over to the door to look outside and see if it were raining, and once this task had been
accomplished, he would be annihilated. Needless to say,
the cloning procedure reduced such excessive periods of
natural labor to a few days, though they remained, essen-
tially, the same.

V

The moment has come, I believe, to do another "translation" of the story I am telling in order to make clear my true intentions. My Great Work is secret, clandestine, and encompasses my life in its entirety, even its most insignificant folds and those that seem the most banal. Until now I have concealed my purpose under the accommodating guise of literature. Because I am a writer, this causes no particular concern.

Marginally, this pretense has afforded me certain mundane pleasures, and an acceptable modus vivendi. But my goal—which in my quest for transparency has become my best kept secret—is typical of the comic-book Mad Scientist: to extend my dominion over the entire world.

I am aware that we have here a metaphorical alibi; "dominion" and "world" are words, and the sentence containing them lends itself to intellectual, philosophical, and paradoxical interpretations ... I refuse to fall into that trap. The dominion I'm talking about wants to be extended across reality, the "world" is none other than the objective, shared world ... The only paradox, if there is one, is that language has shaped our expectations so extensively that real reality has become the most detached and incomprehensible one of all.

The opening of the doors of reality is the infinite pro-legomenon to my Great Work. And I have already made reference to one of these "doors" (an inoffensive meta-phor): perfection. From there to the pool. My brain: the battlefield.

After a certain age, doubt threatens the perfection of the body. Assessing ourselves objectively is difficult because we continue to think of ourselves as adolescent, and others always have a reason to lie. Perfection becomes a longing, sometimes all-consuming. We would do anything to achieve it, we really would: any diet, any exercise. We would not shrink from any effort. But we don't know what that "anything" is and have no way of finding out. If we ask ten people, we get ten different answers. And thus we squander the most genuine of longings. We would do whatever was necessary ... if we knew what that was. But we don't.

As a result, perfection has to find its own way. We can't find perfection. The miracle is that it happens at all. Life is generous that way, it always is.

If the preceding text were a riddle, I would not need to provide the answer, not even written upside down at the foot of this page, because any reader could have guessed it right away: love. Love, the portentous coincidence, the surprise, the flower of this world.

Until now, I have been drawing a portrait of a character who represents me in more or less fair and realistic—even if partial—terms. Until now, he could have been taken for a cold, clear-headed scientist writing a well-reasoned memoir in which even emotions take on an icy edge ... To complete the portrait, though, we would need to paint in a background of passion, so alive and excessive that it makes the rest tremble.

It would be counterproductive to go into too many details, so I won't. I know myself and I know that the triumph of my false modesty when I sit down to write would translate into such absurd fairy tales that I don't know where it would end up. I'll say only what's most basic; better: I'll sketch it out.

Years ago, in this same city, at this same pool, I met a woman and fell in love with her. I couldn't and didn't want to commit myself, so I returned to Buenos Aires and my life there, but I couldn't forget Amelina. I should add that we did not remain in touch, not even epistolary touch, because when I left I forgot to write down her address—a meaningful lapse. To tell the truth, I didn't feel I had the right to love her. She was young enough to be my daughter, she studied literature, and she was innocent in a way that is difficult to describe. As for me, I was married, with children, dedicated to my secret scientific endeavors that forced me into Machiavellian contortions ... What kind of future could we have? The opportunity passed, and by the same token, didn't pass. Amelina's love continued to reside within me and remained a constant source of inspiration. Now, upon my return, I thought of her ... But Amelina didn't appear. She was still living in the city, as

I discovered by accident, and she must have read in the newspapers of my presence, but she kept her distance. She was avoiding me. I understood and accepted. Moreover, I wasn't even sure I'd recognize her if I saw her again. A lot of time had passed, she'd probably gotten married ...

It was an old story, older than she was in reality. When I met Amelina, it was love at first sight, overwhelming, a whirlwind ... This was because the current carried me way back, back to a time when I, too, had loved. By the time I met Amelina, I was already a grown man, I had lost almost all hope, I felt defeated, I believed nothing could bring back my lost youth. And nothing did, obviously. But when I saw Amelina, I miraculously recognized in her features, her voice, her eyes, a woman who had been my great passion when I was twenty. I had loved the beautiful Florencia to despair (ours was an impossible love) with all the madness of adolescence, and I never stopped loving her. It wasn't meant to be, we took different paths, she got married, I did too, we lived in the same neighborhood, sometimes I saw her walk by with her children as they were growing up ... Twenty years passed, thirty ... She gained weight, that delicate and shy girl I had adored turned into a mature woman full of middle-class respectability ... She must be a grandmother by now. How incredible! How life flies by! For the heart, time doesn't pass.

Florencia had been reborn, in all the splendor of her youth, in the sweet Amelina, whom I had had to cross a continent to find. I sensed their resemblance in the smallest of details, in the most intimate folds of their smiles, or of their dreams. The coincidence spanned a lifetime, and in the magical wonder it brought me, I found the justification for my work: during the years following my encounter with Amelina, my Great Work took off, embarked on a definitive direction, and I began to see the fruits of my labor. She was my Muse.

All well and good. On Thursday afternoon, I was dozing in my lounge chair by the pool when suddenly something made me lift my head and look around. At first it didn't seem like anything very special was going on: the few bathers who were often there at that time of day were quiet, some conversed in low voices, several children were playing in the water. In the sky: the omnipresent turkey vultures. Nevertheless, I could feel it: something was stirring in that uneventful calm ... I knew I was in a prophetic state, as if possessed. What was about to happen was already happening. I leapt up, light and heavy at once, a statue made of floating metal, and walked over to the edge of the deck. On the other side of the pool, right in front of me, rose a living statue. I have never felt so naked. It was Amelina, larger than life (or smaller?), in subtle colors that seemed to have been gleaned from the noontime shadows. She looked at me. I understood that I was hallucinating because I saw her as she had been so many years before, almost a child who was discovering me with all the surprise of a romantic adventure. But she was real, or there was something real about her. There's always something real in what happens, no avoiding that. But her skin tone was too strange, as was the light that outlined her figure, which seemed set apart from the atmospheric light. This was due, I noticed with amazement, to the fact that her figure projected no shadow onto the ground. Instantly, in a very rapid psychic sequence, I realized that I also had no shadow and that the sun had disappeared from the sky, which I confirmed when I raised my eyes. The perfectly blue sky of four o'clock in the afternoon, without a single cloud ... had no sun. It had evaporated.

I looked again at Amelina. Monumental transparent shapes in continual metamorphosis were rising from the water in the pool that separated us. I thought it was another Macuto Line, the one of dreams, the private ...

Suddenly, Amelina disappeared, the shapes melded into a horizontal wave, and the sun was once again shining in the sky. My shadow stretched out in front of me once again ... My shadow, in every swimming pool in the Andes.

I couldn't help glancing up at the mountains in the vicinity of where I had left the cloning machine. That gesture had the virtue of returning me to reality. At least I could be sure that what was happening there was not a dream. No matter what strange paths my thoughts might take, the process would continue, independently of me, though subsequently I would take charge of it. That, however, would be a kind of epilogue; in itself, the Great Work consisted principally of me abstaining from all and every intervention, of achieving a parallel trajectory of absolute integrity.

VI

There is another coincidence on another level: that between the velocity of thought and thought itself. This is the same as saying that the Great Work—the creation of the individual—is exactly what is accomplished during a life span at that constant velocity. In a certain sense, velocity is the Great Work; confusion arises about the method. Thus, my Great Work, my secret labor, is highly personal, nontransferable, nobody but I could carry it out, because it consists of the innumerable psychic and physical instants whose sequence confirms my velocity. The velocity at which I unfold through time. By becoming an individual, my work allows me to love and be loved.

The aforesaid occurred to me while I was considering, with amazement, the quantity of things that were happening to me while nothing was happening. I noticed this as my pen was moving: there were thousands of tiny incidents, all full of meaning. I've had to pick and choose carefully, otherwise the list would be endless. But it's normal for more things to happen when you're traveling than during the normal course of habitual life. Not only because they actually happen because one is on the move and actively going out looking for things, but because our perceptions awaken when we leave our habits behind, we see more and hear more, we even dream more. For someone who travels as little as I do, for someone who leads such a routine life, a trip can make an enormous difference; it is the objective equivalent of cerebral hyperactivity.

I am selecting, somewhat haphazardly, the facts I use to carry forward this story of the days I spent waiting while the cloning process was taking place at the top of the mountain, focusing exclusively on the translation possibilities. I should mention that the literary conference I had been invited to attend was taking place concurrently, but I was so detached from it I would not have been able to name even one of the subjects of its sessions and panel discussions. In one, however, I was a participant, and although this participation, fortunately, was passive and indirect, I had no choice but to know about it. It was a marginal activity, attendance optional, held outside the framework of the official sessions; it consisted of the staging of one of my plays by the University Theater Group of the Humanities Department. They had, apparently, already staged other plays of mine, and this time they had chosen one called *In the Court of Adam and Eve*. It was not the one I would have chosen, but I did not object when I saw it on the program they sent me months earlier. As soon as I arrived they asked me to attend the final rehearsals, approve the costumes and sets, meet the actors ... I politely declined. I wished to be merely another member of the audience. That last statement was made out of a sense of obligation, for I didn't care whether I saw it or not, and if it had been up to me, I wouldn't have gone; but it turned out to be true. As far as their request that I speak to the cast about my motivation for writing it, firmer reasons accompanied my refusal. The first one, I considered it inadvisable to explain; the others had to do with the amount of time that had passed since I'd written it, and how totally I had forgotten it. We left it at that, and though they were probably disappointed, they did not seem offended.

Nevertheless, I did intervene on one point. The play would be performed for the general public in a newly built theater, but only those attending the conference would see the preview, and that performance could be held in a different venue, possibly in the open air, thereby taking full advantage of the climate. They asked my opinion, and in this case I felt I did have something to say. They expected me to come up with something unexpected and extravagant, so I chose the airport, which is right downtown because Mérida takes up the entire small valley in which it is situated. They liked that idea, got authorization, and made all the arrangements.

The play dates back to my Darwinian period, but it foreshadows my subsequent work with clones. Within the entire body of my work, it is an exception: I have an aversion to what is now called "intertextuality," and I never make literary allusions in my novels or plays. I force myself to invent everything; when the only choice is to recycle something that already exists, I prefer to take recourse in reality. But I allowed myself this exception because Genesis is a special case, even if only for its title. If inventiveness, or the transmutation of reality, is part of a broader mechanism of literary genetics, Genesis could well be considered the master plan, at least among us Westerners.

Saying that this short play foreshadowed my subsequent scientific work is, to tell the truth, an understatement. The mere idea of Adam and Eve's existence, of humanity (the species) retroactively reduced to a single couple, gives rise to genetics. I would even say that it is as far as the imagination can go in this field. Genetics is the genesis of diversity. But if diversity has nobody on whom to spread itself out, it turns on itself, gets tangled up in its own general particularity, and therein the imagination is born.

I remember how one critic, at the play's debut many years ago, called it "a beautiful love story." In retrospect, I have found in that play the key to my difficulty in speaking about love other than through complex translations of perspectives. The coincidence of Adam with Eve in a world where it was unnecessary to seek each other out through the exhaustive labyrinths of the real is one theory of love. The passage from Adam to Eve under the guise of the fable of the rib was simply cloning. Once both characters were in the scene, cloning collapsed, decisively. The level of the fable guaranteed it would belong to an inaccessible past, a past that could only be captured through the imagination or through fiction. I believe that this myth is what turned the past into a mental construct; if not for its intercession, today we would perhaps be dealing with the past as simply one more reality, like any other object of perception.

As it turned out, sex remained the only path to reproduction. Sex, and the concomitant maneuverings of love.
The scenes with Adam and Eve occurred in such close
proximity to cloning—of which they had been involuntary protagonists—that the fable contaminated their con-
jugal passion. To the same degree I had made *sexuation* a
personal taboo, I approached them with the trembling of
monstrous familiarity.

I now begin to remember in greater detail the period
of my life when I wrote that piece. I understand why I
wanted to obscure it behind a cloud of voluntary obliv-
ion, because it was a dark moment in my life, perhaps the
worst, the most disturbed. My marriage had undergone
some very demanding trials, I was obsessed with divorce,
which, at the same time, seemed the only solution and
caused me unendurable fear. I began to drink too much,
and as my constitution is averse to alcohol, I began to develop rather grotesque symptoms; the worst was a contraction of my left leg, which began to behave as if it were
eight inches shorter than my right; as far as I know, my
two legs are exactly the same length, but for months I was
going around with quite a conspicuous limp. This, on top
of everything else, led me to take drugs (the only time in
my life I've ever done so). I became addicted to proxidine
and so severely abused it that I would have died of an over-
dose if I had not finally found a way out.

Part of my recovery, in any case the testament to it, was
the writing of this play. Which explains my use of a pre-
existent myth. This may seem like excessive justification

for my falling into a literary trap I deplore, but so it goes, that's the way the cookie crumbles. Deep down, the marriage of Adam and Eve was the myth of absolute contingency: sex preceded and made possible by cloning; proxidine produced the same effect in my cells five times a day. But once everything reverted to literature, my recovery was complete.

In another confluent episode, which memory now holds out to me in a gesture that seems to say, "There's more where that comes from," I had a kind of fleeting hallucination, though in the midst of so many perceptual changes brought about by my drug use, I didn't pay much attention to it. Every time I closed my eyes I would see two men hurling themselves against each other, like two swordsmen, but without swords; I would see them in profile, sharply outlined, both dressed in black. The scene had very little depth, almost like an animated painting, but it was infused with a terrible level of violence.

I would immediately open my eyes, and the scene would vanish. The hatred with which those two little optical men hurled themselves at each other filled me with horror. I couldn't stand it, and so made them dissolve by popping open my eyes, reducing the scene to a quick sketch of an unarmed thrust. What happened next? I never found out, but perhaps one day I will.

The performance was on Saturday, late afternoon. I cut short by a little—a very little—my session at the pool, showered, and took a brief nap. I went downstairs after they telephoned me to say that the bus was ready to leave.

My colleagues, both men and women, were all dressed in their Sunday best, as if they were going to the opera. The young female students—conference volunteers—wore fancy outfits, and their dark, heavily made-up faces were crowned by high, elaborate hairdos, topped with silk bows. Two buses were waiting, as well as a long line of taxis and limousines. As always, we were running late. I got on the first bus, whose driver was impatiently honking the horn, and we shot off. To save time, we took the highway that circled the city, and the whole way I contemplated the view of the mountains through my window, absorbed in my own thoughts. If my calculations were correct, that very night the final gong would sound as my cloning machine completed its task and the Genius hatched from his shell. Creation's integuments were undoubtedly already expanding. At dawn, the finished clone of Carlos Fuentes would be making its way down the mountain, and thus the final phase of my Great Work would commence.

At the airport everything was ready for the show, which began as soon as the last invited guests arrived. Though they had reserved a seat for me in the front row, I preferred to watch it from further back, standing up, hidden—one could say—"in the wings," that is, behind the plants, because the show was being staged in a garden surrounded by waiting gates, ticket counters, and the bar of the glass-enclosed pre-boarding area. It was a marvelous garden, though somewhat wild; at those latitudes it is difficult to keep vegetation under control. Bushes with flame-like flowers surrounded the palm trees, the banyan tree spread its eavelike branches in all directions, the fern fronds formed dense screens, and everywhere hung enormous yellow, violet, and blue orchids. The leaves of some of the plants were so large that one was enough for me to hide behind. I enjoyed spying on the audience. Everyone looked like automatons from the very heart of my experiments. I underwent some kind of doubling of the self. I thought: "If they were real, what would they be doing right now?" But the other part of me knew they were real. It was as if reality itself had switched time frames and one had leapt into another … Years ago, in this same place, I had seen Amelina for the last time, we'd said our final parting words, replete with tears and promises. This spot remained pregnant, like objective rapture. I realized I was looking for her but wouldn't see her. How to see through the walls of the present? The garden's exuberance, transparent in its repetition, was reflected in the buildings' enormous panes of glass, and through those ghostly labyrinths passed the airplanes' huge white forms.

It may have had something to do with the time of day. The sun had dropped behind the mountains, which were so high and so close, thereby causing confusion. After disappearing from the sky, the sun's golden glow in the atmosphere intensified.

The moment the first lines of dialogue were spoken—which I remembered better than I would have wanted to—things got stranger. My eyes were drawn, as if magnetically, to Carlos Fuentes, sitting in the front row.

I saw he was absorbed in the play, totally focused, transported to another world. By his side sat his wife, Sylvia, as beautiful as the good fairy of storybook fame, looking relaxed and with a vague smile of interest playing on her lips. Authorial vanity, which never completely fell away, not even at that moment, made me wonder what they would think of my little play. I feared I would come up short in their estimation. But, I told myself, this was inevitable, and anyway, what did it matter at this point?

The laughter surprised me. I had forgotten that an audience could react. I quickly turned my attention back to the actors, who were evolving in the middle of the garden. Eve was lying on a divan, wearing a cumbersome red sultana's dress and holding in her arms a rubber Mickey Mouse doll. She seemed to be waiting for something with great impatience. Two jesters played on harps at her feet. A servant entered and announced:

"Mr. Adam can't come right now. He's busy."

What was all this about? I didn't recognize it, it was too Dadaist. Nevertheless, I had written it. Eve went to his laboratory to get him. Adam agreed to have tea with her, but not to put down his Exoscope, an enormous instrument he carried around with great difficulty. Slowly, I began to remember. Yes, I had written that. Moreover, they were scrupulously following the text, to the very last comma. Gone were any remaining doubts that I had written it, for there were my recurrent themes, my little tricks, and even the dialogues I had lifted verbatim from reality and that carried me back to teas I'd had with my wife on long-ago summer afternoons. But why were they drinking from such oversized five-gallon cups? At that point, I had to remember (which I did) my mental process while I was writing; in this case, remembering meant reconstructing. That detail about the cups meant to suggest that at the beginning of the world there was still no congruency in the sizes of things: this had required a much longer span of evolution. The dialogues, spoken with a Caribbean accent, sounded strange to me, especially when I began to recall their intellectual pulse, but I had to admit they were verbatim.

There was only one innovation in this production: Adam was black. Though this didn't exactly qualify as an innovation. The actor was black, and he was probably the best actor they had. They weren't about to discriminate against him! In Venezuela there are lots of blacks, though many fewer in the Andean region, and even fewer at the university. Those there are tend to be outstanding, so it shouldn't have surprised me that they had given him the main role. They probably pretended he was just another actor, like any of the others, and, to tell the truth, I was probably the only one who realized he was black.

As for the Exoscope Adam carried around with him throughout the entire play, they had, indeed, done a good job, even though they resorted to the simplest and most unimaginative solution. The entire play pivoted on this instrument. In the notes, I had specified only its size (six-and-a-half feet by five feet by three-and-a-half feet, more or less) and that it should look like a scientific-optical device. The idea, which the props person had understood, was that it would be a celibate machine; perhaps he had understood it a little too well, because this Exoscope looked a lot like Duchamp's *Large Glass*.

The plot unfolded one event at a time. The entire drama was based on the mysterious impossibility nested at the very heart of the relationship between the two protagonists. Their love was real, but at the same time it was impossible. Adam's experiments, Eve's courtesan frivolities, all were mere evasions. Love was revealed as an impossibility that seemed either metaphysical or supernatural, but was in reality very simple and even prosaic: Adam was married.

I must confess, I didn't know how to resolve the difficult problem this plot line presented. Because if Adam and Eve were, respectively, the only man and the only woman on the planet, then Adam's wife—the absent wife whose existence prevented him from living out his love with Eve—couldn't be anybody other than Eve herself. The idea (very characteristic of me, to the point that I believe it to be how I conceive of literature) had been to create something equivalent to those figures that was both realistic and impossible, like Escher's *Belvedere*, figures that look viable in a drawing but could not be built because they are but an illusion of perspective. Such a thing can be written, but one must be very inspired, very focused. I fail because of my precipitousness, my rush to finish, and my desperation to please. I was able to sustain it in this play only through the strength of ambiguities and funny repartees. And only for a short time, because very soon things started to happen.

It was then, when the action rushed toward a resolution, after the exasperating teatime dialogues, that the extent of my fiasco fell on me like a mental atomic bomb. Once again I had submitted to nonsense, to the frivolity of invention for invention's sake, resorting to the unexpected as if it were some kind of deus ex machina! Again I had squandered the wise ancient advice adorning the frontispiece of my literary ethic, "Simplify, my son, simplify!" I have managed to write a few good things by following, quite by accident, that advice. What a waste! Only through minimalism is it possible to achieve the asymmetry that for me is the flower of art; complications inevitably form heavy symmetries, which are vulgar and overwrought.

But my mania—to be constantly adding things, episodes, characters, paragraphs, to be constantly veering off course, branching out—is fatal. It must be due to insecurity, fear that the basics are not enough, so I have to keep adding more and more adornment until I achieve a kind of surrealist rococo, which exasperates me more than it does anybody else.

It was like a nightmare (the mother of all nightmares) to watch the living defects of what I had written materialize in front of me. Though my punishment was a kind of poetic justice, because from that point on the logic the play began to obey was the logic of nightmares. Poor Adam's brain began to rebel against him, and in a burst of dementia he murdered Eve ... The scene was full of gruesome details: he decapitated her, and, after performing a few macabre juggling acts with her head, he divided her long blond hair into two locks and tied them around the waist of the corpse, which he left standing. The hair knot hung over her buttocks, and her head hung down in front of her sex, like a codpiece ... then he ran off, still carrying the Exoscope. The police of Babylon got involved, and the inspector in charge proclaimed: We are dealing with a serial killer, there is a pattern, this is the seventh such crime, all with long blond hair, all with the head tied around the waist ... But Adam, by definition, was the first and only man! Therefore, he couldn't be just one among many suspects, he was by necessity the guilty party. And moreover, if Eve were the only woman, how could she be one in a series of victims? Serial killers came later in evolution. I myself didn't even understand it.

In the next scene, in the cave where Adam went to hide, Eve's ghost appeared as an integral part of the glass of the celibate machine. Agents of a foreign power took advantage of the situation to steal the Exoscope from him, without knowing that Eve continued to live inside it ... It was grotesque, repulsive; I was mortified.

VII

Difficult as it is to believe, people liked that crap. It was nighttime by the time it ended. In the last light of day, at the culminating moment of the show, the evening flight arrived; there are two flights a day to Mérida, and both have to land during daylight hours because of how difficult it is to land a plane in this narrow valley surrounded by high peaks. The noise of the engines drowned out a few lines, and shortly thereafter the passengers walked in single file across the stage carrying their bags and suitcases but without interrupting the show. That detail was the most widely discussed during the reception hosted afterward by the airport director. There was a festive atmosphere, almost euphoric; everybody seemed happy, except me. I allowed myself to carry out the bad idea of drinking myself out of my depression. Since my detoxification, ten years earlier, I had not had a drop of alcohol. At least I had the good sense not to mix my drinks, but rum is deceptive, always so smooth, so calming, like a perennial cause with no effect, until the effect shows itself, and then you realize the effect had been there from the beginning, even before there began to be a cause. The hall had a bad echo. Everybody was shouting and nobody could hear anybody else. I accepted the congratulations with the graciousness of a perfect idiot. I watched lips move and smiles appear, sometimes I moved my lips, too, and drank, and smiled again; my face was hurting from holding that grimace for so long. That was even how I received Carlos Fuentes's words.

What happened next is blurred by the fog of intoxication. We boarded buses that took us directly to the hotel dining room for dinner, from there we went to the bar so we could keep drinking, and at midnight we took taxis to a discotheque ... Throughout the many stages of that night I felt, underneath the strong effects of the rum, a discomfort that never let up, undoubtedly because I never managed to put my finger on what it was. I didn't know what was wrong; it couldn't be that I felt out of place, because that was normal for me. In retrospect, I understood what was happening to me: in my semiconscious state I had joined the group of young people: I returned with them on the bus, sat with them at dinner, and continued in their company through all that followed. They were the students who did volunteer work (they called it "logistics") for the convention, almost all of them female, almost none older than twenty. People who signed up for this were not necessarily devotees of literature. My colleagues had done nothing to extricate me from them, on the contrary. They were corroborating the reputation I had forged for myself of preferring "life" to literature. They were convinced that I was pursuing the young women, and they approved; in a certain way it legitimized them indirectly by showing that literature was part of life and passion. As far as the students were concerned, they asked for nothing more than the attention I seemed to be paying them, the fact that I chose them over the famous writers I should have been interacting with, and the chance to be seen in public with the hero of the Macuto Line.

I spent the rest of the night at the discotheque. There were strobe lights, blasting salsa music, and so many people you could hardly move. But I didn't care, I was in the stratosphere. The young people were my drunken bodyguards. The erroneous impression my more mature colleagues got of me could have been seen from a different point of view, which in the end was the same: vampirism. My false maturity could not be seen in any other way. But my vampirism is special, I think.

Vampirism is the key to my relationships with others, the only mechanism that allows me to interact. Of course, this is a metaphor. Vampires, as such, do not exist, they are merely a hook on which to hang all manner of shameful parasitisms that need metaphor to come to terms with themselves. The shape that metaphor takes in me is special, as I said. What I need—which I suck from the other—is neither money, nor security, nor admiration, nor, in professional terms, subject matter or stories. It is style. I have discovered that every human being, every living being in reality, in addition to everything he has to show for himself by way of material and spiritual possessions, has a style he uses to manage those possessions. And I have learned to detect it and appropriate it. Which has important consequences for my relationships, at least for those I have established since I turned forty: they are temporary, they begin and end, and they are quite fleeting, more and more fleeting as I become increasingly skilled at capturing another's personal style. Any other kind of vampirism could lead to permanent relationships; for example, if I extracted money or attention from my victim, the other's reserves would likely become infinite. Even if I were looking for stories, a single subject could supply me indefinitely. But not style. It has a mechanism that gets worn out in the interpersonal transfer. Once in action, I watch my victim quickly dry up, wilted and vacant, and I lose all interest. Then I move on to the next one.

I have now revealed the entire secret of my scientific activity. My famous clones are nothing more than the duplication of style cells. Which should lead me to question my appetite for styles. I think the answer resides in the mere necessity to persist. I have sought an outlet for this need through love, without any success, so far.

We were crowded together on a bench pushed against a wall; next to me, at moments talking to me, sat Nelly, one of my young Venezuelan friends, a graduate student in literature. I admired her and I had a tendency to feel toward her that rare kind of envy that crosses sexual barriers. She must have been twenty-one or twenty-two, but she was the embodiment of an ageless ideal. She was small and thin, her features were unusually pure, and she had enormous eyes and an aristocratic air. Her suit—wide pants and bustier—was made of brown satin; her perfect breasts were almost exposed; she wore very pointy Asian slippers on her feet. Her blond curly hair fell over her shoulders at an angle, covering one eye. Part of her charm lay in her incongruity. She was mulatto, perhaps also with some indigenous blood, but her face was French. Her hair color was recent, judging by the comments I heard from her friends; I had met her as a redhead, years before. One could never guess what she was thinking. In the discotheque she was calm, relaxed, a glass of rum in her hand, her beautiful eyes lost in contemplation. She seemed to be elsewhere. She spoke only when spoken to; when not, she allowed a peaceful, cozy silence to envelop her. She spoke in a whisper, but she articulated her words so well that I could understand her perfectly over the loud music.

"You are enchanting tonight, Nelly," I told her, my tongue heavy with alcohol. "As usual, I should say. Or did I already say that? Every sentence I utter comes out twice, though that's why I feel it twice as strongly, wrapped as it is in the deep truth of its meaning and its intention."

For a moment she seemed not to have heard me, but that was her usual reaction. In that minuscule space between our two bodies, she turned toward me, like the statue of a goddess turning on the altar.

"I dressed up especially in your honor, César. Today is your day."

"Thank you very much. I am enjoying it. But you are always elegant, it's a part of you."

"That's kind of you to say so. You are good inside and out, César." My face must have betrayed my puzzlement at the second statement, because I heard her add, "You are young and beautiful."

The lights were very low, we were practically in the dark. Or rather, the beams and pulses of the colored lights allowed us to see what was going on but not reconstruct it in our minds. This is the astute discovery such night spots have made. Their lighting arrangements reproduce subjectivity thereby nullifying it, a process further assisted by the alcohol and the noise. From the depths of this nullification rose, golden and warm like a houri out of paradise, the beautiful Nelly. I slipped my arm around her waist and kissed her. Her lips had a strange flavor, which made me think of the taste of silk. We were so close, so nearly on top of each other, that every gesture we made required only minimal displacement—almost imperceptible.

"I am no longer young," I told her. "Haven't you noticed how much hair I've lost since my last visit?"

She looked at my hair and shook her head. I insisted with the obstinacy of a drunk. I told her that my imminent baldness terrified me. And it wasn't just out of vanity; there was a very concrete reason. I told her that when I was young I shaved my head in a rapture of madness, then had a message tattooed on my scalp, which my hair then covered when it grew back. If I went bald and this inscription were revealed, it would be the end of the scant prestige I had managed to build up as a fragile defensive shield around me.

"Why? What does it say?" she asked, pretending for a moment that she believed me.

"I can only tell you that it is a declaration of belief in the existence of extraterrestrials."

A violet light that swept fleetingly over her face showed

me her serious smile.

That was why, I went on to explain, I spent a fortune on shampoos with capillary nutrients, and why, not trusting commercial products, I had dedicated my life to chemistry.

A while later, changing the subject, I asked about the ring she was wearing on her left hand. It was a fascinating piece of jewelry, shaped like a crown, with a blue stone whose facets seemed to have been set separately. She told me it was her graduation ring, one of the traditions of the university, though hers had a special feature: they had doubled hers in honor of her having earned two simultaneous degrees, as Professor of Literature and Professor of the Teaching of Literature; it was a fairly subtle distinction, but she seemed quite proud of this double achievement.

She left her silky hand between my paws corroded by the nucleic acid I work with. I lifted it to my eyes so I could examine the ring, which was truly a notable piece for its workmanship and clever design. Each time a ball of strobe light rolled over us, the blue stone lit up brilliantly, and through the two tiny chiseled windows I could see the crowd of young people dancing. The thin gold ribbon that twisted around the stone carried an inscription.

"Look," she said turning the ring around with two fingers from her other hand. "Can you see how the words of the inscription recombine to form other words, spelling out both of my two degrees?"

I couldn't, of course, due to the lack of light and my befuddlement at that late hour, but I could admire the mechanism. I kissed those fingers.

May God forgive me, but I began to doubt the seriousness of the course of studies at that tropical university. All those exchanges and caresses in that discotheque were part of a larger context through which I was taking a measure of Nelly's true intelligence. All my seductive moves, both the innocent and the daring, and even the most impassioned and sincere, have in common the same backdrop: my constant evaluation of the intelligence of the woman in question. I can't help it. Even further in the background must be my adolescent fantasy of having a sex slave, a woman who submits, without any reserve, to the will of my desire. For this, her intelligence must have a very special size and configuration. But intelligence is mysterious. It always gets the better of me, escapes my manipulations—even my literary ones—and remains an insolvable enigma.

I was interested in Nelly for another reason, both more positive and more ineffable. She was Amelina's best friend, her confidante, she knew everything about her ... Among other things she knew where she was hiding. She was in on the secret, though secretive herself, thereby establishing a continuum of love. The two women weren't at all alike, they were almost opposites. Once I had compared them, in jest, to the sun and the moon. There in the disco, in my intoxicated state, I had next to me, throbbing and perfect, a reality that touched all other realities and spread through them until it encompassed the entire world. Nelly's dreamy eyes lost themselves in the night and in me.

VIII

At dawn, things emerged from their reality, as if in a drop of water. The most trivial objects, embellished with profound reality, made me quiver almost painfully. A tuft of grass, a paving stone, a scrap of cloth, everything was soft and dense. We were in the Plaza Bolívar, as lush and leafy as a real forest. The sky had turned blue, not a cloud in sight, no stars or airplanes, as if emptied of everything; the sun should have appeared from behind the mountains, but its rays were not yet touching even the highest peak to the west. The light intensified and bodies projected no shadows. The dark and the light floated in layers. The birds didn't sing, the insects must have been asleep, the trees remained as still as in a painting. And, at my feet, the real kept being born, like a mineral being born atom by atom.

The strangeness that made everything sparkle came from me. Worlds rose out of my bottomless perplexity.

"So, am I capable of love?" I asked myself. "Can I really love truly, like in a soap opera, like in reality?" The question surpassed the thinkable. Love? Me, love? Me, the brain man, the aesthete of the intellect? Wouldn't something need to happen to make it possible, some cosmic sign, an event that would turn the course of events around, an eclipse of a kind...? Inches away from my shoe, one more atom crystallized in a blaze of transparency, then another... If I could love, just like that, without the universe getting turned upside down, the only persistent condition that made reality real was contiguity: that things were next to things, in rows or on plates ... No, it was impossible, I couldn't believe it. Nevertheless ... Plop! Another atom of air, in front of my face, initiating another spiral of splendid combustion. If all conditions can be reduced to a single condition, it is this: Adam and Eve were real.

Nelly and I, sitting on a stone bench under the trees, were as pale as a sheet of paper. My features were as drawn as could be, an old man's face, pale, bloodless, my hair sticking out. I knew this because I was looking at my reflection in the glass of the Exoscope we had in front of us. The actors of the University Theatre had brought it to the disco at the end of the party, to pay me a good-bye homage; we danced around it like savages enacting a rain dance, watching our reflections in miniature and upside down. Afterward, drunk as they were, they left it behind, and I made the effort to carry it to the plaza, thinking that sooner or later they would remember it and come get it—they needed it for the show's official opening.

I had to admit they had done a good job. The dawn was fully reflected in the Exoscope, and in that dawn, the two of us, as if after the end of the world. With great effort I turned my eyes away from the instrument's glass and looked directly at Nelly. Without knowing why, I asked her a stupid question.

"What are you thinking about?"

She remained quiet but alert for a moment, her eyes lost in the void.

"Do you hear that, César? What's going on?"

I could have sworn the silence was absolute, though as a foreigner I was unable to determine what was normal or abnormal within that silence. In any case, it was not the silence that was puzzling Nelly. Awakening from my reverie, I heard shouts of alarm, cars suddenly accelerating, sirens, all in a kind of dull buzz that pulsated around me, still not disturbing the otherworldly peace of the city center, though approaching.

"The birds have stopped singing," Nelly whispered, "even the flies have gone into hiding."

"Could it be an earthquake?" I ventured.

"Could be," she said noncommittally.

A car drove past the plaza at full speed. Behind it came a military truck full of armed soldiers, one of whom saw us and shouted something, but they were driving so fast we couldn't understand him.

"Look!" Nelly shouted, pointing up.

I looked up and saw a crowd of people on the roof terrace of a building, all staring off into the distance and shouting. The same thing was happening on the balconies of the other buildings around that plaza. Right in front of us the cathedral bells began to ring. In a flash the streets were thronging with cars filled with entire families … It seemed like collective madness. As far as I was concerned, it might have been normal: I didn't know the customs of that city, and nothing precluded this from being what happened every Sunday at dawn: the locals coming out onto their balconies and terraces to check the weather, and shouting out joyfully that it was a beautiful day for their outings and sporting events; the cathedral bells, for their part, calling people to morning services; families leaving early for their picnics … If I hadn't been with Nelly I could have taken it as the normal Sunday routine. But she was extremely puzzled, and even a bit alarmed.

It was obvious that whatever was happening was happening far away, and far away in this small, enclosed valley meant the surrounding mountains. We couldn't see them from the plaza, but there were panoramic views from any of the adjacent streets, one of the city's great tourist attractions. I stood up. Nelly must have been thinking the same thing because she also got up and quickly figured out the closest spot where we could find out what was happening.

"Let's go to the archway on Humboldt Street," she said, already starting off. That archway, which I was familiar with, was about one hundred yards away; it stood at the foot of a very long public stairway that was so steep you could see half the valley from there. I started to follow her, then stopped her with my hand.

"Should we leave this monstrosity here?" I asked, pointing to the Exoscope.

She shrugged. We left it and walked off quickly. In the

brief time it took us to get to the archway, just a short distance away, the activity in the streets had increased so much it was difficult to make our way through the crowds. Everybody was nervous, some were terrified, most were rushing around as if their lives depended on it. Everyone was talking, but I couldn't understand a word, as if they were speaking foreign languages, which must be a natural effect of panic.

When we got there, we saw it. It was so astonishing it took a while for me to absorb. To begin with, we saw that the alarm was justified, to say the least. I don't know exactly how to describe it. At first, it was otherworldly; it was still dawn, the sun hadn't yet appeared, the sky was very clear and very empty, bodies projected no shadows ... and colossal blue worms were slowly descending from the mountain peaks ... I'm aware that stating it like this might bring automatic writing to mind, but stating it is my only choice. It seems like the insertion of a different plot line, from an old B-rated science fiction movie, for example. Nevertheless, the seamless continuity had at no time been interrupted. They were living beings, of this I was certain: I had too much experience manipulating life forms to make that mistake. There are some movements no machine can imitate. I calculated the size of the worms: they were approximately one thousand feet long and seventy feet in diameter; they were almost perfect cylinders, with no heads or tails, although their geometric form had to be mentally reconstructed because they were coiling and twisting and changing shape as they moved across the anfractuous mountain terrain. They also looked soft and slimy, but their formidable weight could be deduced by observing them displace enormous rocks along their way, sunder the mountainside, and reduce whole trees to splinters. The most extraordinary thing, which would have been worthy of admiration had the circumstances not added an extra touch of terror, was their color: a phosphorescent blue with watery tones, like an almost darkened sky, a blue that seemed dampened by fresh placentas.

Nelly grabbed my arm. She was horrified. I swept my eyes along the perimeter of this great Andean amphitheater: there were hundreds of worms, all descending toward the city. From the shouts, which I quickly began to understand, I learned that the same thing was occurring in the mountains behind us, the ones we couldn't see from where we stood. I've already said that Mérida is completely surrounded by mountains. This meant only one thing: very soon we would be crushed by the monsters. The landslides they were provoking were cataclysmic; the entire valley shook as stones the size of houses tumbled down the slopes, and there was probably already vast destruction on the outskirts. A simple projected calculation revealed that the city was doomed. Two or three of these worms would be enough to leave no brick standing. And there were hundreds of them! Moreover, with horror and despair I realized that the quantity was indefinite … and increasing. It was as if they kept being born, and the process showed no signs of stopping.

The ones in front were already halfway between the

highest peaks and the valley floor. That's why they were descending: their own multiplication was forcing them downhill. It was an almost mechanical destiny, not one due to any murderous impulse on the part of these strange beasts. In fact, they were much too strange to harbor any agenda. Their size was what would destroy us ... If anyone entertained a hope that their size was an optical illusion, and that they would get smaller as they descended until they appeared as inoffensive as cigarette butts under the soles of our shoes, they would have to dismiss the idea: they were very real, and having one nearby would be a terminal experience.

Any hope regarding the relativity of their size was painfully dispelled a few minutes later, when we witnessed the following episode from where we were standing under the archway. Several military trucks, the one we had seen driving past the plaza and others, converged on a road that rose in the direction of the worms. We saw them stop when they reached the one nearest the city. The soldiers got out and fanned out in front of the blue mass. At that moment denial was no longer possible: the men looked like insects next to the monster—and pathetically ineffectual. This became obvious once they began to shoot at it with their machine guns. They didn't miss their target once (it was like aiming at the mountain itself), but they could have continued for an eternity to the same effect, that is, to no effect. The bullets disappeared into the soft tons of blue flesh like pebbles tossed into the sea. They tried bazookas, cannons, hand grenades, even antiaircraft missiles fired from the hood of one of the trucks, all with the same derisive futility. The climax came when the worm, in the course of its blind march, slid down a steep slope and one section of its body rolled onto the road, crushing trucks and men like an enormous rolling pin, reducing them to laminas. The survivors ran off in terror. The crowd broke their awed silence as they watched the events unfold, and I heard cries and shouts of anguish. Their worst fears were being confirmed. Somebody pointed to another spot, to one side, where another catastrophe was taking place: it was the highway that led across the plateau and out of the valley. Another worm had fallen over a compact line of cars trying to escape, causing innumerable fatalities. Traffic came to a standstill, and people abandoned their cars and ran between the rocks and bushes back toward the city. There was no escape. This was definitive. Eyes turned with fear toward the old colonial buildings around us: the city itself seemed to be the last possible refuge, and it was an illusion to think that its feeble walls could withstand the weight of the worms.

The collective attention turned back to itself, as if to confirm the reality of what was occurring through the reaction of fear. And I was implicated in this reversion. Like so many others, like everybody, perhaps, I have always thought that in a real collective catastrophe I would find the material of my dreams, take it in hand, shape it, finally; then, even if only for an instant, everything would be permitted. It would take something as grand and widespread as an earthquake, an interplanetary collision, or a war to make the circumstances genuinely objective and thus make room for my subjectivity to take hold of the reins of action.

But the subjective was made manifest even in the supremely objective. The examples of cataclysms hereby offered, which in reality are not examples, do not include the invasion of enormous slimy creatures. That would never happen in real life; it rises out of a feverish imagination, in this case mine, and returns to it as a metaphor for my private life.

Here I have again reached the moment to change levels, to make another "translation." But this one is so radical that it comes full circle and reties the plot line exactly where I left it.

The mental process of the character representing me in the previous "translation," from the point at which he was contemplating the benefits of a collective catastrophe, apparently dissolved entirely into fiction, then gathered up all the loose ends and elaborated a generalized reinterpretation, not only of the previous "translations" but of the process itself out of which "translations" arise.

Just as when interpreting a nightmare, I was assailed by a sudden doubt: might it be my fault? A priori, this seemed absurd, an extreme manifestation—exaggerated to the point of caricature—of the lack of proportion between small causes and grand effects. But one thing led to the next, and in a vertiginous process this conjecture became more and more plausible. I went back and reviewed my own "translations" until I found the root of them all, the device from which they had emerged. In my mind, the march of the worms became retrograde, and with the same brutal blindness with which they were descending, they turned and climbed back up, destroying my inventions, from whose crushed cadavers rose little clouds of memory, ghosts of memory.

Because I had forgotten everything. The same system that created my thoughts took charge of erasing them, turning them into sinuous white strips that reached across every level. How can there be so much amnesia in a single lifetime? Isn't this a point in favor of the theory of reincarnation?

Of course, there is such a thing as "blind translation," the act of mechanically transposing one language to another, without passing through the content, which is what professional translators do when they come across a technical and detailed description of a machine or a process ... In order to understand what it's about, they would need to consult a manual on the subject, study something they know nothing about and doesn't interest them ... But that isn't necessary! By translating correctly, sentence by sentence, the entire page, the translation will turn out well, they will continue to be as happily ignorant as they were at the beginning, and they will get paid for their work. After all, they are paid to know the language, not the subject matter.

The inverted vortex of the titanic herd of blue worms was located somewhere in the mountains. They emerged from that spot into the light and began to slither—even before they came fully into view—along the broken horizon of the peaks, like a ball circling the top of the roulette wheel, until they stopped, made their appearance, and began to descend. There were so many and their issuance was so constant that they were all descending at once from all points around the circle (in that particular game of roulette, all the numbers came up at once). I could pinpoint the locus of their emergence, and I was the only person who could: it was the cloning machine. It couldn't be anything else. The years I had devoted full time to the manipulation of cloned materials had so refined my sixth sense that I could recognize it. These worms had all the characteristics; their very excess—where would that come from if not the uncontrolled multiplication of cells that only the cloning machine could generate? Functional beings have inviolable limits. My first thought was that the machine was malfunctioning, had gone haywire. But I immediately corrected myself; that thought was worthy only of a citizen of a consumer society who buys a microwave or a video camera and is overwhelmed by its complexity. This was not the case with me, because I had invented the cloning machine, and nobody knew better than I that it was infallibly rational.

As I have already mentioned, the worms' color and texture were their most noticeable characteristics. They are also what led me to the heart of the matter. Because that color, that very peculiar brilliant blue, immediately reminded me of the color of Carlos Fuentes's cell, which my wasp had brought me ... Though when I saw that color in the cell it did not evoke what it was evoking now that I was seeing it extended over vast undulating surfaces. I now realized I had seen that same color somewhere else, the very same day the cell had been taken, one week before. Where? On the tie Carlos Fuentes was wearing that day! A splendid Italian raw silk tie, over an immaculate white shirt ... and a light grey suit ... (one memory led to another until the picture was complete). And this horrendous piece of evidence revealed the magnitude of the error. The wasp had brought me a cell from Carlos Fuentes's *tie*, not his body. A groan escaped my lips.

"Stupid wasp and the accursed mother who made you!"

"What?" Nelly asked, surprised.

"Don't pay any attention to me, I understand myself."

The fact is, I couldn't blame her. It was all my fault. How could that poor disposable cloned tool know where the man stopped and his clothing began? For her it was all one, it was all "Carlos Fuentes." After all, it was no different than what happened when the critics and professors who were attending the conference found it difficult to say where the man ended and his books began; for them, too, all of it was "Carlos Fuentes."

I saw it with the clarity of the noonday sun: the silk cell contained the DNA of the worm that had produced it, and the cloning machine, functioning perfectly, had done nothing more than decode and recode the information, with the results we were now witnessing. The blue monsters were nothing more nor less than silkworm clones, and if they had been magnified to that absurd size it was simply because I had set the cloning machine to run in "genius" mode. Under other circumstances I would have smiled with melancholic irony upon seeing to what awkward and destructive gigantism literary greatness could be reduced when it was passed through the weave and warp of life.

I came to my senses after having lost myself in thoughts that rushed through me like a hiccup, and I felt an urgency to do something, anything, to prevent the imminent catastrophe. Regrettably, I have no talent for improvisation. But this was the time for action, not regrets. I would think of something. And even if I didn't, everything would turn out well. If I had started it, I could end it. If it had come out of me, it had to return to me. It couldn't be that I would be responsible for the deaths of several tens of thousands of innocent people and the utter devastation—no stone would remain standing—of this old city. The very possibility of the disaster cast over my being a demonic splendor. In my role as a writer, I am inoffensive. What more could I want than to be diabolical, a destroyer of worlds?! But it is impossible. Well reasoned, however, therein lie the benefits of the changes in level, because then I could, in reality, be a diabolical being, an evil monster: such things are fairly relative, as everyone knows from daily experience.

I grabbed Nelly by the shoulder, and we left the group under the archway. The entire crowd was dispersing, women and men moving suddenly and without any apparent purpose. What could they do? Hide in a cellar? Make final arrangements? In the end, they had to do something.

Nelly was in shock. I brought my face up to hers and spoke to provoke a response from her.

"I'm going to do something. I think I can stop them." She looked at me incredulously. I repeated, "If anyone can save the city, I can."

"But, how?" she stammered, looking behind her.

"You're going to have to help me," which wasn't altogether true, among other reasons because I still hadn't devised a plan. But it worked, her eyes recovered a glimmer of interest. She must have remembered that I was the hero of the Macuto Line and that performing feats of historical proportion was not unknown to me.

We didn't have to go far. We literally bumped into an empty car that had its motor running and the door open; its owner must have joined the group watching events from the archway.

"Let's go!" I said. I got in behind the wheel. Nelly sat in the passenger seat. We drove off. It was a taxi, an old Pontiac from the seventies, as long and wide as only cars in Venezuela can be today.

I feared the streets would be blocked, but they weren't. The paralysis of uncertainty persisted throughout the city. I sped up, and we came to Viaduct Avenue. The only solution I could think of was to find a way through the newborn beasts, reach the cloning machine, and turn it off. In this way at least I could stop their emergence. I didn't know if putting the machine in reverse would reabsorb the worms, but I could try. In the meantime, I stepped on the gas. We were soon on the viaduct, where we commanded an excellent view of the blue masses slithering down the mountains.

"Where are we going?" Nelly asked. "I don't think we can escape."

"That is not my intention, quite the contrary. I'm going to try to get to the place where they are coming from," at which point I inserted a tiny white lie, because I didn't want her to guess that I was responsible for the disaster. "What we have to do is close the ... hole they are coming out of, and perhaps make them go back ... underground."

She believed me. It was absurd, but in a certain way it evoked the spring mechanism of the Macuto Line, over which I had already been triumphant, and this lent it a patina of truth.

I kept climbing, driving faster and faster. The old Pontiac vibrated, its panels rattling. Driving helped me recuperate some of my lost coordination; a sleepless night and the alcohol had left every cell in my body dead tired. I was overwhelmed with exhaustion. But the internal adrenalin bath sustained my movements, and slowly I recovered my faculties.

I turned left onto a small, very steep street, shifted into first gear, and floored the gas until the motor roared. In a final effort the clunker carried us onto the highway that circled the city. I turned right, moving in the same direction as the morning breeze; snakes and rats, escaping in terror from the mountains, were scrambling across the asphalt. We could now see from close up what was happening. The blue of the worms filled the windshield. They were everywhere, nearby and far away, and their forward march was inexorable. The route we were taking would be quite dangerous in a matter of minutes, and if not, would become so later on. We heard a few rocks, luckily quite small, falling on the roof of the car. I began to doubt the feasibility of my plan. Reaching the cloning machine seemed like mission impossible. We would have to abandon the car sooner or later, perhaps quite soon; I hoped to drive at least as far as the intersection with the road that continued along the plateau; but I remembered that I had climbed on foot for an hour or more before setting down the machine. And based on the way events were unfolding, this interval would give the worms plenty of time to turn the city into a tabula rasa. That is, if we managed to avoid them and reach our goal. We passed by one that was slithering down the hill about two hundred yards from the road. Seen from close up, they were overwhelming. Their shape, which from far away had seemed so well defined, so worm-like, here turned into a blue mess, cloudlike. Nelly devoured it all with her eyes, in silence. She turned to look back at the city, as if calculating the time left before the inevitable occurred. At that moment I sensed she was remembering something, and, in fact, she let out a choked exclamation and looked at me.

"César!"

"What?" I said, lifting my foot off the gas pedal.

"I forgot about Amelina!"

This surprise completely confused me. At that moment more than ever before, Amelina felt like a myth, the legend of love. I had already resigned myself to never seeing her again, so her name came to me from a distance that was purely linguistic. But Nelly's words carried with them an urgency of reality that forced me to adopt a more practical perspective, as if Amelina really did exist. And, undoubtedly, she did. She was somewhere in the city we saw spread out to our right, small and threatened like the model of a city in the hands of an angry child. The image of Florencia, my childhood love, flitted through my mind, the young and enamored Florencia, whom I felt had been reborn in Amelina thirty years later. Like in a trick diorama, what was far away looked close and vice versa. Love's ghostly stand-ins, which had shaped my life, were spinning around me, forming a tunnel of black light that I was sinking into.

"Where is she?"

"At her house. She sleeps late and very heavily. We must go wake her up and tell her what's going on!"

What good would that do her? None, of course. And us, even less. But the idea attracted me for two reasons: first, I could see Amelina again, and under savage and peremptory circumstances; second, it was the perfect excuse to abandon my impractical plan of reaching the cloning machine. The very instant I made the decision to go, I became possessed by an almost infantile euphoria, because Nelly's words implied that Amelina still lived alone, she had not gotten married, and she, Nelly, continued to think of her in relation to me, and if she had decided to mention her only under this extremity, it was because our love story was real, it carried across all the translations, it would keep its appointment ...

"Let's go," I said. "But you'll have to guide me."

She pointed to the first exit, and I veered off the highway, making the tires screech. We turned our backs on the mountain and the worms, as if to say, "Who cares!" and we returned to the city along a road I didn't know. She told me that Amelina was still living in one of the student apartments in the Nancy Building, the same one where I had visited her years before. It wasn't far away, but nothing was in such a small city.

The traffic got heavier, though it was still moving because nobody was paying any attention to the traffic lights. I wondered where they were all going. From the terraces, people kept looking toward the mountains with the same expectations, the same alarm, the same dismay. They were not taking any measures, but what could they do? The cars were driving like crazy, all in the same direction ...

"Where are they going?" Nelly asked.

Suddenly, I knew: to the airport. It seemed strange that I hadn't thought of that sooner; apparently others had. The only way out was by air. But, even assuming there were still some private airplanes available and that military planes were on their way, many could not be saved, let alone all. The commercial flight arrived at ten and departed at eleven, if they hadn't cancelled it. And if it arrived full of passengers, the passengers themselves would want to remain on the flight back to Caracas.

A Mercedes Benz, its horn blasting like a siren, passed us; I glimpsed Carlos Fuentes and his wife in the back seat, their profiles set in serious expressions. They, too, were on their way to the airport. How naive! Or, perhaps, they had been offered seats on an official plane? The city was the provincial capital, and surely the governor would have one … but I found it hard to believe that in this predicament of "save yourself if you can," literary hierarchies would be respected. No way! Surely they were going to try to somehow wangle a seat, like so many others … I remembered that I had a reservation for the eleven o'clock flight, I was even carrying the ticket in my pocket … If I had been able to catch up with that powerful Mercedes I would have offered them my seat … I've always liked Carlos Fuentes; not in vain had I chosen him for my experiment. I felt like a scoundrel. Everything that was happening was my fault, and now, instead of putting everything on the line to rid the world of this threat (it was the least I could do), I was allowing myself to be carried away by a private, sentimental whim; I was ashamed of my lack of responsibility.

To appease my conscience, I said out loud, "It will take us only a few minutes. Then all three of us will go to the mountain."

She indicated where to turn and continued directing me along a sinuous route. She leaned forward and pointed her finger in the direction I should go. I couldn't avoid looking at her, and I seemed to be seeing her, again, for the first time. Again I discovered her beauty, her youth … a bit excessive for me, but that's what it was all about. To be young again, "good and beautiful," as she had said. She was mysterious, that little Nelly, her serenity and silence shielded some kind of secret that enthralled me …

Here there is a blank in the story. I don't know what happened in the following few minutes. Perhaps we never reached Amelina's place, perhaps we got there and didn't find her, or couldn't rouse her. What I do know is that I suddenly found myself about a hundred feet below street level on the banks of a stream through a deep gorge that crosses the valley and the city longitudinally. Behind me, far above, was the viaduct, the most centrally located bridge connecting the two sides of the gorge. A large crowd had gathered on the other side and was watching me. In front of me, almost perfectly still, was a worm. He was little more than fifty feet away. Apparently the monster had rolled there: his descent had been brutal, judging from what he had left in his wake: fallen trees, houses smashed to smithereens. His congeners must have been surrounding the city in a deadly grip. I looked around. The balconies of the buildings along the edge of the gorge were full of people, eager to witness the confrontation. I recognized the Nancy Building, whose pinkish walls emitted an opaque hue that tinged everybody with their color.

But I had to hurry. The sense of urgency was the only thing that had survived my amnesia. My hands were clutching the vertical bars of the Exoscope, and Nelly was holding the other end. I saw her through the glass panels. How had we gotten there, and with that device? I didn't have time to reconstruct it all, but I could imagine it. Upon seeing the worm fall into the deep riverbed, the lowest level it could reach, I must have thought it would be at my mercy, at least for a few minutes, so I could test an annihilation experiment. We probably ran to the plaza, several hundred feet away, to get the Exoscope, then carried it (this was evident from how every muscle in my body ached) and lowered it from the viaduct: the rope still attached to it was testimony enough.

Whatever the nature of the experiment, I didn't even have to think about it because my brain, in parallel, was already making the calculations ...

"A little more ... here ... slowly ..."

Poor Nelly was panting from the effort. We stood the Exoscope up in front of the worm and carefully turned the glass panels. A fraction of an inch in either direction would make all the difference. I saw the worm's reflection and touched its image in the cold glass with the tips of my fingers. Though threatening, brutal, as lethal as a soft skyscraper come to life, it was beautiful, a masterpiece. I am fascinated by what is huge, excessive. Perhaps never before had such a creature trodden upon the earth, a being made of blue silk, so artificial and at the same time so natural. All its fascination resided in its magnification. It was still a miniature, on which the limitless freedom of size had operated.

I turned to look at it directly. It had moved closer. Though it had no face, it had a vague expressiveness that seemed to speak of its horror at having been born, its feeling of not being welcome, of having landed where it wasn't wanted. I could have stayed there for hours contemplating it. After all, I had good reason to believe it to be my masterpiece. I would never again create anything like it, even if I wanted to. What gave it that particular blue hue was the depth of its materiality, the fact that each cell was composed of reality and unreality. As if my gaze were stimulating it, it began to move, though most likely it had never stopped moving. It covered the distance between us with what was probably, for it, no more than a shudder. Nelly took refuge behind me; the audience held its breath. I lifted my eyes to its formidable mass—the height of a five-story building. It was now or never.

Just as it was supposed to happen, at that instant a ray of sun shone through a break in the mountains and in a straight line onto the glass of the Exoscope. I expertly moved the panels so that the yellow point would draw a tiny square. I knew well the effect this action of the light would have on the cloned cells. And, indeed, the worm began to get reabsorbed into its own reflection in the glass. It was very quick, very fluid, but it was not without incident. The structure of the Exoscope shook, and I was afraid it would fall over. I held one end with all my strength and asked Nelly to do the same on the other. She obeyed me, in spite of her fear. It seemed as if it were going to break apart, but we held firm, and the worm kept going and going … When less than a tenth of its mass was still materialized, it coiled up around us. I closed my eyes. I felt it slipping, almost brushing up against me, and the blue color penetrated me even through my lowered eyelids. When I lifted those lids, it had finished its reentry … Or, rather, it hadn't. One last fragment of blue substance remained, which, perhaps because it was the last, rose up in a violent whirlwind on Nelly's end then quickly got sucked into the glass. The movement made one of her shoes fly off, and I saw that her foot was wounded.

The Exoscope was still. I leaned over to look into the glass. There it was, a transparent blue phylactery dissolving into atoms and mixing up with the golden atoms of the sun in a furious battle, in an inoffensive, artistic game that dispersed in seconds. But one drop of blood on Nelly's foot had splashed onto the glass. In a swish, the atomic beam carried it away into the depth of the transparency.

I stood back. It was over. The audience applauded and cheered, joyous honking began to resound throughout the city. The entire herd of gigantic worms had disappeared, dissolved into the dawn air. People took it as some kind of miracle, but I, of course, knew that clones were like that: one is all.

I examined my friend's foot, which was bleeding profusely. Men and boys were climbing down the gorge, and the first to arrive offered to carry her up; the wound wasn't serious, but she needed to be taken to the emergency room to be bandaged. I climbed up behind them, and when they'd gotten her into the car, I told her that I was leaving on the morning flight, as planned. She promised to come to the airport to say goodbye.

MARCH 8, 1996

ABOUT THE TRANSLATORS

Chris Andrews teaches at the University of Western Sydney. As well as work by César Aira and other authors, he has translated many books by Roberto Bolaño into English.

Katherine Silver's most recent and forthcoming translations include works by Daniel Sada, Horacio Castellanos Moya, Rafael Bernal and Marcos Giralt Torrente. She is also co-director of the Banff International Literary Translation Centre.

He just wanted a decent book to read ...

Not too much to ask, is it? It was in 1935 when Allen Lane, Managing Director of Bodley Head Publishers, stood on a platform at Exeter railway station looking for something good to read on his journey back to London. His choice was limited to popular magazines and poor-quality paperbacks – the same choice faced every day by the vast majority of readers, few of whom could afford hardbacks. Lane's disappointment and subsequent anger at the range of books generally available led him to found a company – and change the world.

'We believed in the existence in this country of a vast reading public for intelligent books at a low price, and staked everything on it'
Sir Allen Lane, 1902–1970, founder of Penguin Books

The quality paperback had arrived – and not just in bookshops. Lane was adamant that his Penguins should appear in chain stores and tobacconists, and should cost no more than a packet of cigarettes.

Reading habits (and cigarette prices) have changed since 1935, but Penguin still believes in publishing the best books for everybody to enjoy. We still believe that good design costs no more than bad design, and we still believe that quality books published passionately and responsibly make the world a better place.

So wherever you see the little bird – whether it's on a piece of prize-winning literary fiction or a celebrity autobiography, political tour de force or historical masterpiece, a serial-killer thriller, reference book, world classic or a piece of pure escapism – you can bet that it represents the very best that the genre has to offer.

Whatever you like to read – trust Penguin.